D1527875

CURSE OF THE PHOENIX

ARCANE IRREGULARS 1

DAN WILLIS

Print Edition – 2021

This version copyright © 2021 by Dan Willis.

All rights reserved. No part of this book may be reproduced or transmitted in any form or by any electronic or mechanical means, including photocopying, recording or by any information storage and retrieval system, without the express written permission of the copyright holder, except where permitted by law.

This novel is a work of fiction. Names, characters, places and incidents are either the product of the author's imagination, or, if real, used fictitiously.

Edited by Stephanie Osborn
Supplemental Edits by Barbara Davis

Cover by Mihaela Voicu

Published by

Runeblade Entertainment
Spanish Fork, Utah.

1

THE PRISMATIC MAN

Danny Pak sat at his desk and stared at the wax paper that contained his roast beef sandwich. It was his third cold lunch this week, and he just couldn't bring himself to unwrap it. He glanced at his metal lunch bucket, but knew it held nothing more for him. When he was a beat cop, his bucket was always full of good things to eat. That had been when his sister Amy lived with him and did the cooking.

He sighed as he realized that those days were over a decade gone. Amy was a nurse in Philadelphia now, married to an accountant.

Danny sighed again and tossed the still-wrapped sandwich back into the metal container.

"You'd think a lieutenant would have time to get a hot lunch," he grumbled as he shut the lid and placed the lunch pail back under his desk.

He'd been a lieutenant at the New York Police Department for almost seven months now and, while he liked the work, the hours left a lot to be desired. When he'd been a detective, he'd spent most of his time in the field, so grabbing a hot lunch on the job was routine. Now he seemed anchored to his desk by mountains of paperwork.

Every report on every case he assigned to his detectives had to be reviewed, annotated, and filed by him. Then there was the never-ending stack of incoming cases that he had to review and assign to the detectives that worked in his division.

The trick to it was matching the case to the detective. Callahan seemed to have a sixth sense about assigning cases. If the last few months were any gauge, it was a skill Danny sorely lacked.

He picked up a folder from the top of the active case stack and opened it. A bicycle manufacturer's showroom had been robbed and half a dozen bicycles stolen. Detective Crenshaw had been nearby when the call went out, so he was the first detective on the scene. Normally large-scale robbery cases went to Division Four, but it looked like an inside job, so Danny didn't want to hand it over if Crenshaw could clear it quickly. Besides, Crenshaw was new, and he could use a few cases in his 'cleared' column.

Danny could use that, too.

He'd inherited Division Five from now Captain Callahan, and it had been one of the most successful and well-run divisions the NYPD had. It was a big responsibility to keep that reputation for success going, and Danny felt the weight of it every single day. So far, it wasn't going as he'd hoped. The case closure rate of Division Five had dropped fifteen percent since he took over. If things kept up this way, Callahan would be forced to demote him back to the bullpen and give someone else the top job.

With a grunt of frustration, he stood and rounded his desk, heading for the bullpen. It was a large, open area where all the detectives for the various divisions had their desks. Division Five was straight across the open floor and Danny headed for it.

"Where's Crenshaw?" he asked Detective Wilson when he reached the cluster of desks.

Wilson was an experienced detective with a large frame, dark eyes, and a droopy mustache. He glanced up from the stack of documents he'd been reviewing and glanced at Crenshaw's desk.

"He said he was going to grab some lunch, then head downtown to interview a couple people about the bicycle robbery," Wilson said with a shrug.

"Must be nice," Danny growled.

"Lieutenant?" Wilson asked with a raised eyebrow.

"Nothing," he said. "What are you working on?"

"That fraud case with the fake investments," Wilson said, holding up the stack of papers. "I think I see a pattern in our bad guy's marks. They're mostly people who are new to wealth, rising business owners, celebrities, that sort of thing."

"That's a pretty upscale crowd," Danny said, rubbing his chin. "How is he meeting them?"

"All the victims were referred by someone they knew. A casual acquaintance, someone they know from a nightclub or the party circuit."

"Description?"

"All of them are different," Wilson explained. "If I had to guess, I'd say there are at least three people involved."

"Hanging out in nightclubs looking for marks isn't cheap," Danny said.

"Based on what I've been able to uncover," Wilson said, "they've raked in over a quarter of a million through their phony investments already."

Danny whistled.

"Keep on it," he said, giving Wilson an approving nod. "Let me know if you find anything interesting."

Wilson smiled, drawing the droopy mustache up on each side of his nose, then nodded.

"Sure thing, Lieutenant."

Danny made his way back to his office. He'd give Crenshaw one more day, then he'd hand off the bicycle case to Lieutenant McClory of Division Four.

With that decision out of the way, Danny returned to his desk and closed the case file. Setting it aside, he reached for the next folder on the stack, but was interrupted by his phone.

"Pak," he said once he pressed the receiver to his ear.

"I have Detective Crenshaw on the line for you," the Central Office operator said.

"Speak of the Devil," Danny mumbled.

"What was that, Lieutenant?" the operator asked.

"Nothing," Danny sighed. "Put him through."

A moment later the young detective's voice came over the wire.

"Lieutenant?"

"What is it, Crenshaw?" Danny asked.

"I got a radio dispatch about some vandalism," he said, a note of nervousness in his voice. "Since I was closest, I responded and..." His voice trailed off as if he were searching in vain for the right words.

"What's the situation?"

"That's just it, sir," Crenshaw said. "I don't even know how to explain it. I think you'd better come down and take a look at this."

Danny was about to chastise his young detective. He didn't want to hold Crenshaw's hand every time things got hard. It was better for him in the long run to learn how to resolve tough situations on his own. Still, there was something in the detective's flummoxed voice that gave him pause.

"Where are you?"

"Two blocks north of New York University," he said. "There's a little art supply store, you know, for painters and such. It's called Pete's Paints."

Danny scribbled the name down in his notebook and stood.

"All right," he said. "I'll be there in half an hour."

He hung up and picked up his suit coat from the back of his chair. Years ago, he'd walked a beat near the university, so he had a pretty good idea where to find the vandalized art shop. He also knew that there were several excellent cafes near the University.

"Looks like I get a decent lunch after all," he said as he shut his office door on his way to the elevator.

When Danny finally arrived at Pete's Paints, he understood why Crenshaw had called him. The art shop was in a small space between a university store and a barber shop. The storefront windows were covered with broad swaths of color from the inside, completely obscuring the glass. As he stepped over the threshold, Danny saw it was more than just the glass; every surface inside Pete's Paints was covered in patterns of swirling colors.

The paint appeared to have been smeared on by hand, but it didn't look random. Danny could see swirls of colors meant to be clouds and trees against a blue sky in one corner. On a display table, the boxes of brushes, paints, and thinners were painted to look like miniature buildings, rendering the table into its own miniature cityscape. Even the floors were splotched with color, though that seemed random, like vandals had carelessly dripped paint as they went.

"It looks like a French Impressionist exploded in here," Danny said as Detective Crenshaw hurried over.

"A what, sir?" the detective asked. Crenshaw was in his mid-twenties with a pale complexion offset by dark hair and eyes. He wore a blue suit with his gold detective badge clipped to his outside breast pocket. Danny tended to think of him as a puppy, rough and uncoordinated, but eager to please.

"Never mind," Danny said, waving aside the question. He looked around at the store, then turned to Crenshaw. "I'll agree this is quite the mess, and I'm glad I don't have to clean it up," he said, "but I don't see why you called me down here."

"Well, sir," Crenshaw said, blushing under Danny's withering look. "It's...well, you'd better come see."

He turned and headed along the front of the store between the painted front wall and the painted display tables. Danny followed him past the last table and then turned to look behind it.

"What the devil is that?" he demanded.

"That's why I called you down here," Crenshaw said in a hushed voice.

On the floor, behind the display table, was what could only be described as an enormous blob of paint. It stood at least ten inches high in the middle of a slowly spreading pool of color. The blob itself was lumpy, as if it weren't made entirely of paint, but rather covered something more substantial beneath it. Dozens of different colors swirled across its surface in wide bands, mixing and forming new colors as they went. The most disturbing thing about the paint blob was that it lay in the shape of a man.

Or rather, most of a man.

It had a head, with the suggestion of a nose, and a sunken area that appeared to be a mouth, open in a wide smile. Below that was a torso with two truncated arms that reminded Danny of the statue of the Venus De Milo. Progressing down below the torso were two thick legs that both ended just below bumps that would have been knees.

"The shop assistant, a Miss Agnus Cornwall, came in for her shift at ten," Crenshaw broke into Danny's observations with a hoarse voice. "She said the owner, Peter Grant, was supposed to open up at eight, but when she got here, the place was closed."

"Was that unusual?" Danny interrupted.

Crenshaw nodded, consulting his book.

"According to the assistant, Mr. Grant was in the habit of staying up late in his studio. Apparently he's an artist himself. Anyway, when Miss Cornwall opened the door, she found all this."

Danny crouched down, being careful not to get paint on his shoes. The paint man on the floor appeared to be slowly melting, spreading out into a viscous pool of color.

"Do-do you think that's Peter Grant?" Crenshaw stuttered, his voice barely above a whisper.

"Did Mr. Grant have a beef with a sorcerer?" Danny asked.

Crenshaw consulted his notebook, then shook his head.

"According to the assistant, everybody liked Mr. Grant. The University has an art school, so the shop was in the black and, as far as she knows, Grant didn't have any enemies."

Danny felt a chill as he looked at the oozing form of the paint man.

"Close up the crime scene," he said, standing up and heading for the door. "Get everyone out for now."

"Where are you going, Lieutenant?" Crenshaw called after him.

"To make a phone call," Danny answered.

There were lots of places where Danny could have made a phone call, including the vandalized art supply store he just left. Despite this wealth of choices, however, he decided on the phone booth in the back of a diner at the end of the block.

"Lockerby Investigations," the voice of Sherry Knox came through the wire.

"Sherry," he said, turning on the charm. "It's Danny, I need to talk to Alex."

"He's in with a client right now," Sherry said. "I can have him call you back in a few minutes, though. What's this about?"

"Remember those weird deaths back around the time I made lieutenant?" he asked. "There was a couple who got electrocuted, and some people burned down a nightclub?"

"Y-yes," Sherry said, hesitancy plain in her voice. Clearly she thought Danny shouldn't know about that incident.

"Alex mentioned it over lunch," he explained. "Said it was because of some concentrated version of Pixie Powder that gave people real magical abilities."

"Limelight," she said. "It was called Limelight."

"Well, I think I've found another death we can attribute to that stuff. Tell Alex—"

"No," Sherry cut in, her voice hard, even angry. "First of all, that's not possible. The alchemist who invented Limelight went mad and so did the one who was making it. The FBI destroyed all the remaining stock."

"And secondly?" Danny prompted when she didn't elaborate.

"Secondly, I wouldn't tell Alex about this if you threatened to throw me in jail," she said, the undercurrent of anger still in her voice. "Limelight boosts the magical capabilities of runewrights and it's highly addictive. Alex had to use some to stop the Brothers Boom from blowing up Grand Central Terminal."

Sherry paused for a long moment, and Danny considered what she'd said.

"I will not even hint to Alex that any Limelight powder survived," she finished, her voice low to prevent it being overheard.

"You think he'd go after it for himself?" Danny asked, a bit shocked that Sherry would think that about Alex.

"I don't know," she admitted. "What I do know is that runewrights and alchemists who use Limelight end up insane or dead. I'm not going to risk any of that happening to Alex."

Danny wasn't sure Sherry was right about Alex. He had more willpower than anyone else he knew. Still, she might have a point. Plenty of otherwise accomplished and intelligent people succumbed to drink or opium or dozens of other things, abusing them until they ended up dead. Danny had seen it over and over as a detective. If this Limelight stuff was really as addictive as Sherry claimed, he had no choice but to keep its existence a secret from his best friend.

"All right," he said. "Does anyone else know about this stuff?"

"Sorsha does."

That wasn't the answer Danny wanted. Sorsha worked with the feds and if they got wind of this case, they'd come sweeping in and take the whole thing.

"And I think Captain Callahan originally handled the case," Sherry added, seeming to sense Danny's reluctance.

"Thanks, Sherry," he said. "I'll give them a try."

"Make sure they know Alex is off limits when it comes to this," she said, a hard edge in her voice.

Danny promised he would pass along her message, then hung up. Fishing out another nickel, he dialed the number of the Central Office.

"Lieutenant Pak for Captain Callahan," he told the switchboard operator when she picked up.

"What's up, Danny?" Callahan's gruff voice asked a moment later.

Danny explained about the call from Crenshaw and the state of Pete's Paints, then he repeated his call with Sherry Knox.

"So, you're thinking the feds missed some Limelight and Mr. Grant got ahold of it?"

Danny shrugged even though Callahan couldn't see him.

"Maybe he thought it would help him paint better?" he suggested. "Based on the condition of the art supply store, and what I assume is Peter Grant's body," he said, "I'd say Grant came in contact with some."

There was a long silence on the line before Callahan spoke.

"Let me see if I've got this straight," he said. "Peter Grant gets ahold of some Limelight and, after drinking it, his body turns into paint and he goes around his shop literally painting himself to death?"

Danny winced. When put like that, it sounded crazy.

"The only thing left of Grant's face was a smile like the one you see on the cat who ate the canary," Danny said. "It looked like he was having the time of his life."

"Right up till he wasn't," Callahan finished. "I want to tell you to get back here and get to work but, and I can't believe I'm saying this, I think you're right."

"I need someone who knows magic to come take a look at this," Danny said. "If the lump of paint on the floor really is Peter Grant, then this just became my top priority."

"Do you think someone could have dumped the paint on the floor and piled it up to look like a body?"

"I don't know," Danny admitted. "But that's an awful long way to go for a prank, and as of right now, we haven't found Mr. Grant."

Callahan sighed.

"All right," he said. "If Alex is off limits for this one, I'll call in a sorcerer to take a look."

"Not Sorsha," Danny said.

"I didn't get to sit in the big chair by being an idiot," Callahan growled. "I know better than to bring in the feds unless we have to. Since we handle all the protection for the New York Six, one of them is always available to us in case we need magical assistance. I'll find out who's on call this week and have them meet you at the art shop."

Danny thanked the captain and hung up. Knowing how sorcerers work, he figured he had at least a half an hour before the captain could round one up. He smiled to himself for his foresight in making this call from a diner, then went to sit down at the counter.

"What'll you have?" a sour-looking waitress with tired eyes and mousey brown hair asked him.

"Something hot," he replied.

2

THE SORCERER

"It's about time you got here," an irritable voice greeted Danny as he stepped inside Pete's Paints. He'd spent the last half hour having lunch and had walked back in plenty of time to greet whatever sorcerer Captain Callahan would send. Danny had worked with a few sorcerers before in his capacity as a detective, but getting their attention usually took hours.

He was surprised, therefore, when he entered the vandalized art supply store and found a thin, gray-haired, older man with a thick, bushy mustache waiting for him.

"Excuse me?" Danny said. "Who are you?"

"John Rockefeller," he said, holding out a hand.

Danny took it somewhat nervously. Rockefeller was one of the New York Six, one of the most powerful sorcerers in the world, and Danny had kept him waiting. It was common knowledge that annoying a sorcerer was something you did at your peril, so Danny affected an apologetic look.

"You must be Lieutenant Pak," he said when Danny failed to speak. "I confess I was annoyed when I got the call from your Captain. The idea that someone would turn a man to paint sounded utterly absurd. Still, now that I'm here, this is fascinating."

"So those are the remains of Peter Grant?" Danny asked, nodding in the direction of the paint blob on the floor.

Rockefeller snapped his fingers and a glowing tube appeared out of thin air hovering in front of his right eye. Squinting through the tube, the sorcerer moved to where the paint man lay. As he moved, the glowing tube stayed in front of his eye.

"No doubt about it," Rockefeller said examining the body. "I just can't figure out who did it."

"Well, that's my job, sir," Danny said.

Rockefeller looked away from his tube for a moment, favoring Danny with an annoyed look.

"Don't be stupid, Lieutenant," he growled. "This wasn't done by a runewright and it's no alchemical experiment gone wrong. This man remained alive for some time after he was transformed into paint. Only a sorcerer could have done that."

Danny opened his mouth to explain about Limelight, but Rockefeller waved at him to be quiet.

"Something like this would have required tremendous power," he said to himself. "To say nothing of the expertise needed. Barton could have done it, but he's too flashy for something like this. If he wanted this man dead, he'd have used lightning."

"If I may," Danny interjected.

"Shush," the sorcerer growled. "I'm trying to think. Now Sorsha hasn't come into her full power yet, and she's too young to have the mental control for work this complex." He stroked his chin for a moment then cocked his head. "She is a woman, though," he went on. "They think differently than men, so it's probably too soon to rule her out. Then there's Henderson, with his surgeon's training, no one understands the human body as well as he does."

"Mr. Rockefeller," Danny said, shifting into his cop voice. "If you'll just give me a moment, I believe I can help."

The sorcerer looked up with an exasperated expression, his brows furrowed over his eyes. After a tense moment he sighed and stood up straight.

"All right, young man," he said. "Impress me."

"About six months ago, the New York Police Department became aware of an alchemical drug called Limelight," Danny began. "Exposure to this substance gives otherwise mundane people magical abilities. It caused several rather exceptional deaths before the source was tracked down and stopped."

"And you believe that this is another such case?" Rockefeller asked.

"We do," Danny said. "You said it yourself, a sorcerer would have to have tremendous power to do this and if a sorcerer wanted Peter Grant dead, they'd use an easier method. What we needed was confirmation that this blob of paint was, in fact, the remains of Peter Grant."

Rockefeller shook his head at that.

"I can't say who it was for sure," he cautioned. "But I do know that it used to be a man."

"No chance it was a woman?" Danny asked, flipping open his notebook.

"I suppose it might have been," the sorcerer said. "But since the torso is more or less intact and he doesn't have breasts, I'm going to go with 'man'."

Danny thought that was a sensible deduction and jotted it down.

"Now," Rockefeller went on. "Tell me more about this Limelight concoction. I've never heard of something that could give regular people magic. It must be very complex and powerful. Can I speak to whoever created it?"

"You'd have to ask Captain Callahan about that," Danny said. "He was involved with the original case."

Rockefeller rubbed his chin as he looked around at the strange, swirling colors and images that now decorated the art store's surfaces.

"Is there any way I can get some of this Limelight stuff?" he said. "I'd like to conduct some experiments with it."

"No, you wouldn't," Danny said. "Limelight grants magic to us mundane folk, but it drives you magical types insane."

"Really?" the sorcerer said, more to himself than to Danny, then he sighed and pulled out a large pocket watch. "Well, as much as I'd love to crack this strange little chestnut, I've got a busy day." As he said it, an appointment book appeared, floating in the air in front of the older man, then it opened itself and flipped to a spot near the back. Rockefeller consulted the book, then nodded. "It's been an interesting experience, Lieutenant Pak," he said, extending his hand again.

Danny shook the man's hand and the moment it was over, the sorcerer evaporated into thin air.

"Good luck with your case, Lieutenant," his disembodied voice said, then it too faded away.

Danny looked around the shop, then shook his head.

"Sorcerers."

The paperwork Danny had so deftly avoided earlier, by going to a crime scene and then lunch, was still waiting for him when he returned to his desk. He spent a few minutes transcribing his notes on the art shop into a new case file before starting in on the rest.

"I figured you would have come to see me when you got back," Callahan's voice interrupted him sometime later.

Danny looked up to find the captain in his doorway, holding a thick folder. The top job seemed to agree with the man, because he looked rested and energetic despite having put on a few pounds since his elevation.

"Sorry," Danny said, setting his pencil aside and sitting back in his chair. "It's been a busy day."

"How did it go with Rockefeller?" Callahan asked, stepping into the office and dropping into one of the chairs in front of Danny's desk.

"He confirmed that the blob of paint on the floor used to be a person," Danny said. "Though he couldn't say if it was the missing proprietor. I told Crenshaw to go to the man's home and see if anyone knows where he might be, then track his movements for yesterday."

Callahan nodded sagely.

"If it was Limelight that did this to him," Danny went on, "that information should give us some idea of where to start looking for it."

Callahan tossed the folder he'd been holding onto Danny's desk with a heavy plop.

"This is everything I have on the Limelight case," he said. "The feds cut me out pretty early, but Lockerby kept me up to speed with their investigation."

Danny picked up the folder and paged through it.

"I reviewed it earlier," Callahan went on. "As near as I can tell, there were only two people who knew how to make Limelight. The first was the alchemist who invented it, Guy Rushton. According to Alex, he's been in a rubber room at Bellevue for years."

Danny scribbled that detail down in his notebook.

"If he was locked up, who was making the Limelight last spring?"

"An upscale alchemist named Olivia Thatcher," Callahan said. "Alex didn't know what happened to her, so you'll have to do some legwork, but we know the Limelight affected her mind like it did Rushton's. She's probably in the same wing at Bellevue."

"All right," Danny said, noting that down as well.

Callahan got up from the chair and headed for the hall.

"Make this your top priority, Danny," he said, turning back as he reached the door. "If someone is making Limelight again, you need to catch them before things get out of hand."

"Understood," Danny answered.

"And this time, Lieutenant," Callahan said with a half-smile. "keep me in the loop."

The captain headed back toward the elevator that would take him up to his office on the tenth floor, and Danny turned his attention to the folder. He didn't relish crawling through it looking for obscure details, but for the moment he didn't have to. Callahan had given him a lead to follow, so he decided to start with that.

A quick call to Bellevue Hospital revealed that Guy Rushton was still a patient there and that, after the last Limelight incident, he wasn't allowed visitors of any kind. Unfortunately, the hospital hadn't heard of Olivia Thatcher, so Danny was forced into the folder to locate her information.

According to the captain's notes, Olivia had run a high-end alchemy shop near the core called The White Rose. The Brothers Boom had blown it up during their notorious crime spree. Callahan's notes suggested that they'd been looking for Limelight.

Danny tried the number listed for Olivia Thatcher, but it had been disconnected. Digging through the file a bit more, he finally came across the name Reginald Andrews. Andrews was listed on one of the lease documents for the space that The White Rose had occupied. When Danny called the number for Reginald, a woman answered.

"I'm looking for Reginald Andrews," Danny said. "Is this his number?"

"That's my husband," the woman replied, her voice smooth and perky. "He's at work right now, though."

"Can I have his work number?" Danny asked. "It's kind of important."

"What's this about?" she asked.

"My name is Lieutenant Pak," Danny said. "I'm with the NYPD and I'm trying to track down the whereabouts of a woman named Olivia Thatcher. I believe she and Mr. Andrews were in business together."

There was a pregnant pause at the other end of the line.

"Olivia is Reggie's sister," the woman said at last. "But...well, you'd better talk to Reggie."

She gave Danny the phone number of a law firm with a core address and hung up before Danny could thank her. Danny called the firm, but the secretary who answered the phone insisted that Mr. Andrews was in a meeting and couldn't be disturbed.

"Have him call me at his earliest convenience," Danny said, after giving the girl his number. She promised to tell her boss and hung up.

Danny set the phone back in its cradle, then steepled his fingers in front of him. Something about the reaction of Reginald Andrews' wife had been off. She'd claimed that Olivia was her sister-in-law, but the mention of the woman's name spooked her somehow.

There wasn't anything he could do at this point but wait to hear from Andrews, so with a sigh, he opened Callahan's file and began to read. Twenty minutes later his phone rang, and Danny scooped it up with enthusiasm.

"That was fast," he said to himself.

When the phone connected, however, it wasn't Reginald Andrews but rather the Central Office switchboard operator.

"You have a call from Detective Miller," she said in a bored voice.

"Put him through."

"Boss?" the detective asked when the line connected. Paul Miller was another of Danny's detectives, a hard-working man who'd come to New York from California. His close rate for cases was decent and his reports were always thorough.

"What is it, Detective?"

"Well, sir...that is, I don't," he stuttered. "I think you'd better come down and have a look at this."

"I'm a little busy," he said, hiding his exasperation. "What is it?"

"I'm standing in the lobby of the New York Public Library," Miller said. "And you aren't going to believe this, but one of the stone lions out front got up and attacked a taxi cab."

Any other day, Danny would have accused his man of drinking on the job. Today, however, he just sighed and stood up.

"I'll be there in fifteen minutes," he said.

When Danny piloted his '27 Ford Coupe up to the sidewalk in front of the library, a significant crowd had already gathered. He wasn't surprised since right in front of him was a taxi with its hood caved in. A grey stone lion stood by the front of the car with a bit of fender clenched in its teeth and its massive front paw on the car.

"Well, there's something you don't see every day," Danny said.

"Lieutenant," Miller called out to him as he exited his car. "Over here."

Danny pushed his way through the gawkers until he reached a clear area around the cab, maintained by several uniformed policemen. Up close, the image of the stone lion tearing a chunk out of the taxi was almost comical.

"Okay," Danny said, not taking his eyes off the surreal scene. "What's the story here?"

Miller flipped open his notebook and checked his notes. He was an earnest young man still in his twenties and his handsome face tended to set people at ease. That usually translated to them telling him more than they otherwise might.

"Well, sir," he said with a shake of his head. "It's pretty much what you see. About an hour ago this lion got up from its pedestal." He turned and indicated the massive granite plinth where the lion usually rested. "It walked down the stairs, then jumped out into the road and took a chunk out of this cab before it stopped moving."

Danny looked around, spotting a thin man in working clothes sitting on sidewalk with his head in his hands.

"That the cabbie?" he asked.

"Yes, sir," Miller replied. "He's a bit shell-shocked at the moment. The woman in his cab went into hysterics, so we sent her to the hospital."

Danny looked around, then sighed. When he'd gotten the call from Miller, he'd had a vague hope that this was some kind of elaborate prank. Now that he was standing in front of the wrecked cab and the triumphant lion, he had to admit that this looked like another Limelight case.

"Damn it," he swore under his breath. Callahan was not going to like this. "Here's what I want you to do," he said to Miller. "Get a dozen more officers down here and push this crowd back. Did you take the cabbie's statement?"

Miller nodded.

"Good," Danny said. "Once the officers get here, go down to the hospital and get a statement from the passenger. Were there any other witnesses?"

"Nobody who stuck around," Miller said.

"All right, get going," Danny said. He waited until Miller was on his way to a radio car before heading up the stairs and into the library. A bank of wooden phone booths stood just to the right of the doors, and Danny took the first available one.

"Callahan," the captain's voice came through the phone once his call connected.

"It's Danny. You'd better call Rockefeller back."

There was a surprised pause, so Danny explained about the lion and the cab.

"Damnation," Callahan growled. "I hoped whatever happened at that art store was going to be an isolated incident."

"It sure looks like someone's making Limelight again," Danny said, "or else they found a stash the Feds missed."

"Either of those is bad," Callahan said. "We're lucky no one was killed this time. I'll see if I can get Rockefeller out there, but who knows how long that will take. Just sit tight."

Danny promised that he would, then hung up and headed for the front doors.

"Here you are," Rockefeller's voice assaulted him when he emerged onto the stone landing. The old sorcerer was standing just a few steps down, leaning against the empty plinth where the lion used to rest. "Are you always late to crime scenes?"

"I was talking to Captain Callahan," he said. "He's supposed to call you, but I guess that's not necessary."

"I heard about this on the radio and anticipated your need," the sorcerer said with a wily grin. "Now, tell me what happened here... beyond the obvious."

Danny recounted the story that Detective Miller had given him.

"That's the most ridiculous thing I've ever heard," Rockefeller said once Danny finished. "Who would animate a stone lion to attack a taxi? What would be the point? Were they trying to kill the woman in the back?"

"Unlikely," Danny said. "This stone is at least twenty yards from the street. It would take the lion time to move down to the street. Whoever brought the statue to life—"

"Animated it," Rockefeller countered. "It wasn't alive, it was just given motion. Bringing it to life is something that's quite beyond magic."

"Okay," Danny said, stifling a sigh. "Whoever animated it wouldn't have been able to see an approaching taxi from here. It seems more likely that the attack was random."

Rockefeller thought about that and gave Danny an appraising look.

"I wondered about you, you know," he said. "I figured for an Oriental like you to make Detective, much less Lieutenant, you must either be well connected, or good at your job. Nice to know it's the latter rather than the former. I hate politics and nepotism."

Danny wasn't sure how to respond to that, so he chose not to.

"Is this something a sorcerer could do?" he asked.

"I suspect so," the old sorcerer said, "but it seems like a prank. Childish. Not something one of us would do."

That was a lie and Danny knew it. Sorcerers had a reputation for doing weird and flashy magical things whenever the mood took them. Of course, they always hung around afterward so everyone knew who had done it. That meant Rockefeller was probably right, and this wasn't the work of a sorcerer.

"You've got me curious," Rockefeller said, starting down the stairs toward the wrecked cab.

"Curious?" Danny said, hurrying to catch up. "About what?"

"Whether or not I could do this," he said.

"You just said a sorcerer could do it," Danny pointed out.

"And I stand by it," the sorcerer said. "But just because someone could do it, doesn't mean I know how they did it."

Danny wasn't sure that made a lot of sense and he said so.

"For the lessers, alchemists and runewrights, magic is a science," he explained. "You use certain ingredients in certain ways and presto, magic."

"And that's not how it works for sorcerers?"

Rockefeller shook his head.

"For us," he said with a sweeping gesture of his hand, "magic is art. We don't have rote ways to use it, we think about what we want to happen and, in our minds, we figure out how to make it happen."

"That would mean every sorcerer in the world uses magic differently," Danny said.

"Of course. That's why we all specialize in different things. I could probably create cold disks like Sorsha or electricity like Barton, but it would be different for me. We tend to specialize in the things that come easiest to us."

"What comes easy for you?" Danny asked. He knew about Rockefeller, of course. Before he got his magic, he'd been one of the wealthiest, most powerful industrialists in the world, building his company, Standard Oil, into one of the biggest on earth. Since then, he was responsible for the crawlers, buses that skittered about on legs of blue energy. He and Barton had even collaborated to make sky crawlers.

They were just like their land-bound brethren, but they ran along elevated rails with purple energy legs.

"I make gizmos mostly," Rockefeller said, running his hand along the mane of the stone cat. "So far the only thing that's really caught on are the crawlers."

"Why is that?" Danny asked before thinking better of it.

"Power. Magical devices require magical power. I can put power into them, of course, just like other sorcerers do to make charms, but that will usually run out pretty quick. What I really need is a way to power my creations over the long term."

That actually made sense to Danny. The street level crawlers only worked when they could syphon electricity from Empire Tower, and if they went too far into the outer ring, they'd stop working.

"Why not get power from Barton's wireless system?" he asked.

"I'd have to put Barton's wireless power receivers in everything for that to work," Rockefeller said, knocking on the stone lion with his knuckles. "Those are big and Barton charges too much for them. Besides, Barton's power network is only a reality here in Manhattan. I need a solution that works anywhere."

Danny started to ask another question, but Barton held up a warning finger. He reached out and tapped the lion on the nose.

"All right, Ginger," he said in the kind of voice one would use with a disobedient child. "You've had your fun, now go back to bed." He pointed up the stairs at the stone plinth.

The lion that had been solid stone a moment before shuddered and dropped the bit of fender in its mouth. The carved muscles rippled under its lithe body and its mouth opened, revealing a row of teeth as big as Danny's thumb. The mane flowed around the statue's neck, and shook as if it were made of actual hair instead of being solid stone.

"Go on, now," Rockefeller admonished the beast.

The lion meowed at him and bumped the old sorcerer with its nose.

"All right," he said, scratching the enormous cat behind its ear. "Now off you go."

The lion leaned into the scratch for a moment, then bounded up the stairs to the plinth. When it reached it, the cat leapt up to the flat surface as if it weighed almost nothing. Turning three times, the cat finally settled down on its bed and stopped moving in the exact position it had been in when it was first installed.

"I thought you said sorcerers couldn't bring statues to life," Danny said.

Rockefeller laughed at that, a sound of genuine amusement.

"We can't," he said. "I just imagined the lion taking on the personality of a cat I used to own, and the magic did the rest."

"Well, thank you for putting the statue back."

"Anything else I can do for you, Lieutenant?"

Danny sighed and shook his head.

"Not unless you can tell me who let the lion loose in the first place."

"Sorry," Rockefeller said. "That's a bit outside my area of expertise."

Danny hated to admit it, but he was feeling the same way. He needed something to go on before someone burned down another nightclub.

3

THE FEDERAL GRIND

Senior Agent William "Buddy" Redhorn had a prime desk in the Manhattan field office of the FBI. Unlike most of the other desks, his faced right out a large window and afforded him a view of the core. He knew it was a good desk, but it had been over a year since he'd even seen it. When he made his way across the field office, he found his well-situated desk covered in files, evidence boxes, bric-a-brac, and dust.

"Great," he muttered to himself as he began to move the larger items from the desk to the floor. Since he'd been assigned to Sorsha Kincaid and her magical crimes task force, he'd been given a desk in the sorceress' swanky offices on the sixty-fifth floor of the Chrysler Building. In his absence, it seemed, his fellow agents had decided to use his desk as a storage area.

"You know, I heard you were back," a nasal voice with a Brooklyn accent said, "but I just had to see for myself."

Buddy turned to find Agent Seth Jones regarding him with a raised eyebrow and a sardonic smile.

"Finally get tired of following the Ice Queen around?" he said, his smile widening. "Who's going to carry her trousseau with you gone?"

Buddy felt a surge of anger, but he resisted the urge to close his hands into fists.

"Keep flapping your gums, Jones," Buddy growled at him. "You'll end up holding your teeth."

"Lay off him, Jonsey," another voice chimed in. "Redhorn here's a ladies' man, you see. He can't get enough at home, so he has to work with 'em too."

Buddy turned to find three more agents watching him. The tall one in the middle was Derrick Unger. He'd distinguished himself about five years back by breaking a smuggling ring for black market potions. Since then, he'd done nothing but ride the wave of his success. The agents who flanked him were Tucker and Vasquez, no account failures as agents who clung to Unger like pilot fish clung to a shark, each of them hoping for any scraps of glory that might fall their way by association. Buddy could have mopped the floor with all of them at once. Instead, he used that knowledge to calm his adrenal system.

"You run your mouth awful freely for a man who hasn't cracked a significant case in half a decade," Buddy said, turning his back on the man in a gesture of disdain.

"At least I'm not playing nursemaid to a couple of skirts," Unger sneered.

Buddy moved the last of the boxes off his desk before turning back to the trio.

"I guess I must be one hell of an agent then," he said, folding his arms across his chest as he leaned against his desk.

"How do you figure that?" Agent Jones said, trying to worm his way back into the conversation.

"I've solved five big cases in the time Unger here has been sitting on his ass," Buddy said with a nod toward the tall agent. "Including retrieving a stolen, top-secret device for the Navy, and preventing the assassination of a member of the President's cabinet. And according to Agent Unger here, I did all that while serving as a nursemaid."

Agent Unger's face screwed up into a look of fury while his hangers-on looked uncertain.

"I heard that was all thanks to the Ice Queen and her boyfriend," Jones said with a sneer.

"You mean the woman I'm supposedly playing nursemaid to...and a private dick?" Buddy chuckled. "You can't have it both ways," he went on. "Either I'm shepherding a bunch of incompetents, in which case I'm some kind of genius, a super-agent...or the ladies on my team are actually good at their jobs." He glared at Agent Jones, then swept his gaze over to Unger and his posse. "So, which is it?"

Agent Unger's face had gone red, and he'd balled up his fists. Buddy leaned back just enough to put him outside Jones' reach. If he wanted to take a swing, he'd have to move, and Buddy would have plenty of time to counter that.

"You listen here," Unger said through clenched teeth, "you—"

"That's enough," a quiet but firm voice interjected. "I believe all you men have work."

Unger's anger vanished and a smile as fake as a three-dollar bill blossomed across his broad face.

"No problem, Director," he said in an oily voice. "Just welcoming Buddy here back to the fold."

He turned and headed back across the open bullpen with his pilot fish in tow. Not wanting to call any more undue attention to himself, Agent Jones had withdrawn, unnoticed, while Unger was speaking.

"How are you, Buddy?" the newcomer asked, extending his hand.

"Director Stevens," Buddy said, taking his hand.

Stevens ran the Manhattan field office of the Federal Bureau of Investigation. He was taller than Buddy with pronounced cheekbones in a thin, clean-shaven face, and sharp, intelligent eyes. A mass of curly hair seemed to spill across the top of Steven's head, shining a coppery red. It was clear to Buddy that the director was in need of one of his regular haircuts again.

"I got a note this morning that you were going to be here for a few days," Stevens said genially. "Is something the matter?"

"No, sir," Buddy said. "Miss Kincaid is out of town for a week or two. The D.C. field office called and wanted her to consult on a case they picked up. The murder of that senator."

Stevens nodded sagely.

"I read about that in the paper," he said. "Nasty business."

"Anyway," Buddy went on, "with Miss Kincaid gone, I figured I'd come back here and catch up on some overdue paperwork."

"And maybe catch a case to work on while Sorsha's gone?" He gave Buddy a conspiratorial wink.

"Well," Buddy said in an offhand manner. "If an interesting case were to come up, I wouldn't object to helping you out, Director. As long as you don't mind my paperwork being late."

"Isn't doing paperwork the reason you have a trainee?"

Buddy chuckled at that. A lot of agents in his position would offload everything they didn't want to do on a junior agent, especially a woman. Buddy had other aims, however. He wasn't thrilled to get a female from the Bureau's pilot program, but he absolutely refused to do anything less than his best training her. It had been a rough ride, to be sure, but he'd managed to mold Aissa Mendes into a capable, reliable agent.

"She's down in the records vault going over some cold cases," he said with a grin. "I want to see if she can find anything the filing agents missed."

"Her probationary period is winding up," Stevens said. "What's your take on her?"

"She'll be ready."

Stevens gave him an appraising look, then just shrugged.

"If you say so, I'll take you at your word," he said.

"You didn't stop by to ask me about Agent Mendes," Buddy said, certain now that Stevens had an agenda.

"No," Stevens said with a sigh, "I didn't. A matter of some...delicacy has come up and I need someone I can trust to see it through."

"You know you can count on me, sir."

"Understand, Buddy, this case could blow up in your face. Governments are involved and there's a real risk of an international incident."

Buddy searched his memory, but he hadn't heard of anything big and embarrassing happening on the world stage.

"This has to do with the government of Brunei," Stevens went on. "About five years ago, the daughter of the sultan married the grandson of a famous sculptor named Jamal Kahar. Since then, the Sultan has bought up all Kahar's work, claiming that they're national treasures."

"Okay," Buddy said, not sure where the Director was going.

"One of the remaining sculptures belongs to an American named Trevor Hardwick. He bought it when he was in Brunei on business a few decades ago."

"And you think the Sultan wants it stolen?"

"Not at all," Stevens said. "The Sultan made Hardwick an offer to buy it and Hardwick agreed, but with one condition. According to the terms of the sale, Hardwick will only relinquish the sculpture upon his death."

"Did someone murder him?" Buddy asked, still not understanding where the director's story was going.

"No," Stevens said again. "But Mr. Hardwick's health has been failing for months, and he decided to turn over the statue to a representative of the Sultan before he dies. Right now, the statue is being displayed at the Devereaux Gallery — it's a private museum in the inner ring. Hardwick wants to turn over the statue as soon as its exhibition at the museum is over."

Buddy decided not to offer any guesses at this stage, but the details of this case were getting complex, so he took out his pad and started making notes.

"The statue in question is called the Jade Phoenix," Stevens explained, "and it was stolen from the Devereaux Gallery last night."

Okay, now it makes sense.

"So," Buddy summarized, "if the statue isn't found, old Mr. Hardwick can't give it to the government of Brunei. They'll blame Hardwick or the city, or maybe even the U.S. for its loss and that will be a P.R. mess no matter how you slice it."

"Just so," Stevens said.

"And I expect," Buddy went on, "that the FBI agent in charge of the case is going to look like a bumbling incompetent if the statue isn't found." It wasn't a question, but rather a statement of fact.

Stevens nodded.

"You don't have to take this, Buddy," he said in a low voice. "I can give it to Unger. He might even pull off a miracle and solve it."

"But you don't want a fall guy, you want this solved," Buddy guessed.

Stevens sighed, then looked around to see if they could be overheard.

"There's more to it than that," he said in a voice that was little more than a whisper. "Someone high up in the Bureau is pushing hard for me to get rid of Sorsha. In fact, I've been getting rumblings out of Washington that someone wants to shut down the whole magical cases task force. They want Agent Mendes out as well."

Buddy Redhorn had been an Agent for over two decades and he liked to think that nothing surprised him anymore. That said, he just couldn't wrap his head around what the director had said.

"We do good work," he protested. "We've stopped no less than three outright attacks on New York by foreign agents, who would want us shut down?"

"I can think of a few names," Stevens said, in a manner that told Buddy that he knew very well who was behind the move, but wasn't going to say.

"What's their reason?" Buddy asked.

"There have been some stories in the news, both here and in D.C. that are claiming Alex Lockerby is the one behind the task force's success."

"You know that's bunk," Buddy growled, his fists clinching involuntarily at the suggestion.

Director Stevens fixed him with a hard look.

"Of course I know it," he growled. "But knowing it and being able to prove it are two different things. Right now the only thing I can do is make sure that you and your protégé don't go down with Miss Kincaid if someone above me makes a decision."

Buddy nodded sagely.

"So if I find this missing statue, Agent Mendes and I get to keep our jobs," he said.

"And if you don't..."

"If we don't," Buddy sighed, "then we'll be forced to resign, and you won't have to fire us."

"That's about the shape of it," Stevens said. "So, do you want this case or not?"

Buddy thought about it for a long moment. He hadn't even been to the crime scene or talked to Hardwick, the statue's owner. For all he knew the statue could be on a boat or on a plane by now. Then again, someone in the Bureau was gunning for him, and not just him, but Mendes too. The thought that some overpaid desk jockey would end her promising career before it started because of her sex, or for some other stupid political reason, really burned him. The hand holding his notepad was clenched so hard he could feel his heartbeat in his fingertips. With an effort of will, he opened his hand and focused his mind.

"We'll take it," he said at last. "I'll show whoever it is that wants me out that he'll have to do better than some hack newspaper articles and innuendo."

Director Stevens took a deep breath and let it out slowly.

"I figured you'd say that. It goes without saying that the entire field office is at your disposal. Take anyone or anything you need, just find that statue."

He offered his hand and Buddy shook it.

"Yes, sir," he said.

The Devereaux Gallery was housed in a stately brick building on East 33rd just down from Lexington Avenue. It was mostly indistinguishable from the commercial buildings around it, except it had bars on its lower windows and a brass plaque on the wall above the door.

"This is it," Buddy confirmed, reading the gallery's address from his notebook.

Agent Aissa Mendes piloted the Bureau-issued grey sedan over to the curb and set the brake. She wore a man's suit, complete with slacks and a vest, though the latter had been specially cut to accommodate her substantial bosom.

"You want me to take statements?" she asked as they both exited the car.

Buddy shook his head as he waited for her to come around the car to the sidewalk.

"This might be touchy," he said. "Let's examine the crime scene first, then we'll interview the staff."

Buddy turned and led the way inside. The foyer of the Devereaux museum was sumptuous, with marble floors and columns that led up to a vaulted ceiling. Cut glass chandeliers hung down, gleaming and sparkling as they cast their yellowish light around the room. As Buddy stepped inside, he was met by a slender man in a silk suit. He had a worried look on his face, but no lines that would indicate it was his usual expression.

"Are you from the FBI?" he asked in a pleasant, sturdy voice.

Buddy got the impression this man wasn't sure what to do, and it was a foreign sensation to him. Everything about the man screamed that he wanted to take charge; he simply didn't know how to do that.

"Agent Redhorn," Buddy said, holding up the thick square of leather that had his official badge pinned to it. "This is Agent Mendes. We were told you had a robbery here, something of significant importance."

Buddy knew more than that, of course, but he always found it was better to let people tell you their troubles from the start. There were often important details left out of official reports.

"You could say that, yes," the man said. "I'm William Devereaux — my family founded this museum."

"Are you the curator?" Buddy asked.

"We don't have an official curator," Devereaux said, "but I'm responsible for getting the exhibits, so I guess I'm your man."

Buddy took out his notepad and began scribbling as William Devereaux related pretty much the same story Director Stevens had told him. The statue known as the Jade Phoenix had been on display in a room at the rear of the building and, at precisely twelve twenty-five the previous night, it had been stolen.

"How do you know it was stolen exactly then?" Mendes asked, taking notes as well.

"We have three night guards here in the museum," Devereaux said. "The man on the main floor reported hearing glass breaking just as he'd registered at the station in the back of the paintings gallery. I checked the watchman clock he carried, and it confirmed that he was at the station at precisely twenty-five minutes past midnight."

"Do all your guards carry watchman clocks?" Buddy asked.

"Of course," Devereaux said. "The objects on exhibit here are owned by private collectors, who loan them to us. They wouldn't do that if they thought our security was anything other than top-notch."

"Is it possible one or more of your guards was in on the theft?"

William Devereaux gave Buddy a withering look, but there was something in his eyes that said he was worried about exactly that.

"I don't see how," he said at last. "They're locked inside the building at night and there's no way out. The doors were all locked when I arrived."

"They called you when they discovered the theft?" Aissa asked.

"Yes, and the police," he added hastily.

"Could they have passed the statue out a window?" Buddy asked. "Maybe through the bars, or lowered it down from an upper window?"

Devereaux shook his head.

"None of the windows here open," he said. "We have cold boxes and radiators in every room to control the temperature."

Buddy turned to his junior agent.

"I know," she said before he could speak. "Go make sure all the windows are shut and unbroken."

She hurried off, the mass of curly brown hair atop her head flying.

"Now, if you don't mind," Buddy said to Devereaux, "I'd like to see the room where the statue was kept."

The museum owner led him through the large central gallery to a room filled with glass cases and stone pedestals. Inside the various cases were all manner of small statuary and busts of famous people. Buddy recognized Ben Franklin and Mark Twain. The statues were of everything imaginable, including animals, flowers, mythological creatures, and even a few buildings. An exquisitely detailed model of Empire Tower had been carved out of some kind of smoky crystal, and there were several, much smaller, versions of Michelangelo's David.

In the center of the room was a credenza made of cherry wood and inlaid with strips of green copper and bamboo. Atop it were a round glass dome that covered a flower that looked to be made of pure gold, and a larger case without a cover. The reason the second case had no cover was immediately obvious, as the shattered remains of it littered the marble floor.

"Is this the Jade Phoenix?" Buddy asked, picking up a picture of a green statue from a stack of programs beside the case.

"Yes, that's it."

The statue was of a tree branch with two birds perched on it. The entire piece had been rendered in exquisite detail and Buddy could hardly help fancying that the birds were about to hop off their perch and take flight.

"They look like robins to me," he said. "Why is it called a phoenix?"

Devereaux just shrugged at that.

"Artistic license, I suppose."

"What is the Jade Phoenix worth?"

"We had it insured when we added it to our collection," Devereaux said. "The appraisal came back at sixty thousand dollars."

That's a lot of motivation to steal it, Buddy thought, staring at the picture on the program card. Something about the photograph pulled at Buddy's attention and he squinted at it as he held it close.

"When was this statue moved into this room?" he asked.

"It's always been displayed in this room," William Devereaux replied.

"Then why does the wall look different in this picture than it does now?"

"Oh," Devereaux said, seeming to suddenly understand Buddy's question. "Our water main broke last month," he said. "It flooded this room and part of the central gallery. We'd only just gotten it fixed last week."

"So you had workmen here, in this room, making repairs?"

"Of course."

"And where were all these statues while that was happening?"

Devereaux looked flummoxed at that question.

"Why, they were returned to their owners during the renovation," he said. "We only just got them all back yesterday."

Buddy's mind was running overtime with this information. Workmen coming in and out of the museum made the perfect cover for a heist, though usually in that case, the heist would have happened during the restoration. That couldn't be though, if all the valuable objects were returned to their owners.

"Where is this water main?" he asked. "The one that broke."

Devereaux pointed toward the corner of the room.

"It's behind that wall," he said. "There's a maintenance door just there."

Now that Devereaux was pointing it out, Buddy could see the faint line of a concealed door.

"I think I want to take a look at your maintenance closet," he said.

"Oh, no one could have gotten out through there," Devereaux said. "It's just a crawl space for the water pipes, and that door is locked at all times."

Buddy gave Devereaux a patient smile.

"I think I'd like to take a look just the same."

4

HIDDEN THINGS

Buddy Redhorn clenched his teeth as he examined the back of the maintenance room's access door. When he heard that the room where the Jade Phoenix was kept had been rebuilt over the previous three weeks, he thought he had the theft figured. One of the workers saw an opportunity and rigged it so they could hide in the maintenance area, then steal the statue and return before the guards arrived.

It was a perfectly good plan too, except the maintenance room was more of a maintenance closet, with barely enough room for one person to squeeze in among the water pipes and the building's main shut-off valve. Additionally, the concealed door to the room was locked with a key and there was no keyhole on the inside. Anyone hiding in the tiny space would find themselves locked in. And then there was the pièce de résistance, there was no way out of the maintenance room other than the locked door that led into it. The room was up against the outside of the building and the brickwork hadn't been disturbed during the rebuilding.

"Damnation," he growled.

"Same here," Agent Mendes called from behind the water main. "These bricks are solid."

"All right," Buddy sighed. "Come on out of there."

"I'm sorry, Agent Redhorn," Devereaux said with an apologetic look. "There's just no way anyone could have used that space to perpetrate this theft."

Buddy hated to admit it as he offered Agent Mendes a hand to help her out of the little space, but Devereaux was right. Once Mendes was free, Buddy started to shut the door but stopped as the light from the room focused down to something sparkling under one of the pipes.

"Did you step in any of that broken glass?" he asked Agent Mendes as he knelt down to reach under the pipe.

"No."

"Then where did this come from?" he asked, carefully picking up a pointy shard of glass and holding it out so Mendes and Devereaux could see it.

"It's probably left over from when the work was done," William said.

Buddy leaned down again and looked under the pipes.

"Everything else is clean. Looks like your construction crew cleaned up after themselves, so I ask again, where did this come from?"

"The thief stepped on it after he broke the glass case," Mendes said, "then tracked into the crawl space on their way out."

Buddy nodded at her, but Devereaux shook his head.

"But you saw for yourself," he protested, "there's no way out from in there. If you're right, then the thief should still be in there."

"You'd think that," Buddy agreed. "But an annoying private dick once told me that when you eliminate the impossible, whatever remains must be the truth. Someone tracked this shard into your maintenance space and it wasn't Agent Mendes or myself, because we stayed away from the broken glass."

William Devereaux looked confused then shook his head.

"But you've already looked in there," he said. "You didn't find anything. What do you propose to do now?"

Buddy raised an eyebrow and looked at Agent Mendes.

"We call the annoying private dick and have him take a look?" she suggested, not entirely sure.

"Exactly. Why don't you do that, he's bound to come running if you call. Tell him to bring his bag of tricks. Meanwhile," he said turning to William, "I want each of your night guards to show me their routes."

"I can't see any of them being involved in something like this," Devereaux protested.

"This case has international consequences, Mr. Devereaux," Buddy interrupted. "As far as I'm concerned, everyone is a suspect. So while we go to your guard room, why don't you tell me where you were between eleven last night and one this morning?"

Buddy cradled his head in his hands as he sat behind the elegant desk in William Devereaux's office. Back in the war, he'd been an army investigator. In that time, he'd heard all kinds of liars; men who stole from their brother soldiers, men who falsified their heroism, men who robbed the dead to line their pockets, and even men who lied to cover their own cowardice. He could always tell. Liars always gave themselves away if you talk to them long enough.

Which was the problem.

He'd interviewed all three of the Devereaux Gallery's night guards and they were either innocent men, or the best liars he'd ever come across. The gallery wasn't big enough for one of them to have perpetrated the theft without being discovered by the other two. That meant that they were all in it together, or they weren't involved. One man might be a good enough liar to fool him, but not all three.

"That bad?" Agent Mendes' voice interrupted his thoughts.

"The guards weren't involved," he said, finally admitting out loud what he already knew. He looked up, expecting to see Mendes with Lockerby in tow, but the man standing behind his junior agent was someone he'd never seen before. He was short with a bowler hat in one hand and a bag like the one Lockerby carried in the other. His face was earnest, with a downward pointed nose, a blond mustache, and his dark eyes were downcast as he shuffled nervously from foot to foot.

"Who's this?"

"Agent Redhorn," Mendes said, indicating the little man, "this is Mike Fitzgerald. He's Alex's protégé."

"Lockerby too busy for us?" Buddy asked. "Or is he on the outs with the boss again?"

"Neither, sir," Fitzgerald said. He had a high-pitched voice and the hint of an Irish accent. "Alex had to go out of town this morning with Mr. Barton."

"Did Agent Mendes tell you what we need?"

Fitzgerald bobbed his head in the affirmative.

"Yes sir." He held up the bag he carried. "If there's anything funny about that crawlspace, I'll find it for ya."

He seemed a bit apprehensive, but eager.

"Fine," Buddy growled, then turned to Agent Mendes. "Show him the room and stay with him."

Mendes nodded, then hustled Fitzgerald out as William Devereaux came in.

"Sorry to bother you, Agent Redhorn," he said, "but can I send the boys home now? They've been up all night, after all."

Buddy regarded Devereaux for a moment. He'd initially suspected the man of having a hand in the robbery, but his genuine concern for his employees went against that. If Devereaux had planned the robbery, he wouldn't have put any of his people under suspicion in the process.

"I'm done with them for the moment," he said. "Tell them not to take any sudden trips out of town."

"Right," he said, turning to leave.

"One more thing," Buddy asked, calling after the museum owner. "Can I see the insurance policy?"

"Of course," Devereaux said. "We carry a policy on every piece of art on loan to the gallery." He crossed to a file cabinet and opened a drawer, moving through the files with his fingers. After a moment, the pulled out a manilla folder and passed it over. "This is the policy," he said.

Buddy flipped the folder open and found a small stack of papers that had been secured together. The header of the first page bore the name of Callahan Brothers Property over an address in the Core.

"Does Callahan Brothers carry all your policies?"

Devereaux nodded, then turned and left.

Buddy paged through the policy, skimming as he went. He wasn't as well versed in insurance forms as some, but this one seemed pretty standard. If the statue was stolen, Trevor Hardwick, as the owner, would be recompensed for the value of the Phoenix at the time the policy was written. According to the document, that was sixty thousand dollars.

Something about that didn't track. From what Director Stevens told him, Hardwick was simply giving the statue away to the government of Brunei.

"Why would anyone just give away something worth that kind of money?" Buddy asked himself. It was a question he would have to ask Trevor Hardwick.

"Boss?" Agent Mendes' voice interrupted his thoughts.

He looked up to find her poking her head in through the doorway. She wore a barely concealed smirk, the corner of her mouth tugging upward as she fought against a grin.

"You really need to take a look at this," she said.

The statuary room looked just like it had when Buddy arrived that morning. The ring of broken glass still littered the floor in front of the empty display case where the jade statue had been. The old doctor's bag Mike Fitzgerald had been carrying sat on the credenza next to the empty case, but there was no sign of Lockerby's protégé.

Buddy regarded Agent Mendes.

"What am I looking at?"

Mendes just smiled and walked over to the hidden door that concealed the maintenance closet. She reached down to the indented edge that served as a handle and tugged on the door. It clicked as the locking bolt kept it closed.

"Okay, Mike," she said, then stood back.

There were several loud clacks and a moment later the door swung open revealing the blond mustache and smiling face of Mike Fitzgerald.

Now Buddy was impressed. He'd been sure that the door couldn't be opened from the inside.

"How?" he said.

"It's a trick door," Fitzgerald said, pointing to the inside panel where a piece of the woodwork appeared to be missing. "Watch."

He reached up, pressing his fingers against one of the wood slats, then he pulled it down, blocking the metal pin that kept the door closed. Next he slid a second piece in place to cover the hole.

"When you open this," Fitzgerald said, "it reveals the pin and you just pull it back with your finger while you push the door open."

Buddy nodded along as the little man opened the secret release again. It was an ingenious mechanism, one that would require very specific skills.

"How did you find that?"

Fitzgerald held up a small telescope mounted to a leather pad and offered it to Buddy.

"Put this over your right eye," he said.

As Buddy complied, Fitzgerald lit a small lamp that reminded Buddy of the kind men used in rail yards. When Fitzgerald shone the light from the lamp on the inside of the little door, Buddy could easily see the two moving boards. They seemed to shimmer a pale blue color against the rest of the wood.

"It's covered in a thin layer of graphite," Fitzgerald said. "That helps it slide."

Buddy reached out and pressed his fingers against one of the boards and, exerting a small amount of force, pulled it sideways. With the strange lens it was obvious.

"Okay," he said, handing the eye-telescope back. "What about getting out of that closet once the thief had the statue?"

"There's a vent fan in the back," Fitzgerald said.

"I remember. It's too small to escape through."

Lockerby's man grinned at him, turning the ends of his mustache up.

"There's a loose brick that pivots if ya push it in just the right place," he said. "Once it's out of the way, the entire fan swings out, big enough for even a fellow like you ta get through."

"I already tried it," Mendes said as Buddy turned to her. "It works just like he said."

Buddy nodded, turning to look at the broken display case. If the thief had opened the secret catch in the door before the guard came in, then moved as soon as the guard left, there would be more than enough time.

Move to the case, smash the glass, take the statue and get back to the crawlspace, he thought, running the scene in his mind. *Close the door, set the lock and wait. Once the guards discovered the theft, they'd begin searching the building. As soon as they're out of the room, open the secret exit and disappear.*

"Good work," he said to Mendes, then turned to Fitzgerald. "You, too."

"What now?" Mendes asked. "We know *how* the thief did it, but we're no closer to figuring out *who* did it."

To his credit, Buddy didn't allow himself to frown. Agent Mendes was a good agent, with good instincts, but every now and again she missed the obvious. He had hoped she would soon be ready to become an independent agent; he'd trained her well, but she still had a bad habit of impulsivity. She still spoke before thinking.

I need to work harder.

"I missed something," Mendes said, reading his hesitation, since he wore no expression.

Buddy allowed himself to smile this time as he looked to Mendes.

"And?"

Agent Mendes turned, sending her curly hair flying as she moved to the little door. Squatting down, she ran her hand around the opening left by the trick panels.

"This is..." she began, "theatric. Like some kind of a magic trick."

"Exactly like a magic trick," he said, nodding.

"There's no way this door was built by some random builder," she said. "This would have taken weeks of work by a master carpenter."

"And?" he prompted again.

"And someone could have snuck this door into the builder's supplies," she said, "but there's no way the builder didn't know about that escape hatch in the back wall." She looked up and gave him predatory smile. "The builder had to be in on it."

"Well done, Agent Mendes. I'd like to have a word with Mr. Devereaux's builder. Go ask him for the man's address, then call the police and have them pick him up. Meet me back as soon as you're done."

"Where are we going?"

"Someone planned this for weeks, maybe months, and it must have cost a fortune," he said by way of answer. "We're going to see Trevor Hardwick. Maybe whoever did all this tried to buy the statue before they decided to steal it."

5

SUSPECTS

The home of Trevor Hardwick was a three-story Victorian monstrosity that looked like it should have been owned by Boris Karloff. It was painted a dark blue that looked almost black, and ancient ivy clung to the walls, trellises, and eaves. Since it was early December, the grass was brown and dead, and the stalks of the rosebushes drooped. The effect made the entire property look as if it were decaying.

"You sure this isn't Lamont Cranston's place?" Mendes said as they mounted the porch. Clearly she was getting the same impression from the home.

"Don't make jokes in the field," Buddy said under his breath, doing his best to keep from smiling. "It isn't professional."

Trevor Hardwick's front door had a massive brass knocker in the shape of a lion with a heavy ring in its mouth. Buddy grabbed the ring and banged it against the strike plate, sending an echoing boom through the interior of the house.

He was about to knock again when the lock clacked as the bolt was drawn back. A moment later the door opened, and they were greeted by a slender, fussy-looking man in an expensive suit. He looked to be in his late forties with a long face and droopy skin that made him resemble a basset hound. The man's complexion was pasty, and he wore a look of disapproval that looked comfortable on his face.

Probably the way he always looks.

"May I help you?" he said after a moment to look them over. His accent was cultured, with a hint of fancy British, but Buddy could tell it was an affectation rather than a result of having lived in England.

"I'm Special Agent Redhorn of the FBI," Buddy said, holding up his badge. "This is my partner, Special Agent Mendes." He nodded to Mendes who held up her badge as well. "We'd like to speak to Mr. Hardwick about his missing statue."

The man at the door blanched, a reaction Buddy didn't expect in response to such a mundane request. The droopy man quickly mastered himself and his look of superior disdain returned.

"For a pair of investigators, you two are rather uninformed," he said.

"What's that supposed to mean?" Mendes growled, leaning slightly forward.

Buddy put a hand on her shoulder, and she immediately backed off. Her Latin temper was something that she had yet to master, but she was much better than when she first started working with him.

"You're absolutely right," Buddy said, taking command of the conversation. "We are rather uninformed." He pulled out his notebook and pencil, flipping the former open. "Let's start with you, what's your name?"

The man blanched again, this time at the thought of having his name written in an official notebook.

"I'm Brent Cooper," he said in an indignant voice. "I'm Mr. Hardwick's butler. And now that's out of the way, I'm afraid you cannot see my employer."

"Why not?" Buddy said, shifting the courteous smile on his face to something more predatory. Surprisingly, that didn't seem to have any effect on the jowly butler.

"Because in order to see Mr. Hardwick, you'd need a medium," Cooper answered. "The master died last night, no doubt after having a premonition about the Jade Phoenix being stolen."

"Trevor Hardwick is dead?" Buddy asked, trying to make sure he understood the officious butler correctly.

The butler nodded.

"I found him this morning when I went to wake the master," he said. "I don't know why you weren't informed. I telephoned the police. The coroner has already been here and collected the body."

That bit of information caught Buddy's attention.

"The police removed the body from the premises?" he asked.

"Yes," the butler said with no hesitation. "They said that in the case of such a wealthy and prominent man, they do an autopsy to ensure the death was entirely natural."

"Is there some reason to think Mr. Hardwick's death wasn't natural?" Mendes asked.

"Of course not!" Cooper almost shouted. "Mr. Hardwick had the cancer, he was a sick man. He's been on his deathbed for months."

"Being his butler, I'm sure you have the name of his doctor," Buddy said, giving the butler an easy smile.

"You don't trust me?" Cooper said with a sneer.

"Of course we do, Mr. Cooper," Buddy said with exaggerated collegiality. "But we have to fill out reports and Uncle Sam likes those reports to be accurate."

Cooper gave him a hard look, obviously judging whether or not he thought he could get away with telling Buddy to take his Jr. Agent and get out. After a moment the butler seemed to decide that discretion was the better part of valor and he stepped back, opening the door.

"Wipe your feet," he demanded as the pair entered. "I'll go fetch Mr. Hardwick's address book."

"Charming fellow," Mendes said with a grin, once Brent Cooper was safely out of earshot.

"Goes with the decor," Buddy noted.

The inside of Trevor Hardwick's house bore a striking resemblance to the outside. The wainscoting was mahogany, and the wallpaper a dreary blue. An ornate and overdone Art Nouveau cabinet stood against one wall with an equally ghastly hall tree opposite, complete with seat and mirror.

"You think it's a coincidence?" Mendes asked in a low voice. "Hardwick dying on the same night someone grabs his sixty-thousand-dollar statue?"

"Maybe," Buddy hedged, "we should check with the coroner once he's completed his autopsy."

"Do we go see Hardwick's doctor next?"

Buddy shook his head.

"First we check with the police," he said. "If they've found Devereaux's builder I want to talk to him first, otherwise we'll go see the doctor."

A moment later, Cooper returned with the address of a Doctor Neilson.

"There," he said, handing it over. "Now if that's all, I must ask you to leave. I have preparations to oversee for the Master's wake."

"There is one more thing," Buddy said, tucking the doctor's address into his coat pocket. "According to Mr. Devereaux, the museum returned the statue here while they were repairing the Gallery. I'd like to see where Mr. Hardwick kept it during the repairs, please."

"The master had the statue placed in his vault," Cooper said.

That struck Buddy as odd. A near-priceless statue that was part of a prized collection, yet Hardwick had chucked it in his vault as if it didn't matter.

Unless he was afraid someone was going to steal it.

"Mr. Hardwick didn't put it in his study or his bedroom?" Agent Mendes asked.

"No," Cooper said.

"Did he have reason to believe that it wasn't safe in this house?" Buddy asked.

"Of course not," Cooper said, aghast. "Why would you even suggest such a thing?"

"Did anyone offer to buy the Jade Phoenix, Mr. Cooper?" Buddy pressed on. "I mean after your employer decided to give it to the government of Brunei?"

The butler's outraged look turned to one of confusion and he seemed flustered.

"Mr. Hardwick has a rather extensive collection of art and sculpture," he said. "Offers to purchase one or more of his pieces came in almost weekly."

"We need to know who tried to buy the Jade Phoenix," Mendes said. "After he promised to give it away, that is."

"W-well," Cooper stuttered. "Any such requests would be filed with Mr. Hardwick's correspondence."

"And you have access to that?" Buddy prompted.

The butler sighed, which made his bassett hound face look even more mournful.

"Of course," he said in a put-upon voice. "Remain here and I will fetch them."

He disappeared into a back hallway again and returned after about a minute with a thin file folder in his hand.

"This is everything we received regarding the Jade Phoenix," he said, handing the folder to Agent Mendes. "Now I really must insist you leave; I have a house full of guests who will be here in a few hours."

Buddy held the butler's eye for a long moment, then smiled.

"Thank you, Mr. Cooper," he said. "The FBI appreciates your cooperation. I'll be in touch if I have any further questions."

He turned toward the door as the butler pulled it open.

"One more thing, Mr. Cooper," he said, turning back. "Who stands to inherit Trevor Hardwick's fortune?"

Cooper hesitated, his eyes downcast for a moment.

"The Master had no heirs," he said after a pause. "Most of his estate will go to charities of Mr. Hardwick's choice and much of his art collection is being donated to museums around the country."

"Who is handling the terms of the will?" Buddy asked.

"The firm of Billings, Andrews, and Milton handle the Master's legal affairs. There will be a reading of the will here as soon as the cause of the Master's death has been certified by the medical examiner."

Buddy thanked the man, then put on his hat and headed out, toward the street.

"What do you think?" Buddy asked Mendes once they were back in their car.

Mendes opened the folder containing the offers to buy the Jade Phoenix and paged through them.

"The butler is a little squirrelly," she said. "Something about him gave me the creeps."

Buddy nodded even though Mendes wasn't looking at him. Brent Cooper had been acting strangely.

"His boss just died, and he has to put together a wake for tonight," he said. "Not to mention he'll be looking for a new job soon. I imagine that's enough to frazzle anyone. Anything in the file?"

"Here's one on the letterhead of the German consulate," she said. "Someone named Otto Von Goring offered to buy the statue on behalf of the German government for eighty thousand dollars."

That didn't sound right, and Buddy searched his memory.

"I thought the statue was only worth sixty thousand."

Mendes shrugged.

"Seems like his government wanted it badly enough to overpay," she said. "My question is why? I mean what would Hitler want with a statue of a couple of birds?"

"I saw something in the Times about the Nazis buying up art from all over the world," he said. "Especially things with religious subject matter."

"I thought a phoenix was some kind of magical creature," Mendes said.

Buddy nodded.

"It's mythological," he confirmed. "They're supposed to burst into flames when they're old and be reborn out of their own ashes."

"How do you know things like that?" Mendes asked, giving him a side-eye stare.

"Reader's Digest."

Mendes continued to look at him as if she didn't believe him, then just shook her head.

"Still doesn't explain why the Nazis want this statue."

"Why does anyone in that file want it?" Buddy pushed back. "As much as I like painting Germans as the bad guys, I don't want to go off half-cocked. Is there anyone else in there that wants the Phoenix bad enough to overpay?"

Mendes chuckled at that as she began pulling pages out of the folder.

"Here's a movie mogul from California," she said. "Here's a museum curator from Chicago, a local businessman, a politician, and the president of the Oriental Culture Foundation. All of them offered more than the Phoenix is worth."

"Fine, we'll start with them," Buddy said as he pulled the car up to the curb in front of the Central Office of Police. "But first let's see if the police have picked up our crooked builder."

Agent Mendes expressed shock when the desk sergeant reported that the police had, in fact, picked up one Hubert Conners, the Devereaux Gallery's builder. Buddy gave her a stern look and she clammed up.

Most agents in the Bureau tended to think of themselves as above regular policemen. Agents like Tucker, Vasquez, and Unger were the worst of the lot, not even bothering to work with the local police. Buddy had learned to be an investigator in the army, starting off as an MP thanks to his size, and working his way up to an investigator with the CID. He'd learned the hard way that if you want to catch criminals and close cases, you had to use every resource available.

With the police, a little respect and courtesy went a very long way. He couldn't count the number of times a word of encouragement to a hard-working officer got him everything he needed and more.

"Thank you, Sergeant," he said to the officer behind the desk. "Where can we find Mr. Conners?"

The sergeant checked one of his many clipboards, then jerked his thumb at a bank of elevators in the corner.

"They're holding him in interrogation for you," the man said. "Fourth floor. Ask for Detective Nicholson."

Buddy thanked the man again and led Mendes to the elevator.

Once they were alone inside, he reminded her of his policy toward policemen and she blushed under the rebuke.

"Sorry," she said as the elevator car stopped at the fourth floor.

"Never give up a possible advantage for a moment of ego gratification," he said as they stepped out into a wide lobby. A reinforced door marked *Interrogation* occupied the wall opposite the elevator. To the right of the door was a long wooden counter with three armed officers behind it. Several chairs lined the wall beside the elevator door, no doubt for attorneys or relatives come to collect someone.

"Can I help you?" a thick-necked policeman said from behind the counter. His voice was calm, even friendly, but the man's posture and expression clearly stated that he was on guard.

Buddy pulled his FBI badge from the outside pocket of his coat and held it up.

"I'm Agent Redhorn, and this is my partner, Agent Mendes. Detective Nicholson is holding someone for us."

In a move reminiscent of the desk sergeant down on the ground floor, the man consulted a clipboard, then nodded at the man nearest the door.

"He's in room seven. Officer Glaser will show you the way and I'll call Detective Nicholson to meet you there."

An officer whom Buddy assumed to be Glaser picked up a heavy ring of keys and moved toward the reinforced door.

"This way," he said in a voice that sounded like he'd been smoking since his sixth birthday.

He opened the door with a large key, then led the way down a long hallway lined with doors. The interrogation rooms were set up in pairs, each with a number and a letter. Officer Glaser turned a corner and finally stopped beside a set of doors labeled 7A and 7B.

"You can wait in there," he said, pointing to 7B.

Buddy thanked the man and he and Agent Mendes went into the observation room. It was smaller than the actual interrogation room next door, visible through a sheet of one-way glass, but it was only designed for a few people.

"So that's Conners," Mendes said, peering through the glass. She spoke softly so as not to alert the man in the adjacent room that he was being watched.

The man in question was younger than Buddy would have thought, early thirties at best, with bushy dark hair he'd parted on the left, a tanned face, and blue eyes. His hands were rough with the scars and scabs of dozens of small cuts covering them, a mute testament to his work with wood.

Before Buddy could comment, however, the door opened and a paunchy, middle-aged man in a rumpled suit entered. There were a few bread crumbs clinging to his tie and a small smear of mustard in the corner of his mouth, evidence that he'd abandoned his lunch to be here.

"Detective Nicholson?" Buddy asked. When the man nodded, he let Agent Mendes introduce herself, then turned to the man behind the glass. "What can you tell me about him?"

Disheveled as he was, Nicholson noticed Mendes staring at his face and he quickly pulled out his handkerchief and wiped his mouth. Next he took a file folder from under his arm and opened it.

"Hubert Conners," he read. "Thirty-two, lives alone but has a reputation as a bit of a ladies' man. He started his own business as a general contractor five years ago; before that he was employed at a cabinetry shop. We picked him up at the address you gave us, which was his office."

Nicholson closed the file as he finished and offered it to Buddy.

"Do we know anything about his personal life?" Mendes asked as Buddy flipped open the folder.

"Not much, I'm afraid," Nicholson said in an easy, professional voice. If he had any misgivings reporting to a woman, they didn't show. "He was surprised when we picked him up, of course, but he didn't protest very much. They always protest," he added with a conspiratorial look.

"You think he wasn't all that surprised to be arrested?" Mendes went on.

"That's my take," Nicholson said. "I don't know why you folks want him, but he's obviously got something to hide."

Buddy kept himself from smiling as Mendes picked the Detective's brain. After all, the man had spent time with Conners and she hadn't, so she was catching up before going into the box, just like Buddy had taught her.

He scanned the page of details inside the folder. It listed Conners' home address as well as his business, along with the name of his secretary and the two men who worked for him as job foremen. There were a few of Detective Nicholson's personal observations on the office where they'd found Conners which were insightful, but not helpful.

At the bottom were three names, The Devereaux Gallery, The Astor Hotel, and Dante.

"What's this at the bottom?" Buddy asked.

"Your boy in there is pretty fond of his clientele," Nicholson said. "He had pictures of the work he did for each of them up on his wall."

With clients like Devereaux and the Astor, Buddy wasn't sure why Conners was robbing museums. He had to be making a good income.

"All right," he said, closing the folder and handing it to Mendes. "I guess we should go talk to Mr. Conners. I'll take the lead," he said to Nicholson. "The evidence at the Gallery says Conners helped out with the theft, but it's circumstantial. I need him to give me something, so I'm going to push him. If he starts getting scared, I want you to jump in and suggest ways he can help himself. Real friendly like."

Nicholson nodded and reached for the doorknob.

"Dante?" Mendes said from behind them. She stood looking into the open folder.

"Agent Mendes?" Nicholson said, not understanding her statement.

"Dante," she said again. "As in Sim Sala Bim? That Dante?"

Buddy had no idea what she was talking about but before he could say so, Detective Nicholson started nodding.

"Yeah," he said. "I guess Conners worked for him too. He had a big color advertisement for him up on his office wall."

Mendes grinned and turned to Buddy.

"Dante," she said, clearly reading the look of confusion on his face, "is one of the most famous stage magicians since Houdini died, and Conners worked for him."

"Why does that matter?" Nicholson said.

"Because, Detective," Buddy said, sporting a grin to match his junior agent's, "what do you think a cabinet maker did for a stage magician?"

"Made magic boxes?" Nicholson said with a shrug.

"Exactly."

6

JADE

Danny resisted the urge to call Alex's office once he got finished with the case of the errant lion. Sherry had made it clear she didn't want him knowing that there might be more Limelight on the street.

He might not have a choice, however. If someone was making the alchemical drug again, they needed to be stopped, and the sooner the better.

Danny pulled his car up to the curb opposite the brownstone his friend shared with Dr. Ignatius Bell. Normally he would have just parked in front of the building itself, but there were already several cars parked there. What's more, the front door to the brownstone was open, something Danny could never remember seeing before.

As he exited his car, a burly man with no discernible neck and a pair of coveralls stepped out onto the stoop and lit up a cigarette. Danny was pretty sure that Dr. Bell was far more formidable than he appeared, but the sight of this strange man having the run of the brownstone set off his danger alarm.

As he set off across the street, Danny reached inside his jacket to make sure the snub-nosed police .38 was loose in his shoulder holster.

"Excuse me," he said, climbing halfway up the stairs to the landing where the man-mountain stood smoking. "Is Dr. Bell in?"

"Beat it, slant eyes," the man said after giving him a disdainful once-over. "The doc don't want to be disturbed."

Danny let the insult slide; it wasn't the first one he'd ever heard, though it was one of the golden oldies.

"I'm afraid I'm going to have to insist," he said with a grin.

"I told you to get lost, little man," no-neck growled, hauling himself up to his full, impressive height.

Danny had dipped into his side pocket as the man spoke and now came up with his police badge.

"That's Lieutenant Little-Man to you, meathead," he said, advancing on no-neck.

No-neck put up his hands in a gesture of peace and backed up as Danny approached.

"H-hey, I didn't mean nothin'," he said. "I didn't know you was a cop."

"What?" Danny said, grinning at the man's discomfort. "Didn't think a slant-eye could make it?"

"Uh," the man said, clearly not seeing an answer that would go well for him.

"You need to get with the times," Danny said, clipping his badge to the front of his coat. "It's nineteen thirty-seven in the greatest city in the world, anybody can be anything now."

"Look," no-neck said, his hands still raised and placating. "I don't want no trouble, it's just that the Doc said he didn't want to be disrupted."

Danny sighed and put his hand to his chin in a gesture of thoughtfulness.

"Nope," he said after a moment. "I just can't take your word for that. Now, are you going to tell me what's going on here, or do I need to drag you downtown?"

"I'm just here to move furniture," the man said, stepping back.

"Is that you I hear, Danny?" Dr. Bell's voice came from inside. A moment later the man himself stepped out onto the stoop.

"Hello, Doc," Danny said, a bit relieved that nothing untoward seemed to be going on. "What's all this?"

Dr. Bell wore a very British tweed suit with a vest and a gold watch chain that ran from the buttons to the pocket. His round face bore a wide, self-satisfied smile and he had a lit cigar clenched in his teeth.

"I'm having some work done," Bell said, taking the cigar out of his mouth. "Speaking of which," he said to no-neck, "you'd better get back to it."

"Sure thing, Doc," the big man said. "Sorry."

That last was directed at Danny and the workman crushed out the remains of his cigarette and headed inside. Bell watched him go for a moment, then turned back to Danny.

"It's time for me to renew the wards on this place and I'm trying something new," he explained.

"And you need muscle for that?" Danny chuckled.

"No," Bell said with an enigmatic look, "but my new method requires all the furniture to be removed from the house. It has to be totally empty, so these gentlemen are moving everything into my vault for safekeeping. I'll redo the runes tomorrow, then have the lads back to return everything to its rightful place."

"Sounds like a hassle," Danny said.

"Oh, it's like most things," Bell said with a shrug. "If it's worth doing, it's worth doing right. Besides, with Alex out of town, this was the perfect opportunity."

Danny did a double take at that.

"Alex is gone?"

Bell puffed on his cigar and nodded.

"Sherry informed me thus this morning," he said. "Apparently the Lightning Lord had business down in your nation's capital and he took Alex along."

"Oh," Danny sighed.

"I take it you need his assistance with a police matter," Bell said.

"Yeah," Danny nodded. With Alex out of the city, he'd need to find someone else who could look at his two crime scenes. Fortunately, help might not be as far away as he thought.

"I know you and Alex talk about his cases, Doc. Did he ever tell you anything about an alchemical drug called Limelight?"

Dr. Bell's eyebrows went up at that.

"Yes, as a matter of fact," he said. "I do hope this is a rhetorical question."

"I'm afraid not." Danny told Bell about his day, starting with the man of paint in Pete's Paints and ending with the library lion running into traffic. "Even if this Limelight stuff is a potent as Captain Callahan says, it sure seems like someone is making more of it."

Bell puffed on his cigar for a long moment while his thick, bushy mustache twitched.

"I dare say you're right," he admitted at last. "The incidents you describe are beyond runewrights or alchemists and I agree with Mr. Rockefeller that a sorcerer would be more creative. That just leaves Limelight."

"Do you think you could come by the library or the paint store and look over the scene?"

Bell shook his head.

"I'm going to be busy here for the next twenty-four hours at least," he said. "For now, I suggest you proceed on the assumption that Limelight is involved. As best I can recall, the alchemist who invented the stuff is locked up in Bellevue"

"Guy Rushton," Danny supplied. "I called the hospital and, after the last incident, he isn't allowed visitors."

"What about the other one, the woman?"

"Olivia Thatcher," Danny said. "I'm still running her down."

"Well, I suggest you get on that, then," Bell said, relighting his cigar. "Limelight was a highly advanced and complex bit of alchemy, and not just any alchemist can make it."

"Do you know what happened to her after her shop burned down?"

"I expect the police picked her up, but I can't be sure."

Danny hadn't thought of checking arrest records for Olivia's name, but if she'd been responsible for manufacturing a dangerous alchemical substance, she might be in jail.

"Thanks, Doc," he said, flipping his notebook shut. "Can I use your phone?"

It was after five when Danny pulled up in front of a ten-story business tower in the core. He knew it was a long shot, but he hoped someone would be burning the midnight oil in the law offices of Evans, Andrews, Philton, and Frank.

The firm was located on the seventh floor and took up one entire corner of the building. When Danny tried the door, it opened on an empty lobby with an unmanned receptionist's desk just opposite.

"Hello?" he called as he stepped in and shut the door behind him. "Is anyone here?"

"Hello?" a man's voice carried down a side hallway.

Danny approached and was met by an older man in a sturdy suit with a pair of spectacles perched on the end of his pointed nose.

"Oh," he said upon seeing Danny. "Miss Wentworth must have left the door unlocked. I'm sorry, young man, but we're closed."

Danny pulled out his badge and held it up.

"I just need to talk to Reginald Andrews for a minute," he said. "It won't take long."

The bespectacled man's expression soured a bit on seeing the badge.

"I'm sure you know," he leaned closer and squinted at the badge, "Lieutenant, that Mr. Andrews can't say anything about any of the cases we're representing, or about our clients."

"I know," Danny replied. "This is about his sister, Olivia, and I only need a few minutes."

At the mention of Olivia, the man's sour expression turned sad.

"All right," he said. "Reggie's office is this way."

He led Danny back along the hall to an exterior office with the name *Andrews* on the door. Knocking, the man opened the door enough to stick his head in.

"There's a police lieutenant here to see you," he said.

After a long pause, he was instructed to show Danny in. The office was ornate and grandiose with shelves full of leather-bound law books on the side walls and an enormous window behind the desk with a view to the south that included the Statue of Liberty in the far distance. Everything in the office seemed to have been made of polished wood, from the desk to the chairs to the fancy liquor cabinet. The man behind the desk was about Danny's age with brown hair that matched the office wood. He had blue eyes and a round face, split by a wide nose.

"Are you Reginald Andrews?" Danny asked, holding up his badge.

"Yes, Lieutenant," he said, standing up as the older man withdrew. "What can I do for you?"

"I'm sorry to bother you, but I'm here about your sister, Olivia."

Reggie recoiled at that, quickly masking a look of surprise.

"Did the police find something of hers they didn't turn over?" The question was mild and confused. Danny knew the police must have picked her up after the Limelight incident, but the record of her arrest wasn't in Callahan's folder.

"Nothing like that," Danny said in his reassuring voice. "I just need to have a word with her. Do you know where she is, currently?"

Reggie's look went from curious to sad and he motioned Danny into one of the chairs in front of his desk.

"I do know where she is, Lieutenant," he said. "But I'm afraid you can't talk to her. She's in a cemetery in Queens next to our mother and father."

That wasn't the news Danny expected to hear, but it wasn't bad news. Dead alchemists didn't make alchemical poisons after all.

"I'm sorry," he said. "I wasn't aware that Olivia had passed. My condolences."

He was about to get back up, but a thought struck him. Just because Olivia was dead, that didn't mean that someone else wasn't carrying on her work.

"Did your sister have an apprentice?" he asked.

"No," Reggie said. "Olivia was too picky. Everyone she ever tried out failed to meet her standards."

"What happened to her alchemical equipment after she died?"

"The police seized everything that the fire didn't destroy," Reggie said. "If you want to see it, it's probably in an evidence warehouse somewhere. What's this about, Lieutenant?"

"Are you aware your sister was manufacturing a dangerous substance called Limelight?"

Reggie's expression hardened.

"Your fellow officers said something about that when they took her equipment," he said.

"Well, some Limelight has just shown up on the street, and I'm trying to figure out where it's coming from."

"My sister is dead because of that stuff, Lieutenant," Reggie growled at him. "She was never the same after the fire, it was like her mind was just...gone. Last month, her body went, too."

"I am sorry, Mr. Andrews, but you obviously understand why it's so important that I find out where this new supply is coming from," Danny said, soothing voice back. "Is it possible something from her shop or her personal possessions contained a sample of the Limelight powder? Or maybe she wrote the recipe down somewhere unusual and now someone else has it?"

Reggie sighed and pinched the bridge of his nose.

"Look," he said, obviously trying to control his temper. "The only things that were left from her shop were some of the lab equipment like tables and measuring spoons. I sold that stuff at auction. Her apartment had furniture, clothing, and a few personal items but nothing to do with her work. Olivia didn't collect keepsakes, she spent almost all her time in the lab."

That tracked with what Danny heard from Jessica...or rather Andrea Kellin. Andrea had to split herself in two just to get the lab time she wanted.

"Do you have a list of Olivia's things that were sold?"

Reggie held his gaze for a long moment, then he sighed and nodded.

"The auction house gave me a receipt." He stood and moved to a polished wood filing cabinet, then squatted down and pulled open the bottom drawer. After a moment he stood up again and returned to the desk with a stack of papers that had been clipped together.

"This is everything that sold and who bought it," he said, handing the papers over.

Danny scanned the front page, then flipped it over. The objects were all ordinary, a desk, some work tables and chairs, a file cabinet. He was about to close up the packet, but the last group of items caught his eye.

"Why did your sister have," he checked one of the entries, "six blocks of varying kinds of stone?"

Reggie actually chuckled at that.

"You know, I asked Olivia that myself, years ago. She told me that some potions require powdered stone or stone chips during the brewing process. She said it was easier to just have a block of the stuff and chip off whatever she needed."

Danny took another look at the list, then a smile crept over his face.

"Do you mind if I keep this for a while?" he asked, holding up the paper.

"Provided you return it," Reggie said with a shrug. "The auction house already paid me but I need it for my tax records."

Danny promised that he would, then stood and shook the lawyer's hand.

"Thank you for your time, Mr. Andrews," he said. "You've been very helpful. Do you mind if I use the phone on your receptionist's desk on my way out?"

Detective Crenshaw and a uniformed officer were waiting for Danny outside Pete's Paints when he pulled up.

"Do you have the key?" he asked as he got out of his car.

"Open it up," Crenshaw said to the uniform. To Danny, he said, "Why are we back here, Lieutenant? I didn't think there was anything left to do but clean up the mess, and that's the owner's job."

"We need to look into Peter Grant's business records," Danny said, stepping inside the art shop and switching on the light. The garish colors and odd landscapes that covered the walls, tables, and merchandise glared happily back at him. Knowing that they were literally part of the dead man's body took a lot of the whimsy out of the scene.

Danny crossed the floor, careful not to step in paint, and pushed aside the curtain to the back room. It was a smaller space than the front area, with a desk and file cabinet in one corner and shelves for stock taking up the rest. Some paint had been smeared around but nothing like the storefront.

The chair in front of the desk had paint on the seat and back as well as the arms. There was a paint handprint on the top of the desk, along with a paint-covered coffee cup, and staggering paint footsteps led from the chair to the curtain.

"Looks like whatever happened to him happened there," Crenshaw observed.

Danny agreed with the detective's assessment and made his way to the desk, avoiding the paint on the floor. He took out his pencil and used it to pick up the overturned coffee cup. As he did, a chunk of the cup fell out from inside.

"What are you looking for?" Crenshaw asked again.

"If the paint blob out front is what's left of Peter Grant, then it's likely he was poisoned with an alchemical powder called Limelight," Danny explained. "You dissolve it in liquid and drink it."

He set the coffee cup on the far end of the desk, then picked up the broken sliver.

"Have this cup added to the evidence box," he said, reaching across the desk to deposit the chip by the cup. As it passed under the still burning desk lamp, however, it sparked a translucent green.

"That's not a piece of the cup, sir," Crenshaw said.

Danny turned the glittering fragment back and forth under the light. It felt like a piece of glass as he rubbed it between his fingers, and Crenshaw was right, it wasn't a broken bit of porcelain from the cup.

"Sir?" Crenshaw prodded. "What is that?"

"Well, don't quote me or anything," Danny said, taking out his handkerchief and dropping the fragment onto it. "I think this is a solid piece of Limelight."

"So do we start looking for someone with a beef against Mr. Grant? Someone with access to this stuff?"

"That's the problem, Crenshaw," Danny said as he folded the green fragment into his handkerchief. "Nobody has access to this stuff anymore."

"Then how did it end up in Grant's coffee cup?"

"Look in the file cabinet," Danny said, returning his folded handkerchief to his trouser pocket. "Find me something official. Something with the business name on it."

Crenshaw was back almost before Danny was done checking the rest of the desk.

"Business licenses," the detective said, handing them over.

Danny took the file and opened to the front page. After a moment, he put the paper on the desk and pulled the auction form Andrews had given him from his coat pocket.

"Just as I thought," he said, pointing to the auction report. "A business with the initials PAS bought three of Olivia Thatcher's stone blocks." He pointed to the entrees marked M, PM, and J. Crenshaw caught on and pointed to the business license.

"And the official name of Pete's Paints is Pete's Art Supplies," he said. "PAS."

Danny turned and headed back into the store proper. Almost all the tools of the artist's trade were covered with the painted remains of the proprietor, but now that Danny knew what he was looking for, it didn't take long to find a nook dedicated to sculpture.

"Got a clean handkerchief?" he asked Crenshaw.

The detective handed his over, and Danny approached what looked like a large, rectangular box. Moving slowly, he wiped away the paint from the side, exposing a chunk of marble with reddish veins running through it. A second box stood next to the first and Danny wiped at that one too, revealing standard grey marble.

"Weren't there supposed to be three of those?" Crenshaw said, accepting his handkerchief back with two fingers.

"Pete must have sold the third," Danny guessed.

"I still don't see how these rocks explain the Limelight in Mr. Grant's coffee cup."

Danny dug the auction page out of his pocket again, indicating the three entries for Peter Grant's purchases.

"This one is marked M," he said, then pointed to the second stone. "Marble."

"Okay," Crenshaw said, "then what's PM and J?"

Danny indicated the first chunk of stone with its pale red veins.

"Pink Marble," he said. He returned the auction sheet to his pocket, then took out his handkerchief and opened it revealing the light green chunk of Limelight. "And J for Jade."

"I thought you said it was that Limelight stuff."

"I'm almost certain that it is," Danny said with a grin. "But you and I are the only ones who know that. To everyone else, this just looks like a chunk of green stone."

Crenshaw nodded as he put everything together.

"So you got me down here to go through Grant's records and find out who he sold his chunk of jade to."

Danny's grin got positively predatory.

"You catch on quick, Detective."

7

FISHING

Danny climbed out of bed and showered well before his six o'clock alarm went off. Growing up, his father had kept a very regimented household, getting Danny and his sister up sharp at six every morning. Being a detective often involved late hours running down clues or poring over evidence, but no matter what hour he managed to drag himself to bed, his body simply wouldn't let him sleep past six. As a detective, coffee became his life's blood.

Now that he was a Lieutenant, however, Danny usually got to bed by ten. After he'd left Detective Crenshaw to pore over the records at Pete's Paints, he'd gone back to the office for a few hours of case file shuffling. Once he had all of his detectives assigned, and the reports were read, he went home, stopping at a café he liked for dinner. He'd given some thought to going by the Lunch Box to talk to Mary, but the more he kept putting that off, the harder it became. There just wasn't anything more to talk about and both of them knew it, so Danny followed his usual routine and was in bed on time.

By the time he up and dressed for work it was six-thirty, so he phoned the Central Office switchboard to see if there were any urgent messages for him. Several of his detectives had left updates, including

Crenshaw, but he only said he'd taken the sales ledger home to go over it.

That didn't bother Danny; Crenshaw was a solid, if not very imaginative detective. If there was a record of the jade block's sale, he'd find it. With any luck, that record would lead them to the source of the new Limelight.

How did the buyer know what it really was? he wondered as he fried a couple eggs for breakfast. He still had the rock-like chip he'd found in Peter Grant's coffee cup wrapped in his handkerchief.

How did it get into Peter's cup?

It seemed unlikely that a chip of what looked like stone could have fallen in the cup by accident. Someone must have put it there, deliberately, but was that Peter Grant, or had someone put it in there without his knowledge?

Probably the latter, Danny reasoned as he ate. *If Grant had known what the jade block really was, he never would have sold it in the first place.*

That thought had disturbing connotations. Given Limelight's history of killing the people that used it, this case might be more than an alchemist getting hold of the wrong recipe. Someone could be using the strange alchemical stone to commit murder.

After washing off his dishes, Danny picked up his coat and put on his hat. His shift didn't start until eight, but he resolved to go in early. He needed to run all this by Callahan.

The detective's bullpen on the fifth floor of the Central Office of Police was never quiet or empty. There was a division specifically dedicated to the night shift, but all detectives were on call should they be needed at any hour of the day. Danny spotted Detective Wilson clicking away at his typewriter as he made his way to his office.

"Lieutenant," Wilson called, looking up as Danny crossed the mostly unoccupied floor.

"How's it coming on that fraudulent investments case?" Danny asked, altering his path to intercept Wilson's desk.

The detective grinned at that.

"I met one of the victims last night," he said. "An up and coming Broadway singer. She has a photograph of herself and a woman she identified as Harriet Mason." He held up a photograph and Danny perused it. "Harriet is the one on the left."

The two women could have been sisters; both were young and pretty with dark hair, wide smiles, and fashionable clothes. Looking closer, Danny noted that Harriet's smile seemed strained and there was no mirth in her eyes.

"Probably an alias," he said, handing the picture back.

"I figured it that way too," Wilson said. "But I hit a few clubs and showed the picture around to some bartenders. One of them recognized her, said she comes in pretty regularly, so I'm going to be staking out the place until I find her."

"Let me know when you collar her," Danny said. "Good work."

He started to turn away, but Wilson called after him.

"The Captain was here earlier," he said, picking up a notepad from his desk and tearing off the top page. "Said he wanted you to meet him at this address as soon as you came in."

The paper had an address down by the east side docks and Danny tucked it in his shirt pocket.

"Did he say why?"

Wilson shrugged.

"All I know is that a tugboat captain dropped anchor near the pier sometime in the wee hours and when he went to leave, his anchor pulled up a party favor. Mob hit, cement shoes and everything."

"All right," Danny said, turning back toward the elevator. "I'll go see what's so important about a dead mobster."

The dock where a tugboat had pulled up a body was easy to find. A dozen police cars were parked on the sidewalk near the warehouse that fronted it.

"Beat it," a uniform growled as Danny approached.

"What was that?" Danny growled right back at the man, pulling his lieutenant's badge out of his pocket.

"Uh, I mean the crime scene is straight back that way, sir," the cop said, pointing at a wide alley between two of the dockside warehouses.

"That's what I thought," Danny said as he passed the man. Danny had been a beat cop, then a detective, and now a lieutenant so most of the officers at least knew of him. Every once in a while, however, he'd run into one who hadn't and couldn't believe that the NYPD would hire an Oriental for anything other than a janitor. It used to bother him, but now he just derived satisfaction at the look of horror in their eyes when they realized their mistake. One word from Danny would be enough to get a beat cop sent back to directing traffic, or worse.

When Danny reached the docks, he found a burly man in a sailor's pea coat and a woolen cap arguing with Callahan. A small boat had been brought alongside the tug where a dead man in what was left of an expensive-looking suit hung from the anchor. It looked like the anchor had snagged on his suit coat, then slipped under his arm. One of the coroner's orderlies and two uniforms were examining the body before trying to get him down.

"Listen, Captain," Callahan said in a rumbling voice. "My boys have to examine that stiff before they cut him free and that's going to take as long as it takes. You give me any more trouble and I'll have the harbormaster pull your license."

The burly sailor looked like he wanted to respond, but he knew that Callahan had the power to make good on his threat. Instead, he turned and stalked away, muttering to himself.

"Looks like you've had a busy morning," Danny said, sidling up to Callahan.

"You're up early," Callahan said, his voice still threatening.

"Keeps me young. How come you wanted me down here?"

Callahan sighed and rubbed his eyes.

"How are you coming with the Limelight case?" he asked.

Danny brought him up to speed about the Limelight rock being sold to Peter Grant, and his selling it to a third party.

"As soon as Crenshaw locates the buyer, that will lead us to the stone," Danny said.

"But?" Callahan asked when Danny hesitated.

"I'm concerned this is more than accidental exposure," he said at last. As the men in the boat finally cut down the body, Danny explained his theory that whoever bought the Limelight block was using pieces of it to kill.

"I found this in Peter Grant's coffee cup," he said, taking out his handkerchief and unfolding it to reveal the little chip of green stone.

"You sure that's Limelight?" Callahan asked.

Danny shrugged.

"A coffee cup would be the perfect place for Limelight," he said. "Wouldn't make much sense to put a piece of normal jade in there."

"You know an alchemist named Charles Grier?"

Danny nodded.

"I was on the crew that rescued him from Torres, that crazy makeup tycoon."

"Good," Callahan said as the rowboat drew alongside the dock. "He helped out with the Limelight last time so he's in the know. Go show that bit of rock to him and make damn sure it's Limelight."

"Is that all, Captain?" Danny asked, wrapping the chip back into his handkerchief and returning it to his pocket.

"Unfortunately, no," Callahan said. "I think your theory about someone exposing people to Limelight on purpose might just hold water."

Danny gave him a questioning look, but Callahan's gaze was fixed on the men in the boat as they hoisted the dead man up onto the pier. He looked to be average height with a fit build but not too burly. His skin was pale white from having been submerged, and his black hair had been cut short. Something about the man looked familiar, but only in an everyman kind of way.

"Take a look at his neck," Callahan said.

Danny crouched down and pushed the dead man's head over to the side. He could clearly see four long slits running diagonally along the neck.

"These don't look like wounds," he said. "And I've never heard of the mob cutting someone's throat if they took the trouble to drown him."

"You do any fishing, Pak?" the Captain asked.

Danny looked up at him to see if he was serious, but the big man's face was set in the same serious mask he always wore.

"No, sir," he said. "The closest I ever got to fish was Mom's cooking."

He hadn't thought about his mother in a long time and a smile came, unbidden, to his lips.

"Well, I was down here on one dock or another every week as a kid," Callahan said. "I can tell you for certain that those marks on his neck...they're gills."

Danny took out the pencil he always carried and used the tip to push open one of the slits. It went through the skin and he could see a reddish white tissue behind it.

"So this guy ingests some Limelight, grows gills, and then..." Danny hesitated, trying to make the chain of events make sense. "And then someone decides to test if the gills really work?"

That didn't make any sense and Callahan said so. Danny rubbed his chin, trying to imagine how the dead man could have come to be here on the dock with his feet in cement and gills in his neck.

"What if he used the Limelight on himself," Danny suggested. "The mob is after him, he gets caught, they send him to sleep with the fishes, and he tries to use the Limelight's magic to escape."

"Now that makes some sense," Callahan said. "Looks like it almost worked, too."

"He must have drowned before the magic finished," Danny said. "I need to know who this guy was. If I'm right, he had Limelight on him and he knew it."

"You think this is the guy who bought the stone from the art shop?"

Danny sighed.

"Maybe, or maybe he knew the guy who did. Either way he's a direct link to that block of Limelight."

Danny turned to the coroner's assistant who had been going through the dead man pockets.

"Did he have an identity card on him?"

The burly orderly passed over a printed card that had been coated in wax to make it waterproof. As Danny turned it over, the reason for such a precaution became obvious: it was a membership card for the plumber's union. Below the long member number was printed the name Andrew Dunbar.

Danny was sure he'd never heard the name Andrew Dunbar before, at least not together. For some reason, though, the names were linked in his mind. He closed his eyes for a moment and tried to concentrate.

Where have I heard that before?

"Andy," he said as it came to him. "Andy Pascal."

"You know this guy?" Callahan asked.

Danny nodded.

"He went missing a few weeks after I made detective," he explained. "His wife came in, Lidia Dunbar Pascal. She was frantic to find him, but everybody knew we wouldn't."

"The mob was after him?" Callahan said. "Even back then?"

"He was a bag man for the Marettis. A street hustler pulled a bag switch on him while he was carrying fifty Gs of family money."

Callahan chuckled darkly.

"That'll put you on the naughty list," he said. "Looks like they finally caught up with him."

"I'll go see where he was hiding all these years," Danny said, holding up the union card. "The union will have his current address. If Andy here is the man who bought the Limelight block from Peter Grant, it's probably still at his home."

"You're assuming the guys who dumped him in here didn't grab it," Callahan pointed out.

"I don't think they would. It would just look like a block of green stone to anyone who didn't know what it was."

"All right," Callahan said as Danny stood up. "I want you on this till it's finished, Danny."

"What about my division?"

"I'll handle all of that. You find this block of magic poison before something really bad happens and we have chaos in the streets."

"I'll want Crenshaw with me."

"Take him," Callahan said. "Just get going."

Danny's first stop was a drugstore where he could use the phone. It was too early for Crenshaw to be in, but he tried the Central Office anyway only to find the detective out. His next call was to the offices of the New York Plumber's Union where he got no answer. Presumably they weren't open yet.

Since he couldn't get Andy Pascal's address until they were open, Danny got back in his car and drove across town to a little shop called The Philosopher's Stone. This particular shop was open and Danny could see several customers being served inside. Over the door was a a painted wooden sigh that declared the proprietor to be *Master Alchemist Charles Grier*.

The bell above the door jingled jauntily when Danny stepped inside. None of the other customers paid him any mind, but the thin, balding man behind the counter noticed him right off.

"Detective Pak," he said, breaking out into a broad smile. "I'll be right with you."

Danny leaned against the wall near a shelf containing pre-bottled potions and waited for Charles to finish with his morning rush. After about ten minutes, a young man in a neat apron came out of the back and took over, freeing up Grier to talk.

"I need to know if this is some form of Limelight," Danny said once the greetings were out of the way. He opened his handkerchief and held it out so the alchemist could see it.

Grier leaned close and squinted at the little sliver of green rock.

"Let's go in the back," he said, turning toward the counter and motioning for Danny to follow. Danny followed through a beaded curtain into the rear of the shop. He'd been here before when Grier had been grabbed by a crazy cosmetics magnate who thought Grier could give him the secret of eternal youth.

"Why would you think this is Limelight?" Grier asked once they were sequestered in the back room.

Danny explained about Peter Grant, Pete's Paints, and finding the jade chip in the man's coffee cup.

"All right," Grier said, sitting down at a heavy oak desk. He switched on a bright lamp, then turned to Danny with a pair of tweezers in his hand. "Let's see what we have here."

Gently picking up the sliver of stone, the alchemist set it under the beam of the desk lamp, the picked up a large magnifying glass.

"It appears to be stone," he said. "Of course, appearances can be deceiving. Let's probe a little deeper."

He opened a drawer in the desk and took out a wooden box filled with glass bottles. Each bottle had a bulb-type rubber stopper and Grier selected one in the middle of the box. Moving deliberately, he pulled out the stopper and used the bulb to transfer a single drop of the liquid inside to the green stone.

The moment the liquid touched the stone, it sizzled and popped as if it were oil dripped on a hot skillet.

Grier pulled back as if he were afraid of being splashed by the smoking liquid. In another second, it had entirely evaporated away, leaving the stone unmarked.

"Was that supposed to happen?" Danny asked when the alchemist didn't say anything.

"You thought this was some form of Limelight?" he said, his voice breathy, as if he'd run a footrace.

"That's the theory." Danny explained about Peter Grant, Andy Pascal, the library lion, and his search for the missing jade block. When he finished, Grier just sat in stunned silence. Eventually he took his handkerchief out of his jacket pocket and wiped his eyes.

"Amazing," he said at last.

"What is?" Danny asked.

"She actually did it," Grier muttered. "She lost her sanity to do it, but she did it ...and I've lived to see it."

"Charles?" Danny said, interrupting his reverie. "What are you talking about?"

"This, my boy," he said, picking up the sliver of stone and holding it up as if he thought Danny had forgotten it. "Do you know what this is?"

"Solid Limelight that looks like Jade?"

"Oh, it's so much more than that," he said, setting the sliver down gently on his desk. "This is a piece of a philosopher's stone."

Danny had heard the term, of course. Grier's shop was named The

Philosopher's Stone after all, though Danny didn't know what a philosopher's stone actually was.

"In the old days, when alchemy was little more than superstition and basic chemistry," Grier said, a wistful look on his face, "men searched for the secret to turn lead into gold. That's one of the things that started alchemy as a proper science."

"Are you saying this bit of green rock can change lead into gold?" Danny asked, briefly considering touching the tip of his pencil to the stone just to see what happened.

"No," Grier chuckled. "Actually turning lead into gold isn't that hard, but the chemicals you need to do it cost more than the gold you'd get out of it. But that's not important, what is important is that ever since those old times, alchemists have tried in vain to create a philosopher's stone."

"Why?" Danny asked. "I mean if it doesn't give you gold, what is it for?"

"It's a magical battery of sorts," Grier said, his smile stretching practically ear-to-ear. "It radiates magical energy."

"Like Empire Tower?"

Grier looked like he might disagree for a moment, then he shrugged and nodded.

"Empire Tower radiates a magical form of electricity," he explained. "A philosopher's stone radiates an energy more useful to alchemists. If you put one in your laboratory, all your potions will come out stronger and it will take less time to brew them."

Danny whistled. Something like that would be worth an awful lot of money to any alchemist on the planet. As he thought about the stone, sitting quietly in some alchemist's lab, he realized something.

"If it just speeds up alchemy, then why is this philosopher's stone killing people?"

Grier's grin evaporated at that, and his eyebrows crouched down over his eyes. He paced back and forth behind his counter, never taking his eyes off the little bit of green stone until he finally snapped his fingers.

"It's a side effect," he said at last. "Every time an alchemist brews a potion, there's always some leftover reagent," Grier explained. "Most of the time it's just toxic junk that we get rid of, but in the case of exceptionally powerful potions, you get a highly concentrated magical substance that will calcify into a solid. We call it slurry stone." He reached out and picked up the green chip again. "Usually it's just a brown, ugly bit of rock, but I've read reports that if you concentrate enough slurry from powerful potions, it creates this," he held up the chip. "Alchemical Jade."

"So this isn't Jade or Limelight?" Danny said. "It's something else?"

"A philosopher's stone," Grier nodded. "As far as I understand, a philosopher's stone doesn't retain any of the properties of potion slurry it was made from."

"You said these stones are made from lots of leftover potion gunk from all different kinds of potions, right?"

Grier nodded.

"What if Olivia Thatcher made this one exclusively out of Limelight runoff?"

"That might explain it, I suppose," Grier said. "Without speaking to Olivia, there's no real way to know."

"Well, we'll have to pass on that," Danny said. "She's dead."

Grier sighed and nodded, more to himself than to Danny.

"That often happens when great strides are made in magic," he said. "People with vision reach too far and end up paying a price they never expected."

Danny knew all too well that he was referring to his former colleague, Andrea Kellin.

"It's remarkable that this little bit of alchemical jade has power in it," he said, holding up the sliver. He held it out and Danny let him drop it into his open palm. Moving to wrap it back in his handkerchief, Danny suddenly felt a cold chill go down his back. Grier said this thing could radiate power and he'd been carrying it in his pocket for over a day.

"Do you think this chip is dangerous?" he asked. He knew if you put it in liquid and then drank the liquid, that was bad, but it wouldn't hurt just to carry it, right?

"Probably not," the alchemist said. "Philosopher's stones radiate power but it's harmless. I suspect this only functions as Limelight if you ingest it."

"If someone did drink some of this, how would it affect them?" Danny asked, holding it up and peering through the glass.

"Limelight seems to give people what they want," Grier said, stroking his chin. "That couple by the cathedral wanted a spark between them."

"And they got electrocuted," Danny finished, remembering Callahan's description of the previous Limelight deaths. "Peter Grant wanted to paint a masterpiece, so it turned him into living paint. It sounds like a genie in one of those old fairy tales."

Grier nodded sagely.

"Indeed," he said. "Be careful what you wish for."

Danny folded the Limelight chip back into his handkerchief, but instead of his trouser pocket, he dropped it in the outside pocket of his suit coat.

"Thanks, Charles," he said. "I'll be careful."

8

OVERLAP

The offices of the Manhattan branch of the Plumber's Union were in a dumpy two-story brick building in the south side's outer ring. Past a battered door inset with a dirty glass panel was a small front office with a single desk, an old couch, and framed newspaper clippings on the wall. A prettyish bottle-blonde looked up from buffing her nails and greeted Danny with a perfunctory smile as he entered. Her look soured considerably when Danny pulled out his badge.

"I need some information on one of your members," he said.

The woman looked nervous, then mastered herself and her smile returned.

"Just a moment," she said, standing. "I'll get someone to help you."

She stood and left through a plain wooden door at the back of the small front room. Less than a minute later, the blonde returned with a short, thick-necked man in a cheap suit that looked more like a mob enforcer than a manager.

No, Danny mentally corrected himself, *a mob enforcer would have a better suit*.

"What do you want, flatfoot?" the man growled.

"Andrew Dunbar," Danny said, holding up the waxed union card. "Tell me where he lives."

"We don't give out member information without a warrant," Thick-neck said. "So get out and don't come back without one."

As power plays went, this wasn't that impressive. The man was technically correct, though the fact that Andy Pascal, a.k.a. Andrew Dunbar was dead made the whole thing a legal gray area. The problem was that this thug in a tie was used to solving things with intimidation. Danny almost smiled at that. No judge in the city would convict him if he just pistol whipped the man until he complied. Still, he'd just cleaned his police issue .38 and he didn't want to have to disassemble it just to get some self-important functionary's blood out of it.

"That only works with live members," Danny said, choosing to smile instead of scowl. "A couple of my boys pulled Dunbar out of the East River this morning." He tossed the union card on the desk. "The mob sent him to sleep with the fishes. Now my Captain wants this solved, but I'm sure he wouldn't mind waiting till after whoever killed Dunbar pays you a little visit."

Thick-neck's look of smug satisfaction evaporated like morning fog in the sunlight. He had to know that whatever got Dunbar killed probably wasn't connected to the union, but he couldn't be sure. That doubt was all Danny needed.

"Well?" he pushed when the man didn't answer immediately. "What's it going to be? I'm a busy man and I don't have all day."

Thick-neck held Danny's gaze for a long moment, then he blew out a long breath and shrugged.

"I'll go get the file," he said, picking up the card from the bottle-blonde's desk.

Danny didn't smile. He'd won the game and lording it over a man who was obviously spoiling for a fight didn't seem like a good idea. Not many regular folks would hit a cop — that was a great way to end up in the hospital — but Thick-neck didn't appear too bright, so discretion seemed the better part of valor at this point.

The secretary sat down at her desk, giving Danny a sullen look. Clearly she'd been expecting her boss to ride Danny out of the office on a rail. He just ignored her and stood facing the door where her boss had disappeared.

Two minutes later, Thick-neck returned with a thin folder in his hands.

"This is Dunbar's file," he said, shoving it at Danny. "Everything we know about him is in there. Now take it and get out."

Danny accepted the file and flipped it open, checking that Dunbar's address was listed on his membership form. Finding everything in order, he closed the folder and nodded at the man.

"The New York Police Department thanks you for your cooperation," he said in a disingenuous voice, then he took a step back, turned, and left the office.

Once he reached the street, Danny headed down the block to a grimy diner on the corner of the block. Several of the diner's patrons gave him an appraising eye as he entered, so he took out his lieutenant's badge and clipped it to the outside breast pocket of his suit coat while he headed for the phone booth on the back wall.

"Lieutenant?" Detective Crenshaw's voice came tentatively over the line once the police operator connected the call.

"How'd you make out with our jade buyer?" Danny asked.

"I found him," Crenshaw said, with a noticeable lack of excitement in his voice. "But I don't think he's the one who slipped Peter Grant the mickey."

"Why?"

"Well, that auction where Grant bought the jade block was back on November fifth. That's six weeks ago, and according to Grant's records, he sold the block five days later to someone named Gilbert Sadler."

"So this Sadler guy had it for five weeks," Danny said, thinking out loud, "but if that's right, why did Limelight symptoms only start showing up two days ago?"

"No idea, but if I had to guess, Gilbert Sadler gave the jade to someone else and that guy is our killer."

Crenshaw's theory made sense and Danny said so.

"I'm glad you agree, but that means we're back to square one," Crenshaw said in a dejected voice.

"Actually, we aren't," Danny said, then he explained about Andy Pascal and his half-formed gills.

"So you think he's the one Sadler gave the Limelight to, and he knew enough about Limelight to try to use it to save his life?" Crenshaw asked.

"If he did, then we'll probably find our missing stone block at his house." Danny gave the young detective the address contained in Andrew Dunbar's file, then hung up and headed back to where he'd parked his car.

The apartment rented by Andy Pascal to live his life as the plumber Andrew Dunbar was exactly the opposite of what Danny expected. The building was a neat three-story brick number in the north side mid-ring. The landlady, Mrs. Lancaster, was the typical wizened old dear that Hollywood liked to put in grandma roles in films. She was dutifully aghast when she found out her tenant had died, and she was only too happy to cooperate with the police by opening his door.

"Thank you," Danny said as she stepped back from the apartment door.

"You find who did this, young man," the old woman said, taking Danny by the hand. "Mr. Dunbar was a good man. He helped out around here all the time, even without being asked; he just saw something that needed doing and he did it."

Danny clasped the woman's hand and gave her a serious look.

"I will, ma'am," he said. He could have told her the truth about the man she knew as Andrew Dunbar, but the truth would only hurt her for no good reason.

Pushing the door open, Danny went inside the small apartment. Like the building, it was neat and clean, though not very large. Just enough for a bachelor's life. The main room was both kitchen and parlor with a sturdy couch in front of a low coffee table on the near wall and the cold box and range along the far wall. A simple table with two chairs stood in the middle and looked well used.

Nothing jumped out to Danny, so he moved to the single door on the left wall and opened it, revealing a small bedroom. The space had barely enough room for the single bed and a dresser. Two curtained alcoves extended from the far side of the room. Danny pulled the first curtain aside to find a small closet. The second curtain hid a toilet, sink, and stand-up shower.

Everything in Andy Pascal's world was neat and orderly. and with so little space, it was obvious that the apartment didn't contain a large block of jade.

"Well, damn it," he said. Unwilling to just give up, he began pulling items out of the closet and setting them on the bed. He'd just made his second trip when he heard a knock at the apartment door. He'd left it cracked about an inch and he heard it creak as someone pushed it open.

"Hello?" Detective Crenshaw's voice came from the front room.

"Back here," Danny called.

Buddy Redhorn felt a strange sense of urgency as he drove north from the Central Office of Police. Hubert Conners had calmed pretty quickly once he realized Buddy knew how the thefts were perpetrated. He and Agent Mendes had sweated the man half the previous night and started in first thing in the morning. Finally, he'd given up the name of his partner, the man Conners claimed was the mastermind behind the entire theft.

Andrew Dunbar.

He had been the plumber on the job, fixing the broken pipes and leaking valves while Conners and his crew repaired the water damage. After hearing the story, Buddy had no doubt that the break in the water main had been set up by Dunbar in advance. With any luck, the plumber would still have the statue on him, and Buddy could wrap up this case.

"This is it," Agent Mendes said, pointing to a well-kept, three-story building.

Buddy pulled the sedan over and parked beside the curb.

"This guy might just be an opportunist," he said as he led Mendes through the building's front door. "But he might be a serious customer, so we're not taking any chances. If he's heard that his buddy Conners was picked up, he might be ready for us."

Mendes reached into her suit coat and withdrew her service weapon, holding it down toward the floor.

"Second floor," she said.

Buddy let her lead the way up the stairs and down the brightly lit hallway. He pulled his own weapon and held it at the ready as they went. Suddenly Mendes stopped and took half a step back.

"The door is open," she said in a near silent whisper.

Buddy stepped around her and approached the apartment belonging to Andrew Dunbar. Sure enough, the door was open about a foot, and he could hear men talking inside. He couldn't make out what they were saying, but there were two of them from the differing tones of the voices.

Holding up two fingers, Buddy leaned around the opening in the door but the room beyond was empty. He reached out and pushed on the door, trying to make enough space to slip inside. Unfortunately the door creaked loudly and the voices in the back room fell silent.

"Go," he hissed to Mendes. He hit the door with his shoulder, bringing his weapon to bear as soon as it was clear.

The men in the back room hadn't wasted any time. The door burst open and two men came charging out with guns of their own.

"FBI," Buddy roared. "Throw up your hands."

"Police," the man in the dark brown suit yelled at the same moment. "Get on the ground."

Buddy's finger tightened around the trigger of his 1911. It was in involuntary response to having a gun pointed at him. At the last moment he realized what he'd heard, and he forced his hand to relax.

"Why, Agent Redhorn," the man in the brown suit said. "What brings you out this way?"

Now that Buddy could hear the voice clearly, he recognized it.

"Lieutenant Pak?"

In the heat of the moment, he'd completely missed the fact that the brown-suited policeman was Oriental. He tried to keep from blushing in embarrassment over such a lapse.

"Hey, Danny," Agent Mendes said with a grin. "I haven't seen you in a while, how've you been?"

"Do you know these people, Lieutenant?" the younger man in the light gray suit asked. His weapon was still raised, and his hands were shaking as they held it.

"Relax, Crenshaw," Lieutenant Pak said. "These are Agents Redhorn and Mendes of the Federal Bureau of Investigation."

The young man lowered his gun and Buddy breathed a sigh of relief. If Lieutenant Pak's man had been a bit more of a greenhorn, he might have started shooting before anyone knew what was going on.

"You working a mob case?" Lieutenant Pak asked as he holstered his weapon.

That took Buddy by surprise. As far as he knew, organized crime had nothing to do with the theft of the Jade Phoenix.

"I'm looking for Andrew Dunbar," he said. "He and a guy named Hubert Conners organized a burglary at a high-end art gallery. They got away with a statue of a pair of birds that belongs to the government of Brunei."

Lieutenant Pak and his Detective exchanged confused glances.

"We're here because a mobster named Andy Pascal was murdered last night," Lieutenant Pak said. "He'd been on the run from the Maretti family for years, but they caught up to him and sent him to sleep with the fishes."

"What does that have to do with Dunbar?" Agent Mendes asked.

"When they pulled Pascal out of the river, there were gills in his neck."

"Gills?" Buddy asked, sure he'd misheard Pak. "You mean like a fish?"

"Exactly like that," Pak said.

"How is that possible?" Agent Mendes asked.

"Limelight," he said.

Buddy felt a chill run down his spine at that. Miss Kincaid had briefed him fully on that magical nightmare powder.

"You and I both know that's not possible," he said.

Instead of answering, Lieutenant Pak reached into his coat pocket and withdrew a folded handkerchief. Opening it up, he took out a bit of green stone and held it in the palm of his hand.

"This is alchemical jade," he said. "Olivia Thatcher made it out of the leftover waste from the Limelight she made. I found this in the coffee cup of an artist whose body was transformed into living paint."

"Oh, God," Agent Mendes exclaimed as her face turned a bit green. "Is he okay?"

Pak shook his head.

"He literally painted himself to death." Turning to Buddy, he picked up the green sliver between his thumb and forefinger. "There's an entire block of this stuff somewhere and Andy Pascal had contact with it."

"That's how he got the gills," Buddy said, nodding to hide the shiver that thought sent down his spine.

"We found one other thing on Pascal's body, his union card. Andy Pascal has been hiding out from the mob as a plumber by the name of Andrew Dunbar."

"Dunbar is dead?" Mendes said, an exasperated note in her voice. "There goes our last lead." She looked from Lieutenant Pak to Buddy, but neither man said anything.

"It doesn't matter," Buddy said at last.

"What do you mean it doesn't matter?" Mendes said. "I thought there would be an international incident if we didn't get the statue back."

"We still need to do that," he amended, "but this lead doesn't matter because the statue Andrew Dunbar, or rather Andy Pascal, stole from the museum was a fake."

"How do you know that?" Pak and Mendes asked in unison.

Buddy turned to the Lieutenant.

"You're looking for a block of alchemical jade, right?"

Lieutenant Pak nodded.

"That statue I'm looking for, it's about eight inches square by eighteen inches tall and it was carved out of jade."

Pak and his detective exchanged worried looks.

"Whoever bought that stone from Peter Grant had it for five weeks," the Detective said.

"More than enough time to make it into a counterfeit statue," Pak agreed.

"It fits," Mendes piped up, "but that doesn't mean that's what happened."

"Yes, it does," Pak countered. "Andy Pascal had the alchemical jade; he couldn't have grown gills otherwise. And, if you're right about him stealing your missing statue..."

"Then the statue has to have been carved from the alchemical jade," Mendes finished, nodding her head in understanding.

Buddy stifled a proud grin as Mendes put everything together. He had a right to be proud, he'd worked long and hard to help her develop her investigative skills. Lieutenant Pak, however, didn't have any reason to feel proud over her successful mental gymnastics, yet there was a look of admiration in his eyes as he looked at her. He shifted his gaze to Mendes and detected the faintest hint of a blush in her cheeks. She'd noticed Pak's attention as well. She'd noticed it and she liked it.

That's a distraction neither of them need, he thought. *I'll speak to Pak about it.*

"So what do we do now?" Medes went on.

"Now our job is going to be dramatically easier," Buddy said. He already had a pretty good idea what had happened, but that was a matter for later. "Unfortunately the existence of Limelight in the wild means we have to change our focus. Whoever has the counterfeit statue is either *in* a lot of danger or *is* a serious danger to everyone around them."

"Does this mean you're taking our case?" Pak's detective asked.

Buddy shook his head.

"No. The only people who know about this are the four of us and, unless I miss my guess, your captain."

Pak nodded so Buddy went on.

"We need to work together to stop this or there will be chaos in the streets."

"So I reiterate," Agent Mendes said. "Where do we start?"

"With the last person to see Andy Pascal alive," Lieutenant Pak said. "Your missing statue isn't here, so Pascal must have sold it to someone, or rather given it to them."

The young detective's eyebrows knitted together at that statement.

"Why would Pascal give away a statue worth sixty thousand dollars?" he asked.

"Didn't you wonder how a man who has evaded the mob for over ten years happened to get caught?" Pak asked him.

Buddy chuckled at that. It was the same Socratic technique he used to draw out Agent Mendes' powers of observation and deduction.

"He gave the statue to his old boss as a peace offering," the detective said. "But then why did they kill him?"

"Maybe Maretti figured out it was a fake," Pak said with a shrug. "Or maybe old Nick is just the kind of bastard to take your offering and kill you anyway."

"Nicholas Maretti is the man who killed Andrew ... I mean Andy Pascal?" Mendes cut in.

Lieutenant Pak nodded.

"He's just the kind of guy to have done it himself."

"Why do you ask?" Buddy added.

Mendes turned to him with a wide smile on her face and the light of triumph in her eyes. She pulled a folded piece of paper from her coat pocket and held it up.

"Because Nicholas Maretti is one of the people who tried to buy the Jade Phoenix from Trevor Hardwick."

"Very good, Aissa," Buddy said, giving her an approving nod. Then he turned to the other two men in the room. "Lieutenant Pak, if you're amenable to working together, I think we ought to go and pay Mr. Maretti a visit."

9

THE ART CRITIC

Danny piled into his car along with Detective Crenshaw and followed Agents Redhorn and Mendes south to a large home in the east side inner-ring. Back in the day, Nick Maretti ran beer to a good chunk of the east side and he didn't want his home to be outside his territory. It was located at the end of a row of brownstones and looked more like a bank than a home, with granite walls that culminated in a triangle façade complete with a frieze, pediment, and raking cornice.

There was no yard to speak of, since the house fronted the street. Tall bushes and shrubs in planters filled in the front so the only part of the ground floor that was visible was the broad stair that led up to an exterior vestibule and the front door beyond.

Danny parked right in front of the place, then made sure his lieutenant's badge was firmly in place and clearly visible on his suit coat before stepping out. Redhorn and Mendes had parked just ahead of him, and they were already waiting on the sidewalk when Danny came around the front of his car.

"Do you know this guy?" Redhorn asked as he approached.

Danny shrugged. He'd done his homework on Nick Maretti and his organization when Lidia Pascal demanded the police find her missing husband, but he'd never met the man himself.

"No," he admitted, "but I know he doesn't have a lot of respect for local cops. Maybe you'd better take the lead."

"How do you want to play it?" Mendes asked.

"That fake statue has half a dozen bodies clinging to it," Redhorn said. "Mob boss or not, that's trouble Mr. Maretti isn't going to want on his doorstep."

That was about the way Danny had it figured, as well.

"If we're right about Pascal giving him the statue to get back in the family's good graces," he said, "then just telling him it's a fake will probably be enough."

"Are we just going to ignore his receipt of stolen property?" Crenshaw asked.

"We need that Limelight statue off the streets," Redhorn said. "That's our priority."

"What if Maretti gets suspicious about why we're so intent on getting it back?" Mendes asked her partner.

"Then we play hardball," Danny answered. "Threaten to look into how Andy Pascal ended up in the East River."

"All right," Redhorn said. "Lieutenant Pak and I will take the lead, you two follow and stay close."

Danny patted his left breast, touching the solid form of his police issue .38. He didn't expect Maretti to do anything stupid; he had a reputation as a schemer, not someone to get emotional and start trouble in his own home. Still, it was always better to be prepared.

He smoothed out his suit coat and followed Redhorn up the long, sweeping staircase to the landing. An arched opening led into an exterior vestibule and Danny noticed a stool sitting in the far corner of the little alcove. Next to it was a small table, no more than a foot square, that held an ash tray with a cigarette laid across its edge.

"Hey," he said in a low voice, putting a restraining hand on Redhorn.

The big man stopped with only the briefest look of annoyance.

"You see something?" he asked, and Danny could feel the muscle in the man's arm tighten.

"Most mob guys have someone watching the approach to their front door," Danny said, keeping his voice low. Then he nodded at the empty stool. "Look at the cigarette."

Redhorn scrutinized the scene for a moment, then nodded.

"Looks like someone left in a hurry," he said. "You reckon they saw us coming and went to warn Maretti?"

"No. If we intended to raid the place, we would have come with a few dozen cops and a paddy wagon."

"Well, something spooked him," Redhorn said. "Everybody keep your eyes open."

They ascended the last few stairs and Redhorn and Danny stepped into the little vestibule at the same time.

"Front door is open," Redhorn said, looking left to where the door stood.

Danny didn't look, he was preoccupied with the cigarette. It had been lit when it was placed in the little divot on the edge of the ash tray, he could tell by the ash trail. Reaching down, he picked it up and tapped the end.

"This cigarette is cold," he whispered. "And from the look of it, it sat in the ash tray for quite a while."

"So whatever spooked the guard dog didn't happen recently," Redhorn concluded.

"Do we knock?" Mendes asked, her voice tense.

Redhorn reached into his coat and drew his pistol, a heavy 1911, then stepped up to the door. Danny followed suit with his .38. The big FBI man leaned against the front wall, put the barrel of his gun against the door, and gave it a gentle push.

From his position, Danny couldn't see inside, but Redhorn could, and his face suddenly went hard.

"Man down," he whispered to Danny. "Take the right side." To his partner and Crenshaw he said, "Watch our backs."

He mouthed counting to three, then pushed the door open and stepped inside. Danny followed right behind, turning and moving along the wall past the door. As soon as he cleared the door, he saw what Redhorn had. A man lay in the middle of the large, open foyer, curled up as if he'd been kicked in the groin. A large pool of blood stained the parquet floor under where he lay, and Danny's nose detected the tell-tale tang of iron in the air. It looked like someone had unloaded a couple barrels of double-ought buckshot into his gut.

Whatever had happened here, the dead man hadn't been defenseless. A Colt 1911 handgun lay on the floor a few feet from the body and Danny noted that the slide was locked in the open position. That meant the man had emptied his magazine and still ended up dead.

"Take cover," he hissed, ducking behind a wooden column that ran up to the ceiling two stories up.

"There's another body upstairs," Mendes said in a low voice as she pointed up at the ceiling.

A large stairway occupied the exact center of the foyer and ran up to second floor balconies that ran around the entire room. A limp hand stuck out between the balusters with blood running along the fingers and dripping slowly into a small pool further into the cavernous foyer.

"What the hell happened here?" Crenshaw said, hiding behind a massive Art Nouveau hall tree.

"Focus," Redhorn said. "Anyone see a hostile?"

Danny leaned out from the pillar and scanned the room. Two doors occupied the right side of the foyer with three doors on the left. A glass wall ran along the back, and he could see a garden with a large fountain beyond.

"Clear," he said.

"Everybody with me," Redhorn said, heading for the first door on the left. "Let's make sure there are no surprises on this floor, then we'll head upstairs."

Repeating the process they'd used to enter the front door, Redhorn and Danny stepped through the first door into an enormous kitchen. There were two bodies in this room, a man and a woman. The man wore an apron and still clutched a heavy cleaver in his hand. The woman wore a maid's uniform and was lying face down.

"I think she tried to run," Crenshaw said, kneeling over the woman.

Danny examined the dead cook. His apron was covered in blood, and it looked like he'd been shot in the neck.

"Let's keep going," Redhorn said.

"Just a minute," Danny said, pushing the cook's chin to expose more of his neck. The wound looked ragged and torn, and he couldn't see any sign of an entry wound. "Hey Crenshaw," he said. "Turn the maid over on her back."

With Mendes' help, the detective managed to turn the dead woman over and Danny heard the pair of them gag when they managed it.

"Her throat's been torn out," Crenshaw managed while Mendes looked at the ceiling and took deep breaths to keep herself from vomiting.

"You expected something like that," Redhorn said, when Danny moved to examine the woman.

"I don't think this is the work of a rival mob or an insane gunman," he said. "Both of these people were killed with wounds to the throat. Usually you see this with dog attacks."

"You think a dog did this?" Mendes asked, doubt clear in her voice.

"It'd have to be a really big one, but yeah."

"What about something exotic?" Redhorn asked. "Like a jungle cat?"

Danny shook his head as he stood.

"Cats disembowel their victims."

"How do you know that, sir?" Crenshaw wondered.

"I worked a circus killing about ten years ago."

"Well, if this is an animal, that makes our job simpler," Redhorn said. "An animal isn't going to shoot back. Let's go."

Buddy Redhorn, eased open the door in the back of the kitchen. Beyond it was a big laundry and storage room. He moved from shelf to shelf, clearing each aisle with his gun as he went. Just because Lieutenant Pak thought it had been an animal that killed the people they'd found so far, didn't mean it would be easy to take down. He'd seen far too many men killed by basic inattention back in the Great War.

From the laundry room, they moved to a small solarium, then across the foyer to a beautiful library full of books. The smell of blood was strong when he opened the door and he held up his hand, bringing everyone to a stop.

"Blood," Pak said, catching the scent.

With the bookshelves in the middle of the room, it was impossible to see the far side of the library.

"I'll go right," Pak said, moving around the door. "Crenshaw, you're with me."

"Yell if you see anything," Buddy said as the detectives passed him.

"If we see anything," Pak said with the mischievous grin he often wore, "you'll probably hear us shooting."

"Good point."

Keeping his gun in front of him, Buddy turned left and went along the wall, checking the spaces between the shelves as he went. At the end of each row was an oil painting in a wall niche, illuminated with a small overhead light. Buddy knew a little about art from investigating counterfeiters during the war, and some of these paintings were worth real money.

"For a mob boss, this Maretti fellow has good taste," he muttered.

"Had," Agent Mendes said from just behind.

When he looked at her, she nodded off toward the end of the room. A raised platform was there, encircled by a railing of polished brass. Inside the area were pedestals holding up sculptures, all surrounding a large leather chair next to a fireplace that had an actual sword and dagger mounted above it. On the floor in front of the chair was a man. He wore a purple velvet smoking jacket, silk slacks, and expensive shoes. A glass of some amber liquor lay beside him, mostly empty, and a bottle of similar liquid stood on a little table beside the chair.

"I'd say that's our man," Mendes said.

"I'd say you're right," Buddy murmured. Still being cautious, he moved past the last bookshelf and climbed the two stairs that led up to the platform. Mr. Maretti was quite dead; the pool of blood under his body told the tale.

"It looks like he was sitting in his chair when he was attacked," Mendes said. "Are we sure Danny was right about this being an animal?"

Buddy didn't raise his eyebrows even though Agent Mendes had referred to the lieutenant by his first name. That was a sign she was thinking of him in familiar terms. She always did that when she liked someone. The lieutenant wasn't a bad guy, in fact, he was pretty damn smart and seemed to be good at his job. Still, Mendes needed to focus on solving this case so she could become a full agent. Buddy resolved to talk to her about her wandering focus later.

"No," he answered her question. "If someone had shot Mr. Maretti, he'd still be in his chair."

"Find any..." Lieutenant Pak's voice greeted him as the policeman approached. He cut off his question when he saw the body.

"I can't say I'm sorry he's dead," Detective Crenshaw said as they both mounted the platform. "But we won't be getting any answers out of him."

"We might not need to," Pak said, looking around the garden of statuary. "I'd say our missing statue was right there."

The lieutenant pointed to an empty pedestal that stood in the direct line of sight from the chair. Pak was on to something. Every other pedestal on the platform held a piece of statuary, all except this one.

"What happened, then?" Mendes asked. "Did someone use a rabid animal to cover them stealing the statue?"

"I don't think so," Detective Crenshaw said. "The only people who knew Maretti even had the statue were his men and Andy Pascal."

"Maybe Pascal arranged the theft," Buddy said.

"That could work," Pak said. "Pascal arranged to have someone steal the statue. But Maretti would have to know it was him. As Crenshaw said, there were only a few people who even knew the Limelight statue was here."

"Was it, though?" Mendes said. "I mean right now we think this Pascal character brought the fake statue here, but what if he didn't?"

Buddy walked around the empty platform as he listened to the discussion. His gut told him that Lieutenant Pak had the right of it, but his gut wasn't evidence. He needed something admissible.

"I'm pretty sure Pascal brought the statue here," he said, crouching down to examine the pedestal's base. "We know Maretti tried to buy it, and I'll bet Pascal knew it too. The statue would be the perfect peace offering to get him out of the plumbing trade and back into the high life as one of Maretti's insiders."

"Just because it makes sense doesn't mean the lieutenant is right," Mendes countered.

"No," Buddy admitted. "But this does."

He stood and held out his hand. A tiny fragment of green stone sat in the middle of his outstretched palm.

"There's a bunch of tiny fragments over here," he said, indicating the side of the pedestal furthest away from the chair. "It looks like the statue was knocked over before whoever was after it took it."

Lieutenant Pak pulled the handkerchief from his coat pocket and opened it to reveal the shard he carried. Buddy dropped the shards he'd recovered next to them.

"Looks identical to me," Pak said. "We'll have to have it tested before we..."

Buddy looked up sharply as Pak's voice just stopped. The lieutenant was staring back toward the library part of the room and as Buddy turned his head, he saw it.

Some kind of massive dog was crouched atop one of the shelves. The creature's fur was the golden color of wheat in the spots that weren't matted with blood. The body and legs were thick and bulging with ropy muscle, and it had a broad upper body that made its back look humped. The thing let out a low growl at having been discovered and the muscles across its broad back rippled.

Buddy didn't stop to think. In one smooth motion, he raised his 1911 and fired. The shot caught the creature in the rear hip, and it roared in fury, baring its considerable teeth.

Beside him, Pak and Crenshaw both fired as one, with Mendes a moment behind. At least one of the shots hit the creature and it flinched, but that only served to make it angrier. It roared a second challenge and leaped off the shelf, charging up the center aisle right toward the raised platform.

"It's not stopping," Mendes yelled, pouring lead toward the incoming animal as it came.

Buddy had wondered why the armed man in the foyer had failed to kill an animal and now he had his answer. A tingling sensation ran down his arms, one he hadn't felt since the war. The monster dog would be on them in two seconds, maybe three. There wasn't time to think.

Dropping his gun, Buddy turned to the fireplace and seizing the long parrying dagger mounted next to the sword, he tore it free from the mounting, spinning back as his companions continued to shoot the beast. It leaped at the young detective, who tried to dodge, only to have the creature lock onto his arm with its massive jaw and shake. The detective was pulled off his feet, but before the dog could go for the kill, Pak fired point blank at the monster's head.

Buddy heard the bullet ricochet off the beast's skull and it dropped the detective, turning to lunge at Pak.

"Hold fire," Buddy shouted, hoping they'd listen as he charged right at the monster.

Lieutenant Pak had said dogs went for the throat to kill, and Buddy desperately hoped the man knew his stuff. Holding the knife low, he tackled the monster, using the force of the impact to drive the eight-inch blade of the dagger into its side.

The creature howled and shook, trying to dislodge its attacker. Buddy was raked across the chest by a clawed foreleg, tearing open his shirt and his flesh, but he barely noticed. As the monster rolled over, he let it take him with it until he was on his back on the floor. At that moment, he pulled back against the knife, sliding it easily out of the beast's guts. It howled again as the blade came free but before it could get to its feet to respond in kind, Buddy plunged the knife back into its torso. He repeated the move as quickly as he could, striking three more times before the monster managed to stumble away.

Buddy rolled after it, but the creature was wary now; it leapt back, just out of his reach, then turned and lunged for him. He'd known that going to ground would make him vulnerable, but he'd hoped that stabbing the monster repeatedly in the vitals would bring it down. Now all he could do was slash at the incoming muzzle and hope to drive it back.

The creature snarled and Buddy could see in its eye that it wouldn't be dissuaded by the knife a second time. It opened its mouth and reared up to strike. Buddy raised the knife to protect his throat, but then the monster's eyes went wide, and its head dropped to the floor, separate from its body.

Lieutenant Pak stood over the dog creature, the sword from the fireplace mantle in his hands. The beast was so focused on its prey that it hadn't seen the policeman step in and deliver a killing blow that had beheaded it.

"Thanks," Buddy said as he gingerly touched the wound on his chest.

"We need to get you and Crenshaw to the hospital," Danny said, dropping the sword onto the floor with a clang.

Buddy winced as he got his knees under him and stood up. The young detective was cradling his mauled arm and Agent Mendes had wrapped her suit coat over the wound to stop the bleeding.

"Take him to the hospital," he told her, tossing her the keys to their car. "I'll stay here with Lieutenant Pak."

"Buddy, you're bleeding."

She almost never addressed him by his name, only when she thought the situation was appropriately dire.

"It's just a scratch," he said. "It's already stopped bleeding. Now get going."

She helped Crenshaw to his feet and the two headed for the gigantic foyer and the street beyond.

Buddy turned back to the dog-monster and found that Pak had taken off his coat and rolled up his sleeves. He was currently using the parrying dagger to open up the dead beast's belly.

"What are you doing?

Pak didn't answer, as he sliced open the creature's stomach, causing acidic goo to erupt from the wound. After a second, he used the dagger to pull something out of the disgusting puddle, rubbed it on the already ruined carpet, and held it up. Even from a few feet away, Buddy could see it sparkle green in the light.

"What is a piece of the statue doing in this thing's gut?"

Pak stood and moved back away from the carcass.

"I think this used to be the family dog," he said. "There was a picture of Maretti with a terrier in the foyer."

Buddy held out his hand and Pak dropped the sliver of alchemical jade into his hand.

"This little bit of rock turned a terrier into that?"

Pak shrugged.

"It's just a guess."

"How did this get inside a dog?

"Dogs will eat anything," Pak said.

"But it would have to have broken it off the statue first."

"I suspect he nipped at the statue and swallowed it."

Buddy shook his head.

"Everyone's a critic," he said.

10

THE SHELL GAME

Danny watched Aissa Mendes as she helped Crenshaw out to her car. The young man wasn't wounded too badly, but his arm would be in a sling for a couple of days while the mending potions did their work.

"What now?" Agent Redhorn's voice cut through his thoughts. Danny smirked as he remembered something Aissa had said. She'd called the big FBI man Buddy. Since it was unlikely that Buddy was a term of affection, Danny had to assume that it was Redhorn's name. That was something he'd never managed to find out on his own. Redhorn was big, imposing, and as formal as a rich man's butler. The idea that his name was Buddy made Danny want to burst out laughing.

"You still with me, Lieutenant?" Redhorn prodded.

"Sorry," Danny said, his mind snapping back to the task at hand. "We need to check the rest of the house for survivors, though since no one responded to our shooting, I'm guessing we won't find any."

"I doubt there are any more killer dogs, but I'm bringing this along just the same." He held up the dagger with the eight-inch blade, gripping it loosely.

For a moment, Danny considered taking the sword, but decided against it since it was all the way back in the library. Out of habit, he patted his left breast and a pang of alarm raced through him as he found his holster empty.

You dropped it when you grabbed the sword, he reminded himself.

"Come on," he said, turning back toward the library. "I forgot to pick up my gun."

"What about the statue?" Redhorn asked as they went.

"I doubt we'll find it here," Danny said with a sigh.

He climbed up the two stairs to the platform with its statuary garden and located his discarded pistol. He also retrieved his dropped handkerchief and made sure to gather up all the bits of alchemical jade, folding them safely inside the cloth.

"Why not? We know it was here last night."

Danny cleared his pistol, dropping the expended cartridges on the floor.

"Look at the chair," he said, nodding at the leather chair by the fireplace as he pulled loose bullets from the left-hand pocket of his suit coat. "It's facing that empty pedestal, and Maretti was clearly sitting here when he was killed."

Redhorn observed the scene for a moment then nodded.

"I see your point," he said as Danny finished reloading. "The only reason Maretti would be here, with his chair oriented like that, is if he was looking at his fancy new statue."

"The bits of jade you found were on the far side of the pedestal," Danny continued as he replaced his .38 in his shoulder holster. "That's consistent with the statue being knocked over."

"The carpet is thick," Redhorn said. "The statue probably survived the fall, so where is it?"

"My guess?" Danny said, nodding at the glass door that led out into the back garden with the fountain in it. "Someone snuck in and grabbed it after Nick Maretti was dead."

Redhorn groaned, rubbing his temples.

"Great," he said. "I sure hope you're right about the statue being a fake. "Agent Mendes is going to be in real trouble if the real Jade Phoenix is in the wind."

That didn't sound right.

"What's it to her if some stolen statue disappears? It isn't hers, is it?"

Redhorn chuckled humorlessly and shook his head.

"No, but losing it could end her career."

He began heading back toward the cavernous foyer and Danny fell in beside him. As they walked, the FBI man filled him in on the office politics that were threatening to end Aissa's career.

"That stinks," Danny said when Redhorn finished.

"Well, we're not licked yet," he said. "I'm pretty sure you're right about this statue being the fake one. If it was the real one, the family dog wouldn't have turned into whatever the hell that thing was by swallowing a bit of it."

"I can handle this," Danny said, feeling bad for endangering Aissa's job. "Go get your partner and track down the real statue."

Redhorn shook his head.

"If we don't find the missing Limelight, my superiors will blame that on Sorsha's absence and the end will be the same."

The FBI man was really between a rock and a hard place with this case, and that meant Aissa was as well. The only door they hadn't opened on this floor was the one next to the library. Beyond they found an elegant and tastefully decorated parlor with a grand piano in the corner.

"Once we get the Limelight, I'll help you find the statue," Danny said as they quickly searched the parlor.

"We'll take care of that ourselves," Redhorn replied in a gruff voice.

"If tracking down the Limelight takes too long, that statue is going to be out of the country."

"I know," the big FBI man growled, his frustration clearly evident in his voice.

Danny focused on clearing the parlor, finding nothing amiss.

"So," Danny said. "Upstairs?"

Redhorn nodded and they made their way to the massive staircase, then up to the second floor. Large windows looked out at the courtyard behind the house, but other than being brown and dead in the winter air, there was nothing to see.

The balcony ran left and right, turned ninety degrees and ran along the side walls. Three doors were visible to the left, along with the dead man whose hand they saw earlier. He lay in front of the furthest door and Redhorn headed that way.

"Poor bastard," he said when he reached the dead man. It looked like his entire throat had been torn out. Danny shuddered at the sight.

Moving quickly, the pair cleared the left side rooms, finding an office, a spare bedroom, a sitting room and two more bodies. Both were hard-looking men and both were armed. No doubt more of Nick Maretti's bodyguards.

"Any ideas how we're going to find the Limelight statue?" Danny asked as they crossed to the balcony, past the staircase to the far side.

"The only people who knew about the museum theft were the man who planned it, your ex-mobster Andy Pascal and his accomplice, Hubert Conners," Redhorn said. "Hubert has been in your lockup since yesterday, and Pascal is in your morgue."

"That doesn't leave us with a lot of suspects," Danny observed as they reached the first door. Beyond it was a large master suite, but no bodies. "The only other person who knew about the theft was Maretti, and he's out, too."

"The way I figure it, there is one person who knew about the fake who's still unaccounted for."

Danny began to nod, catching the FBI man's train of thought.

"The sculptor who made the fake," he said. "His name is Gilbert Sadler, but that's all I know about him."

"If he's got the skill to fake something as elaborate as the Jade Phoenix, I doubt this is the first time he's made a forgery," Redhorn said. "As soon as we're done here, let's pay a visit to whoever handles burglaries for your department."

"That'd be Lieutenant McClory of Division Four," Danny supplied.

"What kind of man is he?"

"Territorial," Danny replied. "But we may not have to involve him. I know an insurance guy who specialized in recovering stolen art...well, Alex knows him."

"This door is locked," Redhorn said, jiggling the handle.

"Look at that," Danny said, pointing down. The paint had been peeled away in long strips and great gouges were missing from the wood where enormous claws had raked the door.

"Go away!" a woman screamed from inside. Her voice was ragged and horse with the edge of hysteria.

"FBI, ma'am," Redhorn said, his voice shifting instantly to soothing authority. "I'm here with the police. We've killed the monster. It's safe now."

"If someone's with you, have them say something," the voice called.

"Agent Redhorn is telling you the truth, ma'am," Danny said. "I'm Lieutenant Pak of the New York Police Department." He knelt down and pushed his badge under the door. "We've secured the house and the creature is dead."

A moment later the door lock clicked, and it was opened about an inch. A blue eye looked out at them through the crack, and Redhorn held up his FBI badge so she could see it.

After a moment to process what she was seeing, the woman sobbed and the hand holding the door started to shake.

"I apologize for my appearance, ma'am," Redhorn said, indicating his ripped shirt and suit coat. Somehow he managed to sound both authoritative and gentle at the same time. "Are you all right? Is anyone in there with you?"

She began to babble, incoherently. Danny wondered just how long she'd been awake, listening for any sound of the monster that used to be a loyal family pet.

"I'll go call this in and get some men out here," Danny said in a low voice. "You'd better keep her in there until I get the bodies covered."

Redhorn just nodded and began trying to engage with the hysterical woman beyond the door.

Hurrying downstairs, Danny went into the kitchen where he'd seen a phone on the wall. He called the Central Office and reported the incident to the desk sergeant, ordering him to get men over here as soon as possible. Then he went back to the laundry room and collected clean sheets from a shelf, beginning the grim task of covering the dog-monster's victims.

Once Buddy had sufficiently calmed the woman behind the door, he found out that she was Nick Maretti's wife, Sofia. When she heard the screams and gunshots start up on the ground floor, she'd run to check on her children who had just been put in bed by their nanny. Sofia had the presence of mind to lock the door and the four of them had spent a long, terror-filled night listening to the creature prowl the halls and scratch at the door.

He was able to confirm that Nick had received a new statue as a gift the previous night. Sofia was surprised when he went out right away instead of sitting in his library to enjoy it. Of course she couldn't know that her husband was fitting his former employee with a set of cement shoes at the time.

"My husband is dead," she said. It was more of a declaration than a question. "Isn't he?"

"Yes, ma'am," Buddy said.

"That must make you happy," she said in a wistful voice.

"No, ma'am," Buddy said. "I didn't know your husband personally or professionally. I am sorry for your loss."

He didn't know what else to say to the woman, but fortunately the police arrived in force just then. He turned Sofia and the others over to a policewoman with a compassionate face, then headed downstairs. Lieutenant Pak was talking with one of the policemen and a man in a white coat who could only be the coroner.

"I wondered where you got off to," he said as he approached.

"Sorry," Pak said, looking a bit embarrassed. "I had to work out some departmental squabbling. Apparently one of the other divisions has been trying to get Maretti for months. They weren't happy to hear that he was dead."

"They need some perspective," Buddy said.

"That's what I told them, but they still wanted every detail when they got here."

Buddy chuckled at that. Explaining what had gone on in the Maretti house over the course of twelve hours would be a neat trick. Most of it was beyond belief.

"I also got us the name of that insurance guy," Pak said, handing over a torn page from his notepad.

"Arthur Wilks at Callahan Brothers Property," he read aloud. "That's quite the coincidence."

"What is?" Pak asked.

"Callahan Brothers is the insurance company that covers the Devereaux Gallery," Buddy supplied. "That's where the statue was stolen from."

"Could the theft be about insurance fraud?"

"And the forger just happened to pick up a block of alchemical jade to make the fake?" Buddy asked.

"It's a coincidence," Pak said with a shrug, "but they do happen — sometimes."

Buddy shook his head to clear it and headed toward the front door.

Stay focused, he chided himself.

"We'll cross that bridge once we've found the Limelight," he said. "Right now, we need to see an insurance man, but first I've got to get out of this ripped-up suit."

The offices of Callahan Brothers Property were at the top floor of a converted hotel, though as Buddy waited for the elevator, he decided it looked more like the Ritz. The place had the kind of expensive elegance that he only associated with the swankiest of society hot spots.

A short elevator ride later and the doors opened directly into the lobby of the insurance company. A pretty woman sat behind a large desk facing the elevator. She had perky features, a bob haircut, and she was admiring the gold band on her left hand.

Obviously a new addition.

"Can I help you gentlemen?" she asked as they approached, her face splitting into a friendly smile.

"I'm Agent Redhorn of the FBI," Buddy said, flashing his badge. "This is Lieutenant Pak of the New York Police. We need to speak with Mr. Wilks about a matter of some urgency."

A look of concern flashed across the woman's face, but she hid it almost immediately.

"Let me see if he's in," she said, rising from her desk.

"Call him," Buddy said, shifting his voice to a more commanding tone. He wasn't sure about this Wilks character; after all, Alex Lockerby seemed to know a fair number of shady people. The last thing he wanted was for this woman to warn Wilks off.

The receptionist did as she was told and a moment later the door to the left of the desk opened and a man built like a fireplug emerged. His eyes swept over the men in the lobby and Buddy could tell he was expecting trouble.

"You boys cops?" he asked.

"He is," Buddy said, pointing to Lieutenant Pak. "I'm with the Federal Bureau of Investigation."

That sent the man's eyebrows up in surprise.

"Well," he said, his voice never losing its smooth, conversational tone. "Why don't you boys come with me to my office, and you can tell me how I can help you."

He knows how to play the game, Buddy thought. He didn't know if he was in trouble, and he wasn't going to do anything to provoke them in case he wasn't.

A minute later Buddy and Pak were sitting in front of Wilks' clean desk. The office was in the corner of the building with a spectacular view from the wall-to-wall windows. The other walls were packed with pictures, mounted newspaper clippings, and awards. No doubt these represented Wilks' career.

"What can I do for you?" the insurance man asked as he sat down.

"I understand you maintain a fairly detailed network among the stolen art community," Lieutenant Pak said, getting right to the point.

Buddy wondered about that long phone call he'd had with his office. Clearly something had happened to make him hurry. He resolved to ask about it later.

Wilks scoffed and shook his head.

"I knew that stupid private dick would sell me out sooner or later," he muttered.

"If you're referring to Alex Lockerby," Pak went on, "he's a friend of mine, and this is a friendly type visit."

Wilks didn't look like he believed that, but he sat back in his chair and folded his hands across his middle, waiting for the other shoe to drop.

"A statue insured by this company was stolen two nights ago," Buddy said. "We have reason to believe it was a fake."

That got Wilks' attention.

"Can you prove that?" he asked, not bothering to hide his interest.

"Not yet," Pak said. "We need to know who would have the skill to forge such a statue."

"There's a few people who do statuary," Wilks said. "But it really depends on the statue."

Buddy reached into his coat and pulled out the program from the Devereaux Gallery. He placed it on Wilks' desk with the color lithograph of the Jade Phoenix facing him.

Wilks picked it up and whistled.

"Now that's a pretty thing," he said. "This isn't one of my accounts," he went on, "but I think I can help you out. The only guy I know of who's good enough to work in a hard stone like jade is named Gil Sadler."

Buddy and Pak exchanged a look. It was only for a second, but Wilks seemed to pick it up.

"You already knew that," he fumed. "If you already knew, why are you in here hassling me?"

"We knew the name," Pak said. "We need to know where we can find him."

"And anything else you can tell us about the man," Buddy added.

Wilks grumbled under his breath and stood. He walked around his desk to a locked file cabinet on the wall next to his office door.

"I've never met the guy," he began as he fished through keys on a large ring. "But I'm told he's an odd duck. A real wiz with a chisel though."

"If he's so good, why is he counterfeiting statues?" Pak asked.

"The way I hear it, he's an ass," Wilks said, finally locating the key he wanted and unlocking the cabinet. "The kind of people who pay big money for art like to have their butts kissed. Like they're doing an artist a favor when they buy something from them."

"And Sadler doesn't play the game," Buddy guessed.

He'd met men like Sadler in the military. Entitled shirkers who believed themselves superior to other men and therefore exempt from the work regular soldiers had to do. Inevitably, he found such attitudes led either to crime, or to the officer corps.

"Here we go," Wilks said, pulling a paper from a bulging file. "Gilbert Sadler, a classically trained sculptor, works in granite, jade, and marble. He used to teach at New York University but got fired. Now lives above his studio down on Thompson Street near Bleecker. Here's the address." He put the paper on his desk facing Buddy and tapped an address at the bottom.

"You sure this is right?" Buddy asked as he jotted the address in his notebook.

"He's got an apartment and a studio in one building," Wilks said with a sneer. "It's near the university and several statue galleries. He's still there. Space like that is hard to come by."

Buddy rose and nodded at Wilks.

"The FBI thanks you for your cooperation," he said, then turned and headed out with Lieutenant Pak in tow.

"Yeah, yeah," he heard Wilks mutter as he went.

11

MANIFEST DESTINY

A weather-stained wooden sign stuck out from the wall of a four-story building of pitted brick. It hung next to an alley between the four-story building and a barber shop next door. The arrow on the bottom of the sign pointed down the alley.

Sadler Fine Art, the sign declared.

"Very classy," Danny said, peering down the alley. Even now, in the middle of the day, it was dark between the buildings.

"That Wilks fellow said Sadler got fired from his university job," Redhorn said. "This is probably the best he could do."

Danny began heading down the alley, looking for the entrance to the studio.

"That doesn't make sense either," he said. "If this guy is good enough to make a forgery of a famous sculpture, why isn't he selling his own stuff?"

"He probably can't. I investigated some stolen art cases in Germany after the war, and you'd be surprised what passes for fine art. It mostly depends on whether or not rich people like the artist or not. If they do, they buy his stuff and tell their friends to buy his stuff, and he does well."

"If not," Danny said, indicating a plain wooden door set into the wall, "the artist ends up in a studio at the end of an alley."

"Wilks did say he was an ass."

"Should we knock?"

"I don't know about you, Lieutenant, but I've never been that lucky."

Danny chuckled as he knocked on the door.

"You work every day with two beautiful women, Redhorn. I'd say you're lucky."

The FBI man made a face that Danny couldn't interpret. It wasn't much, just a slight shift of expression, but he clearly had opinions about his work. Opinions he didn't seem willing to share.

"It's the middle of the day," Redhorn said after a pause. "Maybe it's open."

Danny tried the knob, but it didn't yield.

"Stand aside," Redhorn said, taking a step back.

"No need for that," Danny said, pulling his key ring from his pocked. "One benefit of being a cop." He held up a large key from the ring. "Skeleton key."

A good quarter of the locks in the city were too new for the skeleton key, but Gilbert Sadler's door was old and the key slid right in. With one quick turn, the lock snapped open, and Danny pushed the door aside.

Redhorn drew his weapon and stepped up to the other side of the frame. Danny gave him a quizzical look, but the big man just shrugged.

"Let's not take chances," he said before stepping around the frame and raising his weapon.

"I'm pretty sure we'll be fine as long as we don't drink anything Sadler might offer us," Danny said, following along.

"Did you forget the dog monster we just found in a mobster's house?" Redhorn chided him.

"Point taken," he said, following the FBI man inside. They found themselves immediately in Sadler's studio. There were shelves and workbenches around the perimeter of a fairly large room. In the center of the room was a small, sturdy table directly under four ceiling lights. It was obviously where Sadler did his work. To the casual glance, it was what Danny imagined a sculptor's workshop would look like.

If everything had been made of stone.

Redhorn whistled as he looked around. The benches, the hammers, the carving tools, even the shelves were all made of the same gray granite.

"Since I suspect those chisels had metal tips when Sadler bought them," Danny said. "I'm guessing we're in the right place."

"That's just creepy," Redhorn said, tapping the butt of his gun on the table in the middle of the room, producing a clack instead of the expected thunk.

"If Sadler was affected by the Limelight, why isn't he dead?" Danny wondered.

"Maybe he knew what he was getting into," Redhorn said. "Everyone else developed magical abilities they didn't expect. They ended up dead because they weren't ready for them."

That made sense in a backward sort of way.

"Anything's possible, I guess," Danny admitted, though something about Redhorn's statement bothered him.

Even though the shelves and tables were stone, there were actual statues on some of them and Danny moved close for a better view. Most were birds on perches, probably the reason he was chosen to duplicate the jade phoenix.

"I don't know much about art, but these are amazing," he said.

"Well, you don't get to be a forger if you aren't good at your craft," Redhorn said as he examined some of the stone tools. "I don't see any evidence that a block of jade was carved here," he went on. "There would be a large amount of waste and I don't even see any dust."

"Well, if you're right that Sadler knew what he had, then he wouldn't have wanted to waste any of it, right?"

Redhorn considered that for a moment, then shrugged and nodded.

"There's nothing here," he declared. "Maybe we'll have better luck with his apartment."

As if on cue, a loud clunk came from above. To Danny it sounded like something heavy had been knocked over on the floor. Reaching into his coat for his service revolver, he looked at Redhorn who already had his weapon in hand. Redhorn pointed to an opening in the back wall and Danny could see the bottom riser of the staircase. Moving as quietly as possible, he put his foot on the first step, only to be met with an echoing creak as he transferred his weight to it. The second step wasn't any better and he ground his teeth together in frustration.

"Police," he called up the stairwell. If Sadler or anyone else was up there, they already knew someone was coming. "Anyone upstairs come down and keep your hands where I can see them."

Danny's words echoed away up the stairs and only silence answered him.

"Don't make us shoot you," Redhorn growled. "Come out now."

When there was still no answer after a few minutes, Danny continued slowly up to the top landing, aiming his weapon upward as he went.

"There's a door here," he whispered down to Redhorn.

Since the door would block the vision of anyone inside, Danny went up the last few steps and took a position on the far side of the door. Redhorn moved to the landing and nodded. Since the hinges weren't visible, that meant the door would open in. Danny twisted the knob and pushed the door open in one smooth motion. He expected there to be shots or a shout of challenge, but nothing happened.

Taking a deep breath to steady his nerves, Danny ducked out from the frame, then immediately back. The brief glimpse he got of the room beyond revealed it to be a one room unit with a bed occupying the back wall and the stove and icebox on the right. There wasn't any sign of life.

"Looks clear," he hissed.

Redhorn nodded, then held up three fingers, and began counting down. When he reached one, Danny stepped around and though the door just ahead of the big FBI man. He trained his gun on the right side of the room, but nothing moved. A little round table sat next to a chair, with what passed for a kitchen behind it. A shelf along the wall held half a dozen carved statues of birds, and there were dishes stacked next to the sink, but that was all.

"Clear," he said.

"Same here," Redhorn replied. "You need to come take a look at this."

Danny turned and found Redhorn indicating a workbench that had been shoved in a corner by the unmade bed. Atop it were glass beakers, jars, and graduated cylinders. He'd seen things like this before, in Dr. Kellin's basement workshop.

"He's an alchemist?" Danny asked, coming over to join Redhorn.

"I'd say that's a good bet," the FBI man said. He had picked up a notebook from the bench and was paging through it. "I'm no expert, but these look like formulas to me."

He held it out so that Danny could see it, but the complex notations inside the book didn't make any sense to him either. It did explain why Sadler hadn't killed himself with some errant display of magic, however. Alchemists and runewrights were affected differently by Limelight.

"It looks like he's frustrated with his skill," Redhorn said, "or lack thereof." He continued paging through the book. "There are several attempts at a recipe for a regeneration potion, all crossed out." He squinted for a moment. "Finally he seems to give up. *I should be able to do this*," he read. "*Why is there so much magic for others, but so little for me?*"

"Why does he care?" Danny wondered, more to himself than anything. "He's a master sculptor."

"The grass is always greener," Redhorn said, tossing the alchemy book on the workbench. "Let's keep looking."

Danny looked around at the tiny apartment and shrugged.

"You want to check the cupboards while I look in the dresser?"

He's said it in jest, but Redhorn just nodded and headed toward the kitchen space. Danny turned to the narrow dresser that was crammed in between the single bed and the ice box. Inside were rumpled clothes that appeared to have been simply crammed inside. Many had dust and stone chips still covering them, evidence that Sadler hadn't had his laundry done in some time. There were five drawers, but it didn't take him long to get through them as all they held were clothes. With a sigh, he shut the drawers and turned his attention to the bed.

Crouching down, he found the underside of the little cot to contain only dust. As he stood, Danny grabbed the thin mattress and picked it up, scanning the wire frame that supported it.

All as they should be.

Laying the mattress back down, he picked up the pillow, but nothing was concealed there either. With a frustrated sigh he dropped the greasy pillow back on the bed and looked around the room. There was a shelf against the wall opposite of the dresser, but all it held was a few jars of alchemical powders.

He was about to turn back to the other side of the room, where from the sound of it, Redhorn was looking in the oven, but the sight of the alchemical table stopped him. It was a simple structure made of rough boards that had been nailed together. Diagonal support braces had been added to the legs to keep the top stable, probably by Sadler when he decided to use it for his alchemy. Despite the state of the tiny bedroom, the braces had been expertly installed, fastened with 2 wood screws on each end of the brace.

Reaching in his pocket, Danny took out a quarter and set it down on its edge in the middle of the table. When he released it, it stood for a moment, then fell over. It didn't roll at all.

"It's perfectly level," he said to himself.

It was easy to forget that, as disheveled as Sadler's room was, the man himself was a master craftsman.

And a master craftsman wouldn't hide anything important under his pillow.

Crouching down, Danny looked under the table, but there wasn't anything concealed there. The table was only as thick as the boards that made up the top, so there wasn't any room for a hidden compartment. Standing, Danny scanned the room. Agent Redhorn was going through the icebox, looking for hidden compartments, but Danny discounted that idea. The table braces spoke of a man who was competent with his hands. The kind of man who wouldn't leave the protection of his secrets to the craftsmanship of another.

He glanced at the shelves holding up the alchemy supplies, but they were shoddy and ugly, not the work of an artist. The dresser was similarly impossible, as was the long shelf against the far wall. All of the furniture was drab and plain.

Ugly.

The only beauty in the room were the exquisitely carved birds sitting on their stone perches. There were five of them. Danny never was much of a bird watcher, so all he could tell was that they were all different. The first statue had two small birds cuddling on a branch. The second had something tropical with an enormous beak. The third was carved out of glossy black stone and depicted a crow. The fourth was cut from crystal and depicted three small birds with long beaks they were dipping into flowers.

The last bird was different from the others. The first four statues were all mounted on solid bases, but the last one was in a cage, as if it were a pet. The cage was made of tin and entirely ordinary. The bird was one Danny did know, a parrot, with its large, round beak and upswept plumage. It was so detailed that it looked as if there were tiny spaces between the feathers, as if they'd been carved separately and attached to the bird.

"What are you doing in there?" Danny said, leaning close.

"What are you doing?" the bird squawked.

Danny jerked back from the cage so quickly that he stumbled and fell on his backside. Before he could stand up, Redhorn was standing over him with his gun pointed at the cage.

"It's all right," Danny said, sitting up. "It just startled me."

"Well," Redhorn said, shoving his pistol into his shoulder holster. "Now we know how the lion in front of the library ended up in traffic." He reached down and gave Danny a hand back up to his feet.

"Only artists understand art," the parrot screeched.

"And we know why he's not a better-known artist," Danny said, leaning back toward the cage. "He has contempt for the people who buy art." The bird shuffled its stone feathers and clawed at its perch before going completely still again.

"I'd say this place is a bust," Redhorn said. "The only thing I found was a fresh bottle of milk in his ice box. Means he's been here within the last twenty-four hours. Maybe if we stake the place out, we'll get lucky."

It wasn't a bad idea, but Danny wasn't done with his search yet. He'd been distracted by the strange, ordinary cage the parrot resided in, but now he knew why it existed. Sadler had brought the thing to life and then had to keep it from moving around.

Satisfied that he understood that mystery, Danny turned his attention to the other four statues. The first three had bases made from a solid slab of marble, but the fourth statue had a base of carved wood.

"This one," Danny said.

"Hummingbirds," Redhorn supplied.

Danny gave the man a raised eyebrow.

"National Geographic," he supplied. "My wife is a fan."

Danny didn't know that Redhorn was married. Come to think of it, he didn't really know much about the man at all, apart from his first name being Buddy. That had to stand for something, but Danny had no idea what.

"Notice how all the statues have stone bases except the hummingbirds," he said. He reached out and took a solid grip on the heavy stone that made up the bottom of the sculpture, then lifted it off the wooden base.

"Grab that."

Redhorn took the base out from under the heavy statue and Danny put it carefully beck on the shelf. The FBI man flipped the base over, revealing a cloth strap tacked to the hollow underside. The strap held a thick notebook in place.

"Good catch, Lieutenant," Redhorn said, extracting the book and handing it to Danny while he set the wooden base aside on the tiny kitchen table.

Opening to the first page, Danny fond Sadler's name and the phrase, *Only Artists Understand Art*, written in bold letters. He flipped through a few pages, scanning the scrawled entries as he went. It looked like a journal of Sadler's thoughts, but there were also notes about sculpture and art.

"Anything relevant?" Redhorn asked.

"He seems to hate sorcerers," Danny said, squinting at the messy script. "He says that the reason so many alchemists don't have more magic is that the sorcerers use it all up."

"That's not how magic works," Redhorn declared.

"Sadler thinks it is," Danny went on. "He's suggesting the government kill all the sorcerers to spread magic to the masses."

"Bolshevik nonsense," the FBI man growled. "Skip to the back, maybe he says something about the statue."

Danny flipped to the end of the writing, then back a few pages.

"Here it is," he said after a moment. "He was commissioned to carve the forgery of the Jade Phoenix. He doesn't say who hired him."

"I guess that would have made things too easy. What else does he say?"

"Looks like he figured out that the statue had magical properties but not until he'd passed it on to his client."

"How did he figure it out after the fact?"

"He says he got some of the jade dust in his bourbon when he was cleaning up," Danny read. "I think the Limelight was beginning to affect him, the writing gets worse here. I can't make much out but there's something about giving regular people magic."

"People like the art supply store owner," Redhorn said.

"He mentions Peter Grant, right here," Danny said, pointing to the passage, "Along with something about the *jade's gift*. It's the last thing he wrote."

"We have to stop this guy, Lieutenant," Redhorn said, a look of stoic determination on his face. "If we don't, there's going to be chaos in the streets before this thing is done."

"Chaos!" the parrot croaked.

"What are we going do with that thing?" Danny asked as the stone bird began preening itself.

"Leave it," Redhorn said. "It's not like it needs to eat."

Danny regarded him skeptically.

"You sure about that? Besides, it's evidence."

Redhorn gave Danny a skeptical look back.

"Why do I get the feeling you just want to take it home?"

"Not me," Danny chuckled. "My landlady would have a fit."

Redhorn looked from Danny to the parrot and back.

"Fine," he growled. "My kids have been bothering their mother for a pet. At least this is one I probably won't have to clean up after."

"Kids?"

"A boy and a girl," Redhorn said. He tried to pick up the cage with one hand, but had to resort to both hands to pick up the stone bird. "Let's get out of here before you saddle me with anything else."

12

TRIAL & ERROR

Buddy grunted as he lifted the heavy bird's cage into the back seat of Lieutenant Pak's Ford coupe. Pak had insisted the parrot was evidence, but Buddy couldn't help wondering if the policeman just thought the idea of him keeping it was funny.

The Lieutenant was a bit of a mystery to him. He was smart, observant, and his instincts were top notch, but he engaged in entirely too much levity in the field. With any luck they could track down the errant sculptor quickly and he could get back to his protégé.

"I have an idea about finding Mr. Sadler," Buddy said as he moved the seat back and sat down on the passenger side of the car. "You've got the chip from the paint shop guy's coffee cup, right? Why don't we just have Lockerby's assistant use a finding rune to track down the other pieces? It's a safe bet Sadler has the remaining bits with him."

Lieutenant Pak shook his head as he pulled open the driver's door and sat down.

"The problem is that there are a whole bunch of these chips that used to be part of the block but got removed when Sadler made the statue," he said. "The more pieces something is in, the harder it is for a finding rune to lock on to it. Sadler probably has some of the chips on him, true, but I doubt he's carrying the stature around with him. He's got that stashed somewhere."

"We still ought to try," Buddy responded. "Maybe we'll get lucky."

The lieutenant gave him a speculative look, then shrugged.

"I usually have to make my own luck," he said. "But stranger things have happened. Let's find a phone and you can call Sherry while I check in with my captain."

The nearest public phone turned out to be a block away at one of the skycrawler stations near the University. Since there were five booths lined up in a row, Buddy and the lieutenant were able to call simultaneously. Buddy pulled a thin black contact book from his back pocket and opened it to the letter 'L'. A moment later he was connected with Lockerby's perky, dark-haired secretary. She passed Buddy on to Mike Fitzgerald, Alex's assistant.

"I'm certainly willing to try," he said, a bit of his Irish heritage coming through in his voice. "But honestly, Lieutenant Pak is right about the finding rune, and it's probably worse than he let on. When your suspect carved that statue, there would have been lots of dust and tiny bits that probably got swept up and thrown away. That would make it impossible to track the stone your chip came from."

Buddy resisted the urge to swear. It wouldn't be professional.

"What if I had a piece of the finished statue?" he said. "Could you use that to find the statue itself?"

"Sure," Fitzgerald said. "That'd be easy."

"Great. You stay there, I'll be over to your office in half an hour."

Fitzgerald promised to stay put, and Buddy hung up. When he stepped out of the booth, he found Lieutenant Pak waiting for him.

"You were right," Buddy said. "There's pretty much no chance of finding what's left of that jade block with a finding rune. But you've still got that piece of the fake statue the dog bit off, right? Mr. Fitzgerald says that's a whole different story."

"It'll have to wait," Pak said, giving Buddy one of his rare serious looks. "My captain got a call about half an hour ago regarding a

Hooverville in Central Park that burned down about an hour ago. Witnesses reported a man made of fire running through the camp right before everything went up in flames."

"Damn," Buddy growled, kicking professionalism right out the window. This was turning out to be a much bigger case than he'd anticipated, and much more magical. He wished that Miss Kincaid was here, but calling her away from her case in DC would look bad. "All right," he sighed, bringing his temper to heel. "Let's get over there. Maybe we'll get lucky and our sculptor is still lurking around."

According to the police, the homeless camp was just off Ninetieth Street at Engineer's Gate. Coming from the south side, it took over half an hour to reach the park. By that time a dozen police cars and an ambulance were pulled up to the curb in the vicinity of the gate.

A uniformed policeman in a heavy blue overcoat tried to stop them when Pak pulled his car alongside a black police sedan, but after a moment he recognized the lieutenant and gave him a salute.

"What's the situation?" Pak asked as he got out of his car.

"It's a mess," the officer said. "Half the camp burned down and there's a couple of dozen people dead, a bunch of women and kids mostly." He bowed his head and crossed himself. "They took a few to the hospital too."

"Who's in charge of the scene?"

"Detective Nicholson."

Lieutenant Pak thanked the officer, then reached into the back seat for his overcoat. The weather was decidedly chilly, and Buddy buttoned up his suit jacket. There hadn't been much wind earlier, but out in the open of the park there was a definite breeze. He'd left his overcoat in his car, since he hadn't anticipated being outside for any length of time. Suppressing a shiver as the wind whistled around him, he wished he'd been more prepared.

"Want me to see if I can round up a spare coat?" Pak said once he had his buttoned.

"I'll be fine," Buddy said. He'd learned years ago, in the trenches of northern France, never to show weakness, and old habits died hard.

The lieutenant just shrugged and headed down the grassy slope toward the knot of policemen. Buddy followed him out across the frozen grass to what was left of the makeshift camp. It was nothing more than some wooden structures pieced together from scraps and some tent-like lean-tos. The entire front side of the camp had been decimated by fire, leaving the charred supports of the wooden buildings sticking up from the debris like blackened bones.

Ragged people were gathered around a few metal barrels with fires in them, huddling close as much for comfort as for warmth. A woman sat on a tree stump clutching a wrapped bundle to her chest and weeping quietly. As Buddy passed, he saw that the bundle wasn't moving.

If Lieutenant Pak noticed the tragic scene, he made no outward sign. He led the way through the remains of the burned camp toward a paunchy man in a rumpled suit.

"Hello, Lieutenant," the man said. "I expected them to send Detweiler."

"I'm not taking over," Pak assured him. "The Captain said something here might relate to a case I'm working. Something about the fire being started by a burning man."

The detective, whom Buddy assumed to be Nicholson, looked around as if he was afraid of being overheard.

"That ain't the half of it, sir," he said in a low voice. "I've got three eyewitnesses who said they saw one of their friends burst into flame, then run off laughing. Then there's the girl."

"Girl?" Buddy and Pak said together.

Nicholson didn't speak, just motioned for them to follow as he made for one of the wooden structures that only looked a little burned. The door was covered with a bit of thick canvas and when the detective pulled it back, it revealed a tiny space. Inside was a woman, dressed in ragged, bloodstained clothes. Her hands had been cuffed behind her back and around a heavy support beam that held up the center of the ceiling.

As Buddy looked, the woman turned toward the door. She had

gaunt features that might have been pretty once, and her eyes were dark and unreadable. The wrists that were secured by the handcuffs were thin almost to the point of emaciation and Buddy could see the bones in her shoulders and hips as she sat.

"Did you bring me something to eat?" she said, her voice a bit slurred.

Buddy's first thought was that she might be drunk, but any such analysis disappeared when she smiled. Instead of normal teeth, this woman had rows and rows of triangular teeth in her mouth, like a shark.

"What the devil is that?" Buddy growled.

Nicholson dropped the canvas curtain back into place and looked around again.

"The first officers on the scene said they caught her eating one of the burn victims," he said. "Thank God he was already dead. The cop handcuffed her but she almost managed to escape."

"She slip through the cuffs?" Pak asked. "Her wrists are tiny."

Nicholson shook his head.

"She chewed them right off her wrists," the detective answered.

"What's her name?" Pak asked.

Nicholson checked his notebook before replying.

"Penny Walker," he replied.

"We need to talk to her," Lieutenant Pak said.

"I don't know, Lieutenant," Nicholson said. "She's already tried to bite three of my men, almost succeeded, too."

Buddy dug into his pocket and extracted a leather disk about a quarter of an inch thick. Squeezing it, the top opened, revealing a small group of coins inside.

"Here," he said, handing Nicholson two quarters. "Send one of your men to find a peanut vendor and get as many bags as that will buy."

"Good idea," Pak said with an approving nod.

Nicholson called over a young officer with jet black hair and eager expression, then handed him the money and repeated the instructions. A moment later the young man was off like a shot.

"While we're waiting," Buddy said to the detective. "What story are the witnesses telling?"

Nicholson consulted his book again.

"They're mostly all over the place," he replied after a moment. "The only thing they really agree on is that whatever happened, it started down there." He pointed to a spot on the edge of the camp where several picnic tables stood. In the center of the area was a fire pit, ringed by blackened stones, and containing a heap of still steaming coals.

"It looks like where the residents here did their cooking," Pak said.

Buddy followed his train of thought quickly. If one had to ingest the Limelight for it to work, the mess area would be a prime place to distribute it.

"Let's take a closer look," he muttered back to the Lieutenant.

Moving down the slope to the fire pit, they found seven bodies lined up and covered with coats and bits of canvas. Buddy noted them, but the feeling of pain and sorrow at the death of another human being had been melted out of him in France.

Around the fire pit were spits for roasting, one of which still had a blackened squirrel impaled on it. There were also a dozen or so wooden bowls scattered around on the ground. Realizing what he was seeing, Buddy swept the scene until he found what he was looking for.

"There," he said, putting a hand on Pak's shoulder. He pointed at a large kettle sitting on a flat rock off to one side. "Someone made soup."

"Right," Pak said, moving over to the kettle.

Inside was a thin layer of dark liquid, but the boil line on the inside indicated that it had once held much more.

"You're thinking our man spiked their dinner?" Pak said.

Buddy nodded.

"That would explain everything," he said.

"Hey, Agent Redhorn," Detective Nicholson called as he approached. "Your peanuts are here."

"Good," Buddy said.

"Get someone down here in heavy gloves and a gas mask," Pak said to the detective. "Have them transfer the contents of that pot to a glass jar and seal it with lead. And make sure no one touches it."

Nicholson scribbled quickly in his notebook, nodding as he did so.

"Hey, Detective!" someone called from the camp proper. "I've got someone alive up here."

Pak took off running in the direction of the voice. Taken by surprise, Buddy started after him and only barely managed to catch up when they reached their destination. For a little guy, Pak was quick.

The policeman who had called out stood over another officer who was crouched down next to what appeared to be a burned, naked body. Before he or Lieutenant Pak could speak, the body jolted and sat up.

"Cold," it gasped. "Why is it so cold?"

"Take it easy," the kneeling officer said, putting a hand on the burned man's shoulder. "We'll get you a coat right away."

He looked up at his partner, who immediately began unbuttoning his heavy police overcoat. Before the standing officer could finish, however, the kneeling officer let out a scream of agony and jerked back from the burned man, cradling his hand against his chest. An acrid, stomach-turning smell permeated the air, one Buddy knew all too well.

Burning flesh.

"Get back," he shouted as the sitting man's naked body changed from black to a copper color. Buddy was forced to put his arm in front of his face as waves of intense heat rolled off the man.

Lieutenant Pak reacted fast, scooping up the man with the burned hand and dragging him away. The officer who was unbuttoning his coat, however, was caught flat-footed and he screamed as the intense heat singed his hair and burned his skin.

Buddy didn't hesitate. Pulling his 1911, he fired three shots into the burning man. All three hit, slamming into the torso in a tight group. The screaming man stumbled back, trying to get away from the blistering heat, and fire erupted from the bullet wounds in the burning man's torso. Buddy lowered his weapon, but the man didn't fall. Instead, his head rotated to look at Buddy. He didn't have any distinct eyes, but Buddy would have sworn he was being scowled at.

Without waiting to find out what the burning man would do, Buddy turned and ran. He felt a burst of heat as a flaming blob of something sailed past him and landed, sizzling, on the frozen ground.

More shots rang out and he turned to see Lieutenant Pak empty his police revolver into the flaming man. These had no more effect than

Buddy's shots had, though the creature of fire stopped looking at Buddy and turned its attention to the lieutenant. It stood up, wobbling a bit as it did so, then staggered toward Pak. The lieutenant backed away as he reloaded his revolver; thankfully the fire creature wasn't very fast.

Finished reloading, Pak fired again. This time several of the shots took the creature in the head and Buddy could see lumps of burning lead come oozing out the back to fall on the ground.

Clearly bullets were not going to stop this thing.

Buddy looked around. The camp was next to Engineer's Gate, one of Central Park's fancy entrances, and stood just above the Central Park Reservoir.

"Lead him that way," Buddy yelled, pointing to a spot where the ground fell away sharply.

The burning man sensed that they were toying with him, and he raised his hand and threw a bob of burning magma at Pak, who dodged it easily. Buddy had no fear the agile lieutenant would get hit by a magma ball, so he turned back to the camp. Scooping up a half-burned tarp, he threw it over his shoulder, then grabbed a short wooden plank that had undoubtedly been part of a shanty's wall before the fire. He wanted to look for more, but Lieutenant Pak yelled at him.

"What now?"

"Keep his attention on you," Buddy yelled, as he dropped the plank and draped the canvas over his head and down the right side of his body. He had to hold the top with his left hand to keep it from falling off, but he managed it. Finally, he picked up the thick board and held it across his body, just over his right shoulder.

Several more shots rang out and Buddy knew he was out of time. Leaping into a dead sprint, he hurtled himself through the remains of the camp, down to the spot where the ground began to angle steeply downward. He felt the heat from the burning man even before he was close, and it grew more and more intense as he charged. When he finally thought he couldn't take it anymore, the plank across his shoulder impacted the monster. Heat and fire washed over the wet canvas, drying it instantly and setting parts of it alight.

Buddy threw himself to the side as the fire monster was knocked forward. Hitting the ground, Buddy rolled, intentionally preserving his momentum and allowing it to carry him as far away from the blazing horror as he could get. Before he stopped, he heard the creature cry out, then the cry began to fade.

As he stopped rolling, Buddy tried to force himself to stand but a wave of dizziness swept over him and he hesitated. The creature screamed again, this time from far away and it wasn't a sound of anger, but rather one of agony.

Pushing himself to his feet, he moved over to where Lieutenant Pack was staring down the steep hill. Below, the fire monster was thrashing around in the shallow water at the reservoir's edge. Everywhere the water touched him, steam erupted and the glowing red color dulled. The monster wasn't that far from shore, but it was blinded by panic and rage. After half a minute, the thing stiffened and fell back into the water with a cry of despair. A moment later all that was left of it was the steam floating over the surface of the reservoir.

"That was pretty clever," Pak admitted, giving Buddy an impressed look. "Where'd you learn to do that?"

"In the war," Buddy said, staring down at the now quiet water. "I saw a man charge a flame thrower like that."

Pak whistled.

"That's brave," he said.

"It's stupid," Buddy said. "He didn't survive."

Pak looked stunned at that admission.

"Then why did you imitate him?"

"The same reason he charged the flame thrower in the first place," Buddy said with a shrug. "It needed to be done."

13

STORIES

Buddy Redhorn pulled the 1911 pistol from his shoulder holster, then nodded to the policeman who stood holding the edge of the canvas flap. The man gave him a worried look, then pulled the flap aside, revealing a small, sheltered space. As shelters went it wasn't much, just a wooden frame and walls made of canvas and heavy blankets. Still, Buddy supposed it was better than nothing.

The roof of the makeshift shelter was made of two pieces of corrugated metal, held in place by the wooden frame and supported by a center pole that had been dug into the ground to keep it from moving. Sitting against this pole was a woman with her hands cuffed behind her on the opposite side of the support. As Buddy entered, she looked up at him with a smile.

It gave him chills.

According to the police her name was Penny Walker, but the officers had already started calling her Penny Piranha. Whatever had happened in the Hooverville had affected her. She now had jagged, triangular teeth, like a shark.

When the officer first arrived at the scene, they found her eating a corpse. Buddy tried in vain not to shiver at that thought. He covered the show of weakness by moving inside the shanty.

"Miss Walker?" he said, moving around so he could sit on the shanty's only bit of furniture, a wooden footstool. "My name is Agent Redhorn, and I'm with the FBI."

"I'm very hungry," she said, slurring her words because of the mouthful of flat, serrated teeth she now possessed.

Buddy tried to focus on the rest of her face and ignore the teeth. She appeared to be fairly young, maybe in her mid-twenties, with dirty blonde hair, pale skin, and dark eyes. It was clear that she hadn't eaten well in some time as her body was extremely gaunt.

Except for her belly.

In other circumstances, Buddy would have assumed she was with child given such a bulging stomach, but it was much more likely that she'd simply gorged herself on her most recent meal. That thought made Buddy queasy again and he took a deep breath to steady himself.

"I brought you some food," he said, as conversationally as he could manage.

"Really?" she said, her hellish mouth widening out in a rictus grin. When she smiled, Penny Walker's eyes went completely black, like a shark's when it attacked.

"You see this?" Buddy said, holding out his gun that was pointed right at her heart.

The black circles that were her eyes retreated so Buddy could see a bit of the whites, and she nodded.

"I'm going to have someone un-cuff you so you can eat," Buddy explained. "If you try to bite him, or me, or do anything I think is threatening, Miss Walker, I am going to shoot you in the heart. You'll be dead before your body hits the ground. Do you understand me?"

Her expression was hard to read with the permanent smile the teeth forced on her, but she regarded him for a moment, then nodded.

"All right, Lieutenant," Buddy called.

A moment later, Lieutenant Pak came in with a sack full of hot peanuts and a ring of keys. He handed the sack to Buddy, being careful to stay out of Penny Walker's lunge range, then moved behind her to release her handcuffs. Buddy shifted his grip on the pistol, keeping it pointed toward the afflicted woman's center of mass.

Once her hands were free, Penny started to reach out for the bag but Buddy held up the gun and she stopped. After a moment to make sure she was in control of her actions, he tossed her the bag. Snatching it out of the air, she grabbed a handful of the nuts and shoved them in her maw, shells and all. Her rictus grin widened as she began to chew and her eyes went black again.

"Do you mind if I ask you some questions now?" he asked her.

She grabbed another handful of nuts and nodded before shoving them after the last batch.

"Were you down where the people were cooking before the fire started?"

She nodded again, but slowly.

"Did you see the fire start?"

Nod.

"What happened?"

Penny chewed for a few seconds, then swallowed with a shiver of pleasure.

"Miles caught on fire," she said. "He was just sitting there eating his soup, and then the next minute he was running through the camp burning everything he touched."

"What did you do?"

She looked away for a moment, then met his gaze.

"You have to understand," she said. "I was so hungry. I hadn't found any food in days. Matt Shaw said he'd trade me some for...for a little... companionship, but I'm not that kind of girl."

Buddy resisted the urge to grind his teeth as his jaw tightened in reaction to Penny's story.

"Did you eat the soup?" he asked.

She nodded.

"A man came with a whole basket full of vegetables, broth bones, and even some meat scraps. He said it was for all of us. I had two bowls."

Looks like Pak was right to have the police collect it.

"What happened after Miles started burning the camp?" he pressed. "Did you see anything else that was strange?"

Penny blushed and shoved another handful of peanuts into her mouth so she couldn't answer. Buddy just waited patiently for her to finish chewing.

"I didn't see anything," she said after the silence dragged on for the better part of a minute. "I was...I was busy."

Buddy knew what she wasn't saying. Her hunger had driven her to use her new teeth on one of Miles' burn victims.

"All right, Miss Walker," Buddy said in a gentle voice. "That's all I wanted to know. The police are going to take you to the hospital now. If you think of anything else, tell one of the officers and they'll tell me."

"Something bit me," she declared, clutching the bag of peanuts.

"What do you mean?" Buddy asked.

"Right before Miles burned up," she said in a low voice. "Something bit me on my back."

She reached up and pulled the flimsy fabric of her dress down over her shoulder and turned. Buddy didn't see anything that looked like a bite mark, but she did have a burn mark in the shape of a tree branch.

Miles must have set a tree on fire and it landed on her.

"I'll have the doctors at the hospital look at it," Buddy said. "Thank you for your help." He stood as four uniformed officers entered and handcuffed the woman again. She protested when they took her bag of nuts, but they quickly assured her that she could have it back when they got to the hospital.

Buddy watched as the men escorted Penny Walker up the incline back to the street.

"What do you think?" he asked, turning to the lieutenant.

Pak scoffed and shook his head.

"I think we'd better find Gilbert Sadler," he said, "and fast. At the rate he's going, we're going to be facing down an army of these magically afflicted people."

"Innocent people," Buddy corrected.

"That isn't going to keep us from having to shoot them," Pak growled.

Buddy could feel the smaller man's frustration and he sympathized. He hadn't wanted to dump Miles in the reservoir, but the man hadn't given him much choice. If he and the Lieutenant didn't stop this madman, they were both going to have a lot of innocent blood on their hands.

Well, more innocent blood.

"I don't think there's anything more we can do here," Pak said, looking around at the scene of death and destruction. "Let's go to Alex's office and see if Mike can find our missing statue."

Before Buddy could agree, a heavyset man with thinning hair and a crooked nose approached them. Like Pak, he had a NYPD lieutenant's batch clipped to the outside breast pocket of his overcoat.

"There you are," he said to Lieutenant Pak. "Nicholson said you were over here somewhere."

"James," Pak said to the man with a nod of recognition.

He then introduced the man as Lieutenant James Detweiler. From the interaction, Buddy guessed that this new lieutenant was Pak's senior in the job and that he didn't particularly care for Pak, though that seemed personal rather than the result of Pak's lineage.

"What's the good word?" Pak asked once the introductions were done.

"Callahan wants to see you," he said, then jerked his thumb at Buddy. "You and your Federal pal here."

"Now's not a good time," Pak said, then he turned to Buddy. "Let's go find a phone and I'll call in."

The other lieutenant just laughed at that.

"He said you might feel that way," he said. "So he told me to remind you that he's the captain and when he gives you an order, you jump. He doesn't care how you feel about it."

Pak sighed and gave Buddy a look that was half frustration half apology.

"I guess we'll stop off at the Central Office on our way to Empire Tower," he said.

As Danny Pak got off the elevator on the tenth floor of the Central Office of Police, he had to admit to being confused. Callahan knew what he was doing and why it was so important, so why had he interrupted the case to have him come back to the office? And why had he insisted Danny bring Agent Redhorn along? How did he even know Danny had teamed up with Redhorn?

It didn't make a lot of sense, and that was what bothered Danny.

Still, Detweiler had a point, the Captain didn't care if it bothered him or not, so here he was, heading down the hall to Callahan's office with Agent Redhorn in tow.

When he reached the door, he started to knock, but paused when he heard raised voices. From the sound of it, at least two people were in the office besides Callahan and they weren't happy. Danny glanced at Redhorn, but the big man could only shrug.

Taking a deep breath, Danny rapped on the door and was promptly instructed to come in.

There were two men in Callahan's office besides the man himself, and Danny recognized both of them. The first man was tall and immaculately dressed, with slicked backed hair and a pencil mustache. His name was Arnold Montgomery, the Chief of Police for New York. Seeing him raised gooseflesh on Danny's arms. The Chief had an office on the other side of this floor, but he was more of a politician than an administrator and usually spent his days at a satellite office in city hall.

As concerning as it was to see the Chief in Callahan's office, the second man's presence was worse. J.D. Rockefeller stood on the far side of Callahan's desk with his arms folded and his bushy grey mustache drooping down in a frown. His eyes were hard and Danny could see a vein pulsating in the man's forehead.

"There you are, Lieutenant," Chief Montgomery said in an irritated voice. "What kept you?"

"I-," Danny stuttered, unprepared for the sudden question. "We were at the crime scene in the park, sir," he said finally. "We came as soon as Lieutenant Detweiler gave us your message."

"And now we're here," Redhorn said in an openly annoyed voice, "instead of chasing down a madman on a magical murdering spree. So, let's get to the point."

Chief Montgomery's face darkened as his gaze shifted to the FBI man.

"You'd be Agent Redhorn," he said. "I'll have you know I'm going to be speaking to Director Stevens about this matter presently."

"Tell him I said hello," Redhorn fired back, clearly not concerned about the veiled threat.

"Enough," Callahan snapped before the chief could say anything more. "I didn't call you two yahoos in here for no reason," he said, glaring at Danny and Redhorn. "When I assigned Lieutenant Pak to investigate this case, it was because I knew from experience that I could rely on a certain amount of discretion."

Danny exchanged a confused look with Agent Redhorn.

"Please explain this," Rockefeller said, speaking for the first time. He held up a tabloid with the screaming headline, *Killer Sorcerer on the Loose, Police Baffled*.

"The story," Montgomery explained. "Details of the death of Peter Grant and the incident with the library lion. According to the muck-raker who wrote it, the police are looking for a rogue sorcerer from out of town."

That isn't good, Danny thought. There were always small groups who were against sorcerers in general, but a story like that could whip up anti-sorcerer sentiment in the whole city.

"It goes on," Rockefeller said, reading from the article. "Eyewitnesses said that J.D. Rockefeller, one of New York's most powerful sorcerers, consulted on the case, but withdrew citing concerns for his own safety." He slammed the paper down on Callahan's desk.

And it just went from bad to worse.

"The only way anyone could have known that I even knew about this was if they were at that paint store yesterday," Rockefeller fumed. "The only people there, Lieutenant, were you, your detective, and a couple of beat cops."

Danny was about to object, but something in the story made him hesitate.

"When you and I first spoke," he said to Rockefeller, "you suggested that the death of Peter Grant might be the work of a sorcerer."

"This is not my fault," Rockefeller fumed.

"I don't think he's suggesting it was, Mr. Rockefeller," Redhorn interjected. "You and the police weren't the only ones to know about that event, after all. Someone called it in to the police in the first place, and there were police cars out in front, probably for hours."

"And there was Peter Grant's assistant, Agnes Cornwall," Danny added. "My point is that this story sounds like someone got their information by loitering outside the art shop after you arrived."

"I notice they didn't mention anything about that Limelight stuff," the sorcerer countered.

"Likely because I showed up and scared them off," Danny said, thankful that he'd been late by grabbing breakfast.

Rockefeller sneered at that explanation, but didn't object further. He exchanged an irritated glance with the Chief, then folded his arms.

"This story is a concern," Captain Callahan said, picking up the paper long enough to drop it in the wastebasket beside his desk. "It could start a panic if this case isn't wrapped up soon. So, how are we coming with that, Lieutenant Pak?"

"We believe that the man responsible for these incidents is a sculptor named Gilbert Sadler," he began, then walked the Chief, Callahan, and Rockefeller through their investigation from Nick Maretti, to the stone parrot, to the burning man, to Polly Piranha.

"This is getting out of hand, Lieutenant," Chief Montgomery said when Danny finished. "The way you describe it, anyone walking by the park could have seen you and the burning man. Not to mention that the death of Nick Maretti is going to be front page news by tomorrow at the latest."

Callahan nodded in agreement.

"What's your next step?" he asked.

Danny started to answer, but the Chief cut him off.

"Put someone else on this, Callahan," he said. "Several someones, I want this Sadler maniac off the streets tonight."

Callahan's fists clenched for a moment, then he looked up at the Chief standing over him.

"I already have my best man on this, Chief," he said. "And before you object, understand that Danny here is the only one who really understands what is going on with the Limelight and how dangerous it is. Anyone else I bring in would have to be read in on that and the more people who know about Limelight, the more chance there is that the next tabloid story will tell the city all about it."

"Right now," Danny added quickly, "the only people in the department who know about Limelight are in this room."

"You should probably keep it that way," Redhorn added.

Montgomery chewed his lip, then looked from Callahan to Danny.

"Do you have any way to catch this sculptor?" he asked.

Danny pulled the chip of the fake statue from his pocket and dropped it on Callahan's desk.

"As long as Sadler hasn't destroyed his fake Jade Phoenix statue, this piece will let us use a finding rune to locate it."

"And Sadler broke into a mobster's house to get that statue," Redhorn said. "He's not going to be far away when we find it."

The Chief chewed on his lip for a moment, then looked to Rockefeller, who just shrugged.

"All right," he said at last. "You two get out of here and find that madman. I don't care what it takes." He reached into his pocket and produced what looked like a short, thin cigarette case. Popping the lid open, he withdrew a pristine white business card and handed it to Danny. "If anyone gives you a hard time, have them call me directly."

"Yes, sir," Danny replied, tucking the card into his shirt pocket. He gave Callahan a thumbs up, then turned and followed Agent Redhorn out of the office.

"That was close," Danny said as he headed down the hall.

"I hate politics," the FBI man growled.

"I never would have guessed," Rockefeller's amused voice cut in from behind them. "You hide it so well."

Danny turned to find the sorcerer coming up behind them.

"Did you need something, sir?" he asked.

"I just wanted to ask you a question on your way to the elevators," he said with a twinkle in his eye. "Were you serious about that piranha woman?"

"Penny Walker," Redhorn supplied. "And yes, she has what looks like shark teeth."

"That's amazing," the sorcerer said in a voice that clearly indicated he was excited. "I wonder why the magic did that?"

"She was hungry," Danny said. "From the look of her, she hadn't eaten in weeks."

"From what we can tell," Redhorn elaborated, "exposure to this Limelight stuff gives people magic to suit their current wants or desires."

Rockefeller nodded at that, then turned to Danny.

"You said the police took Miss Walker to the hospital," Rockefeller said. "Any idea which one?"

14

MEDIUM EXPECTATIONS

Empire Tower had originally been conceived as an office building, but Andrew Barton had purchased it, lock, stock, and barrel, before the building was even finished. As a result, the building's interior tended to resemble the eccentric sorcerer himself. The first two floors were just the lobby, which mostly consisted of the public elevator up to the observation deck on the eighty-sixth floor. There was also a public relations office for Barton Electric where a company spokesman would outline the Lightning Lord's plans to bring wireless power to the globe.

Up from there was Empire Station, a massive open space that transected the building, allowing access to the skycrawler lines that were rapidly expanding all over the city. Above that were business offices up to the twentieth floor, a vast open space that housed Barton's Etherium Generators, then a dozen floors of exclusive residence apartments for Barton's key employees. And on the top, of course, the offices of Barton Electric, topped by the residence of the man himself.

Anyone wanting to reach the residence floors or the offices above had to go through a security checkpoint in Empire Terminal, but people wanting the lower business offices could take a public elevator.

Since Danny had his own car, he entered Empire Tower from the street and headed for the small public elevator off to the side of the massive doors that granted access to the observation platform elevator. He and Redhorn had conferred and decided to split up in order to cover more ground. Redhorn took a cab south to New York University to see if the art department had a picture of their former professor, while Danny went to Mike Fitzgerald to see if he could locate the fake Jade Phoenix.

Arriving at the business elevator, Danny pushed the button marked twelve and smiled as he realized the building didn't actually have a thirteenth floor. Many of the city's hotels lacked a thirtieth floor because superstitious patrons would often refuse to stay on an unlucky floor.

I guess business owners can be superstitious too.

When the elevator chimed and the doors opened, Danny turned left and went down to a solid wood door at the end of the hall. Gold lettering in an Art Deco typeface declared, *Lockerby Investigations*, and underneath in smaller lettering, *The Runewright Detective*.

Danny absently wondered when Alex had added the Runewright Detective bit back. He'd given that tabloid moniker up when he'd moved into Empire Tower.

Turning the solid brass handle, he took off his hat and walked in. The front room of Alex's office was just as elegant as the rest of the building, with comfortable couches on the side walls slanted slightly toward a gleaming desk in front of a massive window.

In front of the window and the desk stood Alex's secretary, Sherry Knox. She was shorter than Alex's former secretary, Leslie Tompkins, and not quite as tall or curvy, but that wasn't really a fair comparison. Leslie had been a beauty queen when she was younger, and time had been good to her. Sherry looked to be in her late twenties, maybe early thirties, with dark hair and blue eyes. Unlike Leslie who was perfectly pale, Sherry had a skin tone that made her look like she had a perpetual tan. Not as brown as Danny, but something vaguely Latin.

Of course it was useless to speculate about Sherry's origins as they were literally lost to history. Sherry might look to be about Danny's age, but she was very much an older woman. Three thousand or so years older. To be fair, for most of that time, she'd been a mummy, magically preserved until a triggering spell returned her to life. There had been a time when Danny wouldn't have believed such a story, but Sherry wasn't even the strangest thing he'd been exposed to since meeting Alex.

Danny shut the door behind him just as Sherry looked up from a notepad where she'd been scribbling. She sat on the edge of the desk with one leg up and crooked slightly and her back ramrod straight. Leslie Tompkins had that posture from her beauty queen days, but Sherry didn't have that training. Clearly she'd chosen this pose for effect, twisting her hips just enough to tug the hem of her skirt an extra inch up her thigh while showing off her upper body in profile.

Clearly she meant to impress someone.

She can see the future, you dunce, he chided himself. The implications of that raised his eyebrows and he couldn't keep the smile off his face.

"Why, Detective Pak," she said with a somewhat mocking smile. "It's been over a month since you've been by. I...we were starting to think you'd forgotten about us."

"Perish the thought, Miss Knox," Danny said, moving to the desk and dropping his hat on it. "But you did warn me to keep away last time I called."

She smirked at that, and a genuine smile spread across her face. Danny noticed that up close she had faded freckles on the bridge of her nose and across her cheeks.

"I did say that, didn't I?" she said. "Well, Alex is out of town right now, so I guess it's okay that you're here. Did you come to see me then?"

"Absolutely," Danny lied. "I desperately need your help." He dug into his pocket and pulled out the broken bit of the fake Jade Phoenix, tossing it on the desk. "You think you can use your powers of persuasion to get Mike to find the rest of this?"

Sherry's smile grew positively predatory as she slipped off the desk and sauntered around to the far side. She was giving Danny ample opportunity to admire her figure and he didn't waste it. By the time she reached the intercom box, Danny felt like he needed to take off his suit coat due to the rise in the room's temperature.

"Mike," she said after pressing one of the keys on the front of the box. “Lieutenant Pak is out front and he’s got something he wants you to trace.”

A moment later the side door on the right opened and Mike Fitzgerald emerged

“How are you, Lieutenant?” he said, inclining his head in a brief nod.

“He wants you to find the rest of this,” Sherry said, picking up the bit of statue. “Owch!” she exclaimed, dropping the bit of green stone back onto the desk and pressing her thumb against her lips.

“What’s the matter?” Danny and Mike asked at the same time.

“It’s got a sharp edge,” she said, pulling her thumb away long enough to look at the small cut that was oozing blood.

Danny picked up the piece, turning it over in his fingers. There was a sharp edge where the stone had broken off and he turned his hand to cup the piece of statue loosely.

“Sorry,” he said.

“What is that thing?” Mike asked.

“A broken bit of a missing statue,” Danny said, handing it over.

Mike took it carefully, not wanting a repeat of Sherry’s experience, and held it up.

“Pretty thing,” he said, then turned back toward the door. “Come on back, Danny. If this is the only broken piece of your statue, we should be able to find it easy.”

Sherry watched them go until the door was closed, then she sat down at her desk and pulled a bandaid out of the bottom drawer. Wincing, she wrapped the little bit of adhesive fabric around the wound. It wasn’t the cut that made her wince, however, it was the numb ache that suffused her thumb and tried to crawl up into her hand and forearm.

Something was very wrong with that little bit of green rock.

She took several deep breaths, trying to calm the feeling of dread that accompanied the throbbing chill in her thumb. She’d only touched the stone for a moment, but that had been enough for a dozen images to wash across her mind's eye. It happened so quickly that she hadn't been able to understand what she'd seen, but two things were perfectly clear from the vision; blood and death would follow that stone wherever it went.

Her eyes darted up to the closed door leading to the back offices.

It had taken Sherry a long time to trust Alex, after she'd come to work for him. On the surface he was a lovable cad, a wisecracking private detective making his way in the world by his considerable wits. Sherry dismissed that image right after meeting him. Alex was highly skilled as a runewright, beyond anyone of whom she knew in this time. In addition to that, he had a way of attracting power to himself. Sorcerers, politicians, and industrialists seemed drawn to him, through no action or even desire of his own.

The first time she'd done a reading for him, she'd drawn two cards to represent him, the Emperor and the Magician.

That reading had terrified her.

The Emperor represented authority and control, everything her former boss had been, and the Emperor inverted represented tyranny. In her experience it wasn't that hard for people to flip to the worst version of their nature.

The Magician wasn't a bad card on its own; it represented willpower and creation. Paired with the Emperor, however, it foreshadowed the kind of man who, given enough power and time, could rule the world. To people in this time, that might sound fantastic, but Sherry had lived in a world like that, a world controlled by the accumulated power and indomitable will of one man.

Ironically, what had eventually convinced Sherry that Alex was one of the good guys, was the connections he made. He accumulated men and women of power, it was true, but he also accumulated people like Danny. Sherry had done readings for all of Alex's associates, looking for potential weak links that might try to corrupt him. When she read Danny, only one card came up for him, Justice. The card represented clarity and truth. As long as Alex had Danny in his life, Sherry was certain he wouldn't fall to the darkness that waited hungrily to consume all-powerful men.

Sherry stared at the closed door, as if the act alone could compel the solid wood to become transparent and let her see into the rooms beyond. Almost unconsciously, she squeezed her injured thumb against her forefinger, causing the ache she felt to blossom into pain.

She didn't know how the green rock was cursed, but she knew for certain that the blood and death she'd seen revolved around Danny.

Ooooo, the voice in her head cooed with menacing delight. *Just imagine what will become of Alex without dear Daniel to steady his moral compass.*

"Shut up," Sherry growled.

Just an observation, it said in a flippant tone. *It really was stupid of you to let Alex discover the truth about you*, the voice went on, dripping with malice. *When he finally takes his rightful place as Pharaoh, he'll never let you go.*

Sherry had heard this all before; whatever the voice in her head was, it seemed to take great delight in torturing her. It would regularly bring up the horrors she had suffered as a slave to her previous boss, a tactic that had been effective when she inhabited her former body, which bore the scars of that abuse.

She shivered, clutching her forearm and running her fingers along the smooth skin to reassure herself. The past was the past and her past was three thousand years gone. It was the present that concerned her.

Too bad you can't warn that handsome lieutenant, the voice hissed. *You could try, of course, but you know what happens when you do that.*

Sherry ground her teeth. In this case the voice was right. She could give hints and do readings, even give people veiled advice, but if she ever tried to warn someone of a specific danger, it would usually end up worse than her visions predicted. It was the reason she used vague instruments like dice or bones or, in this century, tarot cards to make predictions.

"No," she declared, standing up. She had to try something, maybe a reading when Danny came out of the back office. There was no way she would let him...

"Wait a minute," she said aloud. She'd seen a lot of garbled images, and she'd seen Danny's face, but the blood and the death weren't images, they were impressions. It was the way the images had made her feel. What if Danny wasn't in danger at all but rather the focus of those forces?

That's not very likely, the voice said. *Is it?*

Likely or not, it meant that Sherry didn't have any direct danger to warn Danny about. That meant she could take a hand.

As if on cue, the door to the back offices opened and Danny and Mike emerged. They were both smiling, and Danny held a small tin compass in his hand. That meant the finding rune had worked.

"I'll come with you," Mike was saying. "In case you need another one of these."

Sherry swept any trace of emotion from her face, then put on the warm smile she used for greeting clients.

"I'm afraid I need you here," she said to Mike, picking up a small stack of folders from her desk and handing it to him. "I've got three new clients for you, and you should be able to get them done by the end of the day."

A look of profound disappointment swept over the little man's face, but he banished it quickly. Whatever Danny's case was about, he was clearly interested.

"Sorry," she said as he took the stack.

"Apparently I'm blessed with work," he said, turning to Danny. "Just give a call if you need anything more."

He stuck out his hand and Danny shook it.

"Thanks, Mike," he said, then he turned to Sherry. "Be sure to bill the department for this." He held up the little compass. "I'll bring this back when I'm done."

Sherry suppressed the self-satisfaction that threatened to creep into her professional smile when she heard the eager tone in Danny's voice. He wanted to come back, and that meant he had been paying attention after all.

And I wasn't even flirting that hard.

No doubt he intended to return around closing time, when he'd be available to drive her home or maybe get some dinner.

Very smooth, she thought.

She nodded and he turned, heading for the front door as Mike went back to the map room. As soon as Danny shut the office door, Sherry darted into the back office.

"Hey, Mike," she called. "Where did that finding rune send Danny?"

"Out to the Aerodrome," he said. "Why?"

"I wanted to put it on the invoice," she lied. "I'm going to go get a sandwich before I do that, though, so lock up if you go out."

Mike said that he would, and Sherry shut the door. Darting to her desk, she grabbed her handbag, then headed out of the office into the hallway. Ahead of her, Danny had just pushed the button for the elevator and she heard the bell ring as the car arrived.

"Hold that," she called as she hurried down the hall.

Danny looked confused and pleased as she approached, stepping back so she could enter the elevator before him.

"Where are you headed?" he asked as he entered the car and pushed the button for the ground floor.

"To the Aerodrome," she said, forcing her voice to be casual and earnest.

Right on cue, Danny's face clouded over.

"Why are you going there?" he asked, his voice thick with suspicion.

Sherry shrugged and shook her head.

"Don't know," she said. "I just got this sudden feeling that I needed to be there."

"Do you often get feelings like that?" he asked.

"Sometimes. I find it's best if I don't question it."

"I don't think this is a coincidence, but that's where I'm going."

"Oh," she said, putting on the most innocent look she could manage under the circumstances. "Well, in that case, give a girl a lift?"

Danny held up the tin compass.

"If this thing is right, there's a very dangerous man at the Aerodrome."

Sherry's smile didn't slip a bit.

"Well then," she said, "it's a good thing I'll have you along to protect me."

15

TARGET RICH

The New York Aerodrome was a large complex of terminals, fields, support buildings, warehouses, and giant airship hangers carved out of the Lower East Side. Without Mike Fitzgerald, Alex's finding rune, and the little tin compass, Danny would have no chance to find a lone madman with a stolen statue in all of that.

The fact that he was searching for someone so morally bankrupt that he poisoned a group of homeless people that very morning made Danny glance at the seat next to him. Sherry Knox sat there, holding the tin compass in her hand, staring down into it.

"This is exciting," she said when the needle began to turn as they approached the Aerodrome.

"How did I let you talk me into bringing you along?" he groused.

Sherry grinned at him, glancing out of the side of her eye.

"Simple," she said. "I asked and you, being such a gentleman, said yes."

Danny didn't roll his eyes, but he wanted to.

"Do you have any idea where you need to go when we get there?" he asked, hoping he could leave her somewhere safe while he tracked down Gilbert Sadler.

Sherry cocked her head, as if considering her answer, then just shrugged.

"No idea," she said. "I'll just stick with you until I feel some direction."

Danny maneuvered his car into a parking space in front of the Aerodrome's main terminal, then set the brake and shut off the engine. As Sherry reached for the door handle, Danny grabbed her hand. She turned to him, but he released her, then pulled his service revolver from his jacket. He opened the cylinder, checked that the weapon was fully loaded, then tucked it back into his coat.

"This guy I'm looking for is dangerous," he said, giving her his 'serious cop' stare. "I want you to keep an eye on that compass and stay behind me. Got it?"

"You know you can count on me," she said in a placating tone. "I won't get in your way."

"My first stop is going to be their security office. If you give me any trouble, I'll have them detain you there until I find my man."

Sherry raised her right hand in a promissory gesture, but Danny got the impression she was trying very hard not to smirk at him.

"Cross my heart," she said, giving him a ridiculously serious look. "Can we go now?"

Danny stepped out of his car and went around to open the door for Sherry. As he shut the door behind her, she made a point of standing just behind him, something a gentleman normally wouldn't allow. She was doing it to make an exaggerated point, so he just rolled his eyes and went along, moving to glass doors that led into the main terminal.

Inside, the terminal was filled with people moving between the ticket counters and the hallways that led to the various gates where airships were waiting for them. Looking around, he spotted a guard in a brown uniform with a silver badge on his shirt and he headed that way.

"I'm Lieutenant Pak of the NYPD," he said, pulling his lieutenant's badge from his pocket. "I need to speak to someone in charge. Where is your security office?"

"Uh," the guard said, not reacting quickly. "It's, uh, down that way," he said finally getting his thoughts together. "On the left side. Ask for Richard."

Danny thanked the man, then turned to Sherry.

"Down that way," she said, checking the compass, then pointing the same direction that the guard had indicated. "Will you know this guy when you see him?"

"No," Danny said in a low voice. "So if that needle starts turning like we're walking past him, tap me on the shoulder."

He turned and started to move down the terminal, watching the crowd as he went, looking for anyone out of the ordinary.

"Won't he run when he sees you?" Sherry asked, keeping close as he went.

"That's the upside," he said back over his shoulder. "The bad guy doesn't know who I am either."

You hope, he thought. If Sadler had been hanging around the Hooverville earlier, he might very well know who Danny was, or at least that he was a cop.

The Aerodrome security office was located behind a simple wooden door with the word, *Security*, printed on it in silver lettering. It concealed an office only marginally bigger than Danny's own with a single barred cell set into the back wall.

These people would be in trouble if they had to detain a large family, he thought. *To say nothing of an open brawl.*

Two men occupied the office, a tall, beefy man sitting behind a desk and a thin man on a stool, reading a newspaper back near the cell. The beefy man looked as if he'd once been a bouncer or a footballer but had let his athletic figure go soft. He had watery brown eyes and a neck that bulged around his collar.

"Can I help you?" he asked after a moment of silence. The man in the back didn't even look up from his paper.

"I'm looking for Richard," Danny said, holing up his badge.

The beefy man at the desk stood up quickly.

"I'm Richard, Lieutenant," he said. "Is there a problem?"

"I'm tracking a dangerous man," Danny said. "And thanks to a finding rune, I'm fairly certain he's here." He turned to Sherry and held out his hand, and she dropped the compass into his palm as if she'd expected the move. "I'm going to need as many men as possible to help me bring him in without incident."

"Uh," Richard said, mimicking the guard Danny met in the hall.

"How many men do you have in this terminal?"

"Eight," Richard said. "There are two at each end of the terminal and one by each of the main doors."

Danny consulted the compass, then pointed along its indicated path.

"What's in that direction?"

"The north terminal," Richard explained. "There's a passenger waiting area there."

Just like the Hooverville. He's picking heavily populated areas.

"All right," Danny said in his best 'command' voice. "You come with me; you," he turned to the man in the back, "grab the two men by the doors and follow us."

Without waiting for a response, Danny turned and headed back out into the terminal. A quick look toward the north showed a wide hallway branching off from the building.

"Is this guy armed, Lieutenant?" Richard said as Danny headed that way with Sherry in tow.

"I don't know," he admitted. "Right now the only thing I've got is this compass. It's linked to a valuable object in the suspect's possession. I don't even know what the man looks like, so keep your eyes open and look for anything suspicious."

The wide hallway out of the main terminal went on for what must have been fifty yards before it opened up into another hub. Unlike the main terminal, the north terminal didn't have ticket counters along the wall. Instead, it had a small barber shop, a shoe-shine booth, a little café, and a news stand. The room was roughly triangular with a set of glass doors on the points of the triangle. Outside the doors, Danny could see a walkway into an open field.

Beyond the northernmost of the doors, an enormous airship was visible, secured to the ground by heavy ropes. Teams of workmen were loading it with luggage and supplies while passengers milled about to watch the process.

"That way," Sherry said, leaning around Danny to look at the compass. She pointed to the far wall of the room, away from the airship and her passengers.

In the center of the north terminal were rows and rows of benches where travelers waiting for their flight could gather. Danny slowed his walk as he reached it, scrutinizing the travelers as he passed. None of them looked like a crazed sculptor with a statue made of solid Limelight, or at least what he imagined that might look like.

There were plenty of businessmen and several families with young children, most carrying travel bags and suitcases. Now Danny understood how Gilbert Sadler was managing to walk around with a jade statue in public; he'd just put it in a suitcase.

You should get the civilians out of here.

He started to turn to Richard, but Sherry cut him off.

There," she said, pointing to the back wall between the newsstand and the barber shop. There wasn't anyone there, but Danny saw where Sherry's train of thought was going right away. Several dozen transit lockers lined the wall in a double row.

Danny wanted to curse. Crooks had been using transit lockers to stash things they didn't want to be caught with for a long time. It was usual for security at the various stations to clear them out once a week to discourage the practice. If Sadler left the statue here, all Danny would get out of it was a fake statue that wasn't any use to anyone.

At least it won't be in Sadler's hands, he reminded himself.

"You have your skeleton key?" Danny asked Richard as he moved toward the lockers.

"Right here," the security man said, pulling a jingling key ring from his pocket.

Danny moved down the line of lockers until the needle turned as he passed one. Moving back to it, the needle pointed to it exactly.

"Open this one," he said, stepping back.

The head security guard moved to comply, flipping through his keys for the right one. As he found it, the other three security men arrived, looking nervous. The newspaper-reading guard had clearly told them why Danny was there.

At least they'll be alert.

"Uh, Lieutenant?" Richard said as he pulled the locker door open.

Something in the tone of the man's voice was off. He'd gone from mildly interested to actively scared.

When Danny turned, he found out why. The counterfeit copy of the Jade Phoenix was indeed in the locker, broken tail feather and all. That wasn't what was drawing Danny's attention, however. The statue stood in the middle of the space with at least a dozen brown cylinders packed in behind it. Wires ran from the cylinders to a mechanical alarm clock that had been tied to a large battery and the clock gave off soft ticking sounds.

"What is that stuff?" Sherry asked, trying to lean in for a better look.

Danny grabbed her quickly and pulled her back.

"Dynamite," he whispered. He waited until she nodded her understanding before letting her go. "Richard," he said, keeping his voice low. "I need you to get everyone out of the terminal quickly and quietly. Whatever you do, don't cause a panic. If any of this dynamite is unstable, running people might just set it off."

The big man nodded, his eyes as wide as saucers.

"You," Danny said, pointing at the newspaper reader, "go back to your security office and call this in to the Central Office of Police. Tell them to send backup."

"Are you okay?" Sherry asked Richard, who had turned a bit green.

"Pull yourself together, Richard," Danny chided him before he could respond. "Get these people out. Now."

"Tell them it's a fire drill," Sherry said, patting the big man's hand.

"Thanks," he said, relief flooding his voice. He turned and began to walk out into the waiting area, announcing loudly that this was a fire drill and everyone needed to evacuate the terminal.

Danny looked at Sherry and she winked at him.

"Good call," he said as the waiting passengers began to gather up their belongings and head for the doors.

"Sure," she said, glancing back at the open locker. "Now, what are we going to do about this?"

"You are going out with the other civilians," Danny said.

"Do you know anything about bombs?" she went on, seemingly oblivious to his instruction. "Can you disconnect it?"

Danny had studied up on bombs during the Brothers Boom case, but that still wasn't much information.

"I know that he's wired that battery to the alarm clock," he said. "If it makes electrical contact with the wires running to the dynamite there won't be enough left of us to pick up with tweezers."

"So just pull out that wire," she said.

Danny shook his head.

"He might have booby trapped it. I could set it off just by touching anything in there."

He turned to look at the terminal and found it empty. The security people had even gotten the barber, the newsman, and the shoeshine boy out.

"Time to go," he said, turning back to Sherry and giving her a steady look. "We'll wait outside for the bomb unit like everyone else."

She smiled at him, and he thought she was about to say something clever, but her face suddenly blanched and she launched herself into him. Sherry wasn't big, but neither was Danny and she'd caught him completely flat-footed. With a grunt of surprise, he fell backward onto his rear.

At the same moment, a shot rang out, echoing off the walls of the empty terminal. Sherry cried out as she fell on top of him, and another shot boomed. This time Danny saw it slam into the locker next to the open one. Apparently Sadler had hidden himself somewhere to watch what would happen when his dynamite propelled shards of the Limelight statue into a crowd of travelers.

Rolling Sherry off him, Danny grabbed his pistol and rolled up to his knees. A wooden bench stood nearby, and it was blocking his view of Sadler. It was also why Sadler wasn't shooting at him.

He scrambled to the bench as another shot boomed, this time hitting inside the open locker. Danny closed his eyes, expecting to be blasted to kingdom come, but nothing happened.

This time.

Danny lunged up, over the top of the bench, bringing his .38 to bear. Across the terminal stood a wild-looking man holding a pistol. Behind him was the open door to a restroom, clearly where he'd been hiding. The man's aim shifted as he caught movement, but Danny fired first. He sent three shots in Sadler's direction but missed, though he did send the man scrambling for cover.

"Give it up, Sadler," Danny called, waiting for the man to pop up from behind the bench where he'd taken cover. "Police will be here any minute."

"No," Sadler screamed. His voice was high pitched and raw. "Magic must be freed from the grip of the sorcerers." He popped up slightly to the left of where Danny expected him and fired two shots. Instinctively Danny ducked but the bullets slammed into the lockers rather than the bench he was using for cover.

"Magic belongs to everyone," Sadler yelled just as Danny popped up to take another shot at him. This time the bullet hit closer, but it still missed.

"You'll see, detective," Sadler called. "I'll make you see."

He jumped up, firing wildly at the open locker. Danny took careful aim and fired, hitting the deranged man in the leg. There was a crack and a ricochet and Sadler didn't even flinch. He fired again and Danny was suddenly aware of the sound of an alarm clock ringing. Without hesitation he flung himself down on top of Sherry, clutching her to him and trying as best he could to shield her.

The alarm clock continued to ring until Danny could hear it winding down.

"Aren't you supposed to at least buy me dinner first, Lieutenant?" Sherry said. Her usual mocking tone was present, but her voice seemed stretched taught.

"Sorry," Danny said, getting quickly off her. Only then did he notice that she was bleeding from her hip.

"It's not bad," she gasped, reading his face.

Danny wanted to find out just how bad it was, but right now his back was exposed to a crazed gunman. Darting back to the bench, he peeked over the top. As far as he could tell, the rest of the terminal was empty. Gilbert Sadler had seen his chance to flee and he'd taken it.

Cursing under his breath, Danny moved back to Sherry, shoving his gun into its shoulder holster.

"Let me see," he said, reaching for her hand that was pressed against her side.

"Check the bomb first," she said, her voice horse. "It won't matter how badly I'm shot if it blows us to kingdom come."

Danny stood and moved to the locker. Three bullets had hit inside the metal box, one in the back, one just below the alarm clock, and one right into the battery. If Danny had to guess, he'd say that was the crippling shot because it had pulled the battery free from one of its wires. When the alarm clock went off, there wasn't any power to ignite the dynamite. Miraculously, the fake statue hadn't been hit at all.

"It's fine," he said, kneeling beside Sherry again. "Now let me see that wound."

Sherry pulled her hand away and slid the top of her skirt down to expose her hip. The bullet hit her just below her hip bone, punching through the meaty part of her upper thigh and out the back of her leg.

"It doesn't look too bad," he said. "The bullet went straight through, and I think it missed the bone." He took out his handkerchief and shook out the Limelight jade shards into his hand, then dropped them in his coat pocket. Satisfied the evidence was secure, he pressed the handkerchief down on Sherry's wound. "Keep pressure on it and you'll be fine."

She groaned as she pushed down with his handkerchief.

He stood and shouted for Richard the security guard. After he yelled a second time, the man came charging in with most of his men behind him. Unlike the last time Danny had seen the man, he was now armed with a shotgun, and his men had hand guns.

"I heard shooting," he said, a bit out of breath.

"The gunman is gone but Miss Knox has been hit," Danny cut the man off. "Send someone to call for an ambulance, secure this terminal, and put a man on this locker. No one touches anything until the police arrive."

To his credit, Richard simply turned and began giving his men orders without question. Danny went back to where Sherry leaned against the bottom of the lockers.

"You shouldn't have knocked me over," he said, kneeling down again.

"Lucky I did," she said. "He might have got you right in the back."

"Nevertheless, you deliberately put your life in danger with that stunt," he growled at her. "Don't do that again."

"As opposed to your jumping on top of me so the explosion might not kill me?" she challenged him.

"That's different and you know it," he countered. "Protecting people is my job."

Sherry actually smiled at that, though it was quickly replaced by a grimace of pain.

"Come on," Danny said, slipping his arm around her back and under her left arm. "Let's get you to the hospital. I can get you a bed next to Detective Crenshaw."

Danny stood, lifting Sherry to her feet as gently as he could until she could get her arm around his shoulders and hold on.

"If I'd let that man shoot you, your best friend would have my hide," Sherry said as she leaned on him, grunting with each step.

"What do you think he'll do to me when he finds out I took you to a crime scene where you got shot and almost blown up?"

She tried to smile but gasped.

"Don't make me laugh," she managed. "And let's make a deal."

"Don't tell Alex?" Danny ventured.

"Don't tell Alex."

16

THE LEGWORK

Buddy Redhorn got out of a taxi in front of the administration building for New York University. Agent Mendes had taken his FBI-issued car to get Detective Crenshaw's bite wound treated and Redhorn had been relegated to Lieutenant Pak's Ford coupe ever since.

He didn't like that.

It wasn't the car that bothered him, though, it was not being the driver. It also bothered him when he took cabs.

Leaning in through the passenger window, Buddy paid the cabbie, making sure to tip the man well, since it wasn't his fault that Buddy liked to drive himself.

After he and Lieutenant Pak had been grilled by his superiors, they'd agreed to split up and attack the problem of Gilbert Sadler from different angles. Since Pak had an actual piece of the missing Limelight statue, he went to try to locate it with a finding rune while Buddy was tasked with finding out more about Sadler, including what he looked like. That task had brought him to New York University. Since Sadler had been a professor here for several years, there would be colleagues who would know what kind of person Sadler was and there would be a faculty photograph of the man.

Glancing up and down the street, Buddy shrugged. He'd hoped Agent Mendes would already be here with his car, but she was coming from the FBI's field office and that was further away from the university than the Central Office of Police. She'd gone back to the field office once she learned that Buddy and Pak had left the Maretti crime scene. This was standard procedure for a separated team as he'd taught Agent Mendes himself.

Looking up and down the street again, Buddy decided he didn't want to burn more time waiting. She knew where he was going, so Agent Mendes would just have to catch up. Turning from the street, Buddy headed for the large brick building that housed the university's administrative offices. A helpful receptionist in the main lobby directed him to the art building a block away and ten minutes later, Buddy found himself outside a heavy oak door that had been polished to a high shine. A brass plaque, gleaming in the hallway's overhead magelights, read *Hugh McNaughton, Dean of Art*.

Buddy knocked, then opened the door. As expected, there was a small reception area inside. The dean of a college department wouldn't be expected to answer his own door. A young woman with brown hair and a fashionable blouse sat behind a sturdy desk, glaring at a typewriter. Her face took on an exasperated look when Buddy came in, but it was clear she was frustrated with the machine, not the interruption.

"Can I help you?" she asked in a frazzled voice.

Buddy held up his badge and introduced himself.

"I need to speak with Dean McNaughton," he said. "It's urgent."

Before the woman could respond, the office's side door opened and a thin, balding man with a handlebar mustache and a monocle stuck his head into the room.

"Aren't you finished with that report yet, Miss Maxwell?" he demanded in an officious voice. "I must have an accurate list of expenses for my meeting with the Gladstone Foundation."

Buddy caught the young Miss Maxwell rolling her eyes at that. It seemed Dean McNaughton was having her creatively adjust his expense reports.

"Dean McNaughton?" he asked.

The man seemed taken aback that someone had spoken, as if he simply hadn't seen Buddy standing in his outer office, right in front of his secretary's desk.

"Are you from Gladstone?" he demanded, his thin face taking on an indignant visage. "I was told you wouldn't be here until tomorrow. I'm far too busy to speak with you now." He waved his hand in the manner of shooing a fly and shook his head. "Go away and come back tomorrow when you're supposed to be here."

He started to turn away, but Buddy cleared his throat loudly.

"I'm not with the Gladstone Foundation," he said, holding up his badge again so the Dean could see it. "I have a few questions for you."

Buddy assumed that the presence of an FBI agent in his office while he was having his secretary fabricate expense reports would give the Dean pause, but no sooner did he focus his eyes on the badge than his face drooped into a look of scorn.

"If you're no one important, I simply don't have time for you," he said, making the shooing gesture again. "Make an appointment with Miss Maxwell. I can probably fit you in sometime after the holidays."

He started to withdraw, pulling the door closed behind him. Buddy took a big step toward the door and stuck his foot inside the jamb. When the door didn't close, McNaughton turned back. He noticed Buddy's foot in the door, then fixed him with a sneer. Before he could speak, however, Buddy grabbed the door and pulled it open, jerking the knob out of the Dean's hand.

"Apparently I didn't explain myself properly," Buddy said, his voice low but polite. "I'm with the Federal Bureau of Investigation. I'm investigating a case with international implications that involves several murders, and I have questions for you. Now."

McNaughton took half a step back, his eyes wide, but not with fear. To Buddy's utter shock, the man wasn't afraid, or even intimidated. He seemed genuinely shocked that anyone would speak to his august person in such a manner. His eyes hardened and Buddy could tell he was gathering himself for some long-winded declaration of outrage, so he decided to just skip to the end.

"Or," he said, raising his voice to cut off the outraged professor, "I can arrest you for interfering with a federal investigation. You can spend tonight in the FBI's holding cells while I fill out paperwork, then I'll ask my questions in the morning."

Dean McNaughton might be an arrogant academic, but he wasn't a complete fool. He didn't want to believe that an agent of the government would have him arrested, but he knew just by looking into Buddy's eyes that the FBI man would do it — and that he'd enjoy it.

An obsequious smile crept across the Dean's face, and he stepped back with a sweeping motion of his arm.

"I'm sorry, Mr..."

"Agent," Buddy corrected. "Redhorn."

"Won't you come in, Agent Redhorn," he said. "I've been under some stress lately and I apologize for my outburst."

Buddy didn't smile. That would be unprofessional.

Officious, self-important, little twit.

"Thank you for your time, Dean McNaughton," he said. "I need to ask you about a professor who used to work here by the name of Gilbert Sadler."

The Dean's carefully composed expression soured, and he shut his door.

"What's that fraud done this time?" he said, not bothering to hide his contempt as he made his way to a magnificent mahogany desk.

"He's wanted for questioning in the counterfeiting of art," Buddy said, keeping the details salacious enough to be interesting but vague enough not to give anything important away.

McNaughton's scowl somehow got more pronounced. It seemed as though he took something about that statement very personally.

"Well, he certainly has the talent to forge sculpture," the Dean admitted after a moment. "How did whoever hired him drag him away from his chemistry set long enough to forge something?"

That must be his alchemy equipment, Buddy thought.

Out loud, he said, "What chemistry set?"

McNaughton looked like he might not answer, but after a moment, he just sighed.

"Gil was a brilliant sculptor," he said, settling in for a long story. "I admit that I was excited when I got him on staff here at the university. There were several schools that wanted him, you know. But I got him."

Buddy scribbled notes in his book as the Dean spoke.

"You have to understand, Agent Redhorn, Gil was one of the great ones. His work practically came to life as he chiseled them from the stone. His compositions were dramatic, his details were exquisite, and his ability to mimic things like cloth were simply magical."

Dean McNaughton signed again and looked across his inky black desk to where Buddy was still taking notes.

"That was his problem, of course."

"He was too good?" Buddy said, looking up from his notes.

"No," McNaughton said. "Magic. Gil fancied himself an alchemist. To be fair, he did have a small amount of talent in the discipline, but it was nothing compared to his sculpture. Yet every time I would find him missing from his lectures or the practical classes, I'd find him in the alchemy building pestering their professors."

"Why?" Buddy asked, genuinely interested this time. "Why would a gifted sculptor want to be a mediocre alchemist?"

"Gil only tolerated sculpture, Agent Redhorn," the dean said. "As far as he was concerned, his real calling was alchemy. He became obsessed with it. It wasn't too bad while his mother was alive, but she died about a year ago and after that, Gil changed."

"What was her name?" Buddy asked, more out of habit than any desire to know.

"Alvida Grossman," the dean responded without even a pause. "I went to her funeral just to make sure Gil attended," he explained. "Apparently he didn't like Aaron Grossman, the man she'd married after his father died. I always thought that was strange, since he was an alchemist of some repute."

"Is Mr. Grossman still alive?"

Dean McNaughton shook his head.

"He died about ten years back. Anyway, after Alvida passed, Gil was never the same. I don't know if it was his mother or his failure at alchemy, but whatever caused it, Gil went mad."

"Sadler isn't sane?"

"Oh, he's not that kind of crazy," McNaughton said, with a dismissive gesture. "Just obsessed with magic to the exclusion of all else. You said he'd forged some sculpture, and he's certainly talented enough, but

I'm shocked anyone could get him to focus long enough to do the work."

"Is that why you fired him?"

McNaughton nodded then held his hand up with his finger and thumb spread wide apart.

"I've got a file on Gil this thick," he said. "All complaints."

"From who?" Buddy asked.

"It'd be shorter to tell you who wasn't complaining."

"Humor me."

"Mostly it was his students," the dean said. "But there were plenty from the other professors, both in the art department and from the alchemy professors as well. Gil had this theory that the reason regular people didn't have magic was because sorcerers were keeping it all for themselves."

"Even I know better than that," Buddy said.

"Don't mention that to Gil," McNaughton said with a chuckle. "Not unless you want to hear a half-hour screed on how if there weren't any sorcerers, everyone could have magic."

"Sounds like he's a zealot," Buddy said. "Did he have any followers?"

The dean shrugged but then shook his head.

"Not really. The students liked him well enough when he talked about sculpture and carving, but once he started obsessing about magic and sorcerers, they all lost interest. Most asked to be transferred to other classes, and the rest just dropped out. Finally, the dean of the alchemy department sent a letter to the board of directors. After that, I had no choice but to let him go."

"How did he take that?"

"He didn't care," the Dean said, bitterness in his voice. Clearly he had difficulty believing that anyone would take the job of professor so lightly. "By that point all he cared about was developing his magic."

"Was he getting better with magic?"

"Not according to the alchemy department," McNaughton said. "That was part of their complaint, that Gil kept bothering them about the same things over and over. You had it right before, he was a brilliant sculptor and a poor alchemist."

"One last thing, Dean McNaughton, do you have any pictures of Sadler? Maybe a faculty photograph?"

"Ask Miss Maxwell on your way out," he said. "We made some brochures for the art department a few years ago, and as I remember it, Gil's was in those."

Buddy stood and thanked the dean. He may have had to bully the man to get him to talk, but it was never too late to be professional.

"How did it go with McNaughton?" Miss Maxwell asked when Buddy exited the office.

She didn't call him Dean McNaughton and, based on how he'd spoken to her earlier, Buddy could understand her disdain. He asked her about the art brochures and she managed to find one in a cabinet in the back of the office.

"Do you know which one is Gilbert Sadler?" Buddy asked as she handed over the folded paper booklet.

"No, but the names are underneath the picture."

Buddy peered at a group of men in blue robes with square hats. According to the list, a dark-haired man with broad shoulders and spectacles was the elusive Mr. Sanders.

"Is that him?" Agent Mendes voice came from beside him.

Buddy was surprised that she'd managed to sneak up on him. He wanted to be irritated, to complain that it took her long enough to get here, but he was proud of how far her skills had come.

"Third from the left," he said, passing the brochure over. "How is Detective Crenshaw?"

"He's fine," she said. "The doctor at the hospital fixed him up and sent him home. Where's Lieutenant Pak?"

"He dug a broken bit of the fake Phoenix out of that dog monster's stomach," Buddy explained. "He's over at Lockerby's trying to locate the rest of it."

"So he might have our man already?" she protested.

Buddy just shrugged.

"Every part of an investigation is important," he said, taking the brochure back from her. "Even if the Lieutenant has rounded up a bunch of suspects, we're the ones who can tell him which one is Sadler."

"Assuming he'll need that," Agent Mendes groused.

"Well, it will probably be an hour or two before we'll know if the Lieutenant is successful," Buddy said, putting on his hat and leading the way back into the hall. "Let's not waste the time."

"Where are we going?" Agent Mendes called after him.

"To the hall of records."

It didn't take long for Buddy to pilot his government car east to the Hall of Records. The building was sheathed in white marble and looked exactly like the monument to bureaucracy that it was. It was the depository for all the various filings, permits, and deeds of sale generated by New York County.

A long, white stair led up to the building from the street and etched glass doors opened into a massive rotunda.

"Where can I find land records?" Buddy asked an older woman in a cardigan sitting under a sign that read, *Information*. She peered up at him through glasses that made her eyes look too large, then smiled pleasantly.

"Ownership records or building permits?" she asked in a wheezy voice.

"Ownership."

"Third floor in the back on the left side of the building."

Buddy was about to ask if it was his left or hers, but the woman pointed toward his left side where a long stair ran up the side wall with landings on the second and third floors. Agent Mendes grumbled as they ascended, but she was in good condition and wasn't too winded when they reached the top.

"Remind me why we're here," she said, panting a bit from the climb.

"According to Dean McNaughton of New York University's Art Department, Sadler didn't start to become unstable until after his mother died," Buddy explained as they headed for a door marked *Title Records*.

"So?" Mendes groused.

"So, Lieutenant Pak and I searched the little apartment over top of Sadler's workspace. It didn't look like he'd been there the previous night."

Agent Mendes nodded, picking up his train of thought.

"If he's not staying at his apartment, then where is he sleeping?" she asked.

"McNaughton said that Sadler's stepfather was an alchemist and that he died before Sadler's mother."

"So if she left him her house, then he's probably holed-up there." Mendes nodded with a grin.

"How can I help you?" a bored-looking man in a rumpled suit coat asked. He had a cigarette drooping from his fingers and he was leaning heavily on the sturdy counter that separated the front area from the back.

Buddy put his badge on the counter, then cleared his throat.

"I need to know the address of any property owned by Aaron or Alvida Grossman," he said. "It might be listed under Alvida Sadler."

"Well, you don't want much," the man said, dropping his cigarette into a nearby ashtray. "Wait here."

With that he slouched away toward a large card catalog cabinet that filled an entire section of the side wall. With nothing better to do, Buddy watched the man go from card box to card box in his quest for any records of Alvida Grossman's property. For her part, Agent Mendes leaned against the counter and lit up a cigarette to wait.

As it turned out, they didn't have to wait long. The man in the rumpled suit coat came back with a note in his hand.

"According to our records, she owns a small piece of property right there." He handed over the paper, and then tapped it with his finger.

The address was on the east side in the mid-ring and Buddy grinned when he read it. It was actually fairly close to the FBI Field Office.

"Mrs. Grossman passed away about a year ago," Buddy said. "Is it possible to see if the property was sold after that?"

The clerk sighed, but didn't protest as he made his way back to the large card catalogue. He'd left the drawer with Alvida Grossman's record open, so he spent no time finding it again to copy something from it. After that, the man shut the drawer and headed off down the end row of a long bank of shelves.

"Why don't they keep the information in one place?" Agent Mendes asked after several minutes had expired.

Buddy had no idea why the information might have been broken up the way it was, but 'keeping file clerks employed' was definitely on the list of possibilities.

This time the clerk was gone for almost ten minutes, long enough for Buddy to have smoked a cigarette of his own, if he hadn't given up the practice during the war.

"I checked the title to the property," the clerk said when he finally returned. "As far as this office is concerned, the house is still owned by the Grossmans, though it is possible that the land has been passed to a family member who simply hasn't updated the title record."

Buddy thanked the clerk, then headed back into the hall with Mendes in tow.

"You wanted something to do," he said, handing her the paper. "Let's go see if anyone is home at Sadler's mother's house."

17

THE MAD SCIENTIST'S RESIDENCE

The home of Alvida Grossman turned out to be a fairly well-kept older building on a small lot in Brooklyn. It had the simple design of many homes built before the turn of the century, with a bedroom, front room, and kitchen making up the entirety of the space.

As Buddy climbed out of the car, he noted that the grass didn't appear unduly long and there were the remains of flowering plants along the front of the house. Since Mrs. Grossman had passed away a year ago, it meant that someone was living there and had kept up the grounds before the inevitable devastation of winter. A simple brick path led from the street to the front door with no driveway or sign of a vehicle.

Three windows faced the street, all with their curtains drawn. As they approached, Buddy kept a careful eye on them, looking for any sign of movement.

"See anything?" Agent Mendes asked as they headed up the walk. She'd been watching too.

"No," Buddy said, his voice low enough that it wouldn't carry. "Wait till we reach the door, then get out your gun. Don't stand right in front of the door, either," he added.

It wasn't likely that Gilbert Sadler would shoot through the door when they knocked, but in their line of work, you lived much longer by being careful.

Mendes did as she was told, drawing her .38 revolver just as they reached the door. She stepped right, so Buddy went left as he drew his 1911. Mendes gave him a nod to show she was set and ready, and Buddy reached out with his left hand and knocked in the center of the wooden door.

The knock went unanswered, so Buddy tried again.

"Sounds like no one's home," Mendes said.

"Let's go around back," Buddy said. The bulk of the house was to the left, so he moved past Mendes and led the way around the side of the house. He didn't want people seeing him with a weapon, but Sadler was too dangerous to take lightly, so he held the gun low and at the ready.

The back yard was small and although the front showed signs of basic maintenance, the back was much more unkempt. The hedges that separated the yard from those of the neighbors had been allowed to go untrimmed and several rose bushes were growing wild. Based on the placement of the bushes, they had been objects of pride for Mrs. Grossman, but now they were reedy with untamed stalks pointing out at every angle.

A porch, made of the same red brick as the front walk, stuck out from the house into the grass. There was a heavy wooden table in the center with four simple chairs around it, and a door led from the porch into what Buddy assumed would be the kitchen.

As they approached the door, Buddy's nose picked up an acrid smell. He thought it was coming from the kitchen, but a quick check revealed a partially open coal chute that seemed to be the source of the odor.

"What does that smell like to you?" he asked Agent Mendes.

"An alchemist's lab," she confirmed after leaning close to the chute. "One that's working."

"Mr. Sadler must be using his step-father's equipment."

Mendes nodded as Buddy gave her an inquisitive look.

"So we should definitely go in," she said. "Sadler is a fugitive in possession of a dangerous magical artifact, and he may be trying to alter that artifact with alchemy. The danger to himself and his neighbors could be extreme."

"That's how I see it," Buddy confirmed. He nodded toward the back door. "Do you want to do the honors?"

Mendes glanced at the door, then a wide grin split her face. She moved to the door, holding her gun low. Shifting her weight back, she lashed out with her right foot, hitting the door just beside the knob where the force would be transferred to the bolt. Mendes did it perfectly but even so, she had no chance of shearing off the metal door bolt. The wooden jamb that held the bolt, however, was another story.

With a meaty crunch, the jamb shattered, and the door swung inward. Mendes raised her weapon and darted through the now-open door. Buddy followed, turning left inside as Mendes looked right.

He found himself in a small kitchen, facing a sink piled high with dirty dishes. A cutting board full of crumbs and bits of what appeared to be carrot sat to the right with a range next to that on the side wall. The aroma of dirty dishes hung in the air, but it wasn't too pungent, so Buddy knew they hadn't been in the sink for too long.

"Clear," he said. The space on the left side of the door wasn't much to begin with, but protocols were there for a reason.

"Clear," Mendes said. "Opening on the left with a hallway going back to the bedroom."

"Watch the hall," Buddy said, turning and moving past her to the opening that presumably led to the front room.

He swung around the frame, leading with his 1911, but found no one. The front room was neat and tidy but with dust covering every surface.

Clearly Mr. Sadler doesn't spend his time in here.

They moved down the small hallway to the bedroom and found it unkempt and lived-in like the kitchen. Buddy went through to the little bathroom and found a tub, a sink, and a toilet. A towel hung from a bronze bar on the wall and a razor sat on the side of the sink. Running his hand over the towel, Buddy found it damp. In New York's humid climate, it would take at least a day for a bath towel to dry out.

"Sadler's been here recently," he reported, moving back into the bedroom. Agent Mendes had taken up a position outside a simple wooden door in the hall. Since they'd been everywhere else, she'd wisely assumed it led down to the basement.

Moving beside her, Buddy aimed his gun at the door while she quietly twisted the handle. Once the bolt was free, Mendes opened the door quickly. Buddy didn't know if he expected to find Sadler on the other side or not, but all that greeted him was a dark and empty stair leading down.

Moving quickly and cautiously, the pair descended the stairs, finding themselves in a cramped basement with a low ceiling. Most of the space was taken up with a coal burning furnace. It had an electric regulator, but Sadler must have turned it off so it wouldn't burn coal while he was away.

Beyond the furnace were boxes, stacked up neatly. A quick check revealed them to contain mementos and knick-knacks. Lastly, at the far end of the room was an alchemist's table. Glassware and instruments had been laid out on it and several of the jars contained colored liquids. A burner connected to a fuel tank by a rubber hose sat under one of the larger flasks, but it was unlit. It looked like Sadler had been working on something and either got the result he wanted, or gave up.

A thick leather book sat on one side of the table and Buddy picked it up. As he expected, inside were pages and pages of alchemical notes. Unlike the book they had found at Sadler's studio, this one seemed to belong to Aaron Grossman. It had many more recipes in it than Sadler's book, and Buddy paged through them despite not understanding what he was seeing.

"Here," he said, when he reached a page that wasn't like the others. This recipe had been originally written in Mr. Grossman's neat hand, but the page was absolutely scrawled with notes from a different author. "Looks like whatever Mr. Sadler is doing, it has something to do with this." He held out the book for Mendes to take a look. "I only wish I could make sense of any of it."

"Can I take a whack at it?" Mendes asked with an enigmatic grin.

Buddy shrugged and handed the book over. He'd never heard her talk about alchemy in any way to suggest she knew anything about it, but if she wanted to try, he had no objection.

Taking the book, Mendes looked at it for a moment, then shut it.

"That was fast," Buddy said, not expecting her to give up so easily. "What now?"

Mendes' grin got wide and conspiratorial.

"Now," she said with a wink, "I'm going to call in a pinch hitter."

Almost an hour later the sun was starting to set and the sky was beginning to turn red with streaks of purple clouds low on the horizon. Buddy supervised the local police whom he'd called to take charge of the crime scene. Agent Mendes had spent a quarter of an hour on the phone, then went down into the basement to ensure none of the police touched Sadler's alchemy setup.

Finally a taxi pulled up behind the police cars and a balding older man stepped out and headed for the house. Buddy squinted through his spectacles, finally recognizing the man as he approached.

"Mr. Grier," he said, extending a hand to the alchemist. Charles Grier was one of the few people Alex Lockerby and Sorsha Kincaid had trusted with the knowledge of The Legion. Dubbed The Arcane Irregulars by Lieutenant Pak, the group held monthly meetings to look for potential activity from the group of rogue runewrights.

So far, they hadn't found any.

"I told you, Buddy, you must call me Charles," the alchemist said.

"Sorry," Buddy said, resisting the urge to be irritated by the informality of the entreaty. "I have to be formal on the job."

"Yes, yes," Grier admitted, "but you're formal all the time."

Buddy shrugged at that.

"There's always work to do in the FBI," he said. It was his typical excuse when people pressed him to be casual.

Grier laughed at that, a sound of genuine amusement.

"You work too hard,' he said. "Now why don't you tell me what your trainee found? She was a bit vague on the phone."

Buddy started to explain about Sadler and the Limelight statue, but Grier stopped him before he got too far.

"I thought Danny was on this case," he said.

Clearly the lieutenant had already availed himself of the alchemist's experience. Buddy hoped they weren't just going round in circles, bringing Grier out to the crime scene.

"With a big chunk of Limelight on the loose, we're pooling our resources," he said. "We found an alchemy setup in the basement of this house along with a notebook, though it looks like this one belonged to the suspect's step-father. We'd appreciate it if you could take a look."

"Lead on."

Aissa Mendes waited impatiently in the basement for her ace in the hole to arrive. She really didn't understand Gilbert Sadler's motivations, but as far as she understood the effects of Limelight on the magically gifted, he might not actually have motivations that could be understood. What she guessed was that he desperately wanted to do something alchemical with the solid Limelight he'd been given. If she could figure out what he was doing, she might be able to figure out what he would try next.

"Agent Mendes," the voice of Charles Grier washed over her as she stood, "what have you got for me today?"

Aissa turned to find the alchemist approaching with Agent Redhorn in tow.

"Your partner tells me that your missing sculptor is trying to do something alchemical."

Aissa nodded, stepping back from the setup on the table.

"There isn't much here," she admitted, "but he was clearly doing something." She handed the alchemist the thick recipe book, holding it open to the page with all the scribbled, handwritten notes.

Charles took the book, then moved to the overhead light shining down on the alchemy table. Setting the book down, he leaned over, focusing on the book for a good five minutes while Aissa and her partner waited patiently.

"Well, well," he said, paging quickly through the rest of the book. "Mr. Sadler seems to have been all through this book, but you were right to focus on this one page." He held up the book so they could see the page with the hand-scrawled notes.

"So, what is that recipe?" Aissa asked.

"Paradoxically, it's a recipe for what we alchemists call a catalyzer," he said. "This allows us to make a serum that can be added to a finished potion along with another ingredient. The catalyzer allows the potion to absorb the new ingredient as part of itself."

"Why?" Redhorn asked.

"Usually, it's done by alchemists with medical degrees," Charles said. "Using a catalyzer allows them to tailor a baseline potion for an individual patient. Depending on the component added, the potion could be targeted at an organ or area of the body, it could be made to have a lesser effect but over a longer period of time, that kind of thing."

"Then why is Gilbert Sadler interested in it?" Aissa asked.

Redhorn shrugged and spoke before Charles could formulate an answer. "Limelight isn't a potion, but it is alchemical. Mr. Sadler wants to make it affect more people."

"I'm afraid I have to agree," Charles said. "I found a note here about soaking the Limelight stone in what I'm going to assume is catalyzer, and then exposing the stone to extreme forces."

"How extreme?" Aissa asked.

"Dynamite for one," Redhorn said. "When I called in the police, I asked about our friend, Lieutenant Pak. He tracked Sadler down to the aerodrome where he'd left our fake statue in a locker along with a dozen sticks of dynamite."

Charles whistled and shook his head.

"That would be an extreme force," he agreed.

"Did Danny get him?" Aissa asked.

Redhorn shook his head.

"No," he said. "Sadler shot at him to keep him from disrupting his bomb, but he fled when the bomb didn't go off. Lieutenant Pak didn't manage to get a good look at him either," he added, "so our picture of Sadler turns out to be valuable after all."

"Okay," she said, trying to keep the exasperation out of her voice. "Every part of the investigation is valuable."

She did blush a bit. Redhorn was always trying to teach her something, showing her by example and precept how to be the best FBI agent possible. Even when they ate lunch, he would be engaging in observation exercises, trying to teach her the extra vigilance he'd developed fighting in trenches in the war. Aissa tried to learn, but the one thing she did figure out was that without the motivation of imminent sudden death, those skills could be frustrating to perfect.

Other agents had been trained by Redhorn and from what Aissa had learned, most of them ended up hating the man. They viewed him as some kind of zealot, an automaton who ate, slept, and breathed the FBI procedural manual. She felt sad for those agents. Buddy Redhorn was, by far, the best agent she'd ever worked with. Frankly he was the best agent she'd ever seen. His constant training, his ever-present little tests, those were to make her the best agent she could be. Once she figured that out, she'd done everything she could to learn what Redhorn was trying to teach. She did everything she could to measure up.

Maybe you're becoming a bit of a zealot yourself, she thought. *Now focus.*

Snapping her mind back to the task at hand, she quickly went over what she knew about Sadler and his motivations.

Turning to Charles she asked, "What kinds of 'extreme force' is Sadler likely to try next?"

"I couldn't say," he said after a moment's thought. "Dynamite is extreme in both impact and heat, so maybe he's looking at elemental forces."

"Might just as easily be extreme trauma," Redhorn said.

"True."

"So, where would Sadler be able to expose people to those kinds of extreme forces?" Aissa asked.

"Places where people gather," Redhorn supplied. "That's why he put a bomb in an aerodrome locker."

"So where are people gathering?" she pressed. "Baseball is done till spring and the Macy's parade was three weeks ago."

"He's already tried a Hooverville," Redhorn said, musing out loud.

"That doesn't mean he won't try another one," Charles said, "but he did move up to a public terminal. That had to be more difficult than trying another Hooverville."

"So, he wants a better class of test subject?" Aissa asked.

"It might be just that simple, yes," Charles said. He picked up the recipe book and held it up. "I might be able to tell you more if I look at this some more."

"Take it," Redhorn said, startling Aissa.

Allowing evidence out of FBI custody required a mountain of paperwork. It was definitely not something a field agent could just authorize on a whim.

"All right," Charles said, dropping the book in his briefcase. "Call me tomorrow morning. Hopefully I will have learned something by then."

Redhorn thanked Charles and shook his hand again. Aissa gave him a smile and a hug along with her thanks and the alchemist withdrew.

She expected Redhorn to comment on her hug as not being professional, but he let it slide.

"So, what do we know right now that we didn't know before?" he asked.

"We know Sadler is targeting large groups, but we don't have any way to know where he'll strike next," she said. Then she gave him a level look and a grin. "We also know that Lieutenant Pak recovered the missing statue."

"The missing fake statue," Redhorn reminded her.

"You said that Danny found it from a broken piece, right?"

Redhorn nodded, and Aissa went on.

"We still need to get the original statue back, right?" She asked. "Even with Sadler running around with the bits he removed when he carved the fake, we still have to get the original back to the Brunei government."

"Sadler is the priority," Redhorn said. "American lives are at stake."

"I think I have a way to recover the original Jade Phoenix," she said. "How about you let me do that, and you and Danny can go after Sadler?"

She expected him to hesitate. She expected Redhorn to wave her off; after all, he'd been right when he said that Sadler's reign of terror had to be their priority.

"All right," he said, breaking her expectations of him for the third time in as many minutes. "I'll find out where Lieutenant Pak is and we'll meet up in the morning. I'll give you until Saturday to find the Jade Phoenix. If you require help, pull in anyone you need. You're the lead."

An excited smile blossomed across her face. She couldn't have stopped it if she'd wanted to.

"Thanks, boss," she said. "I won't let you down."

"I have faith in you," Redhorn said, his voice low and serious. "Impress me."

"I have to get going, then," she said. "I need to make some calls before it gets too late."

With that, she turned and ran up the stairs, heading for a policeman with a radio car.

18

DIVISION OF LABOR

The automatic elevator chimed its arrival, and the inner door opened automatically. Danny pulled open the sliding outer door and then took Sherry's arm to help her out of the car.

"I'm really all right," she said, wincing a bit as she moved. "The doctor said it was just a flesh wound. I'll be right as rain in a few days."

"Fine," Danny said, not loosening his grip. "I'll let you walk on your own in a few days."

She made an exasperated face at him, but there was gratitude in her eyes. The gouge out of her side looked pretty bad when he'd seen it in the aerodrome terminal, so he wasn't exactly sure he agreed with the doctor who'd tended to Sherry's wound. To keep the bill for his services low, he'd stitched the wound closed and used a regenerative ointment to help it heal. The ointment would cut the time it would take the wound to mend down to just a few days, but a regeneration potion would have healed it completely in just a few hours. Dr. Bell would have used a regeneration potion, of course, but they wanted to keep Sherry's misadventure from Alex, so he hadn't been an option.

Danny didn't like any of it, but since in the end it wasn't his call, he just shut his mouth and helped Sherry down the hall toward the door of Lockerby Investigations.

At least he was managing to make this trip serve double duty. Just before the doctor had finished with Sherry, Danny had called the Central Office to check in. There had been a message from the FBI to meet him at Alex's office and to bring the broken bit of the fake Jade Phoenix.

"Looks like Mike is still here," Sherry said as they approached the closed door.

Since it was well after business hours, they'd expected to find the office empty. The only reason Danny had allowed Sherry to come along was that Mike was likely already gone home and Alex was out of town. Now a light clearly shone out from under the door.

Danny stepped ahead, still holding Sherry's arm, and opened the door. Mike was indeed still at the office, and he was currently standing in front of Sherry's desk regaling Agent Mendes with a tale about finding a lost engagement ring.

Danny had heard that one before.

Mendes' partner sat on one of the waiting room couches with his legs crossed and his hat resting on his knee. A large wooden crate sat on the floor next to the couch and Danny could see packing straw sticking out from the open top. Redhorn appeared asleep, but he roused as Danny helped Sherry inside.

"What happened?" Mike demanded as soon as he saw Sherry.

"It's nothing," she said, blushing slightly. "I zigged when I should have zagged."

Agent Redhorn rose immediately, dropping his hat on the couch, but before he could move to Sherry's other side, she waved him off.

"I'm okay, really." She blushed again as Danny helped her to the chair behind her desk. "Just tell me why you needed me here."

"We didn't," Aissa said. There was a hint of frost in her voice that Danny couldn't explain, but he gave it a pass. He doubted her day had been any better than his.

"I've got this covered," Mike said with a smile. "Why don't you go home and put your feet up?"

Sherry gave him a sly grin that Danny would have sworn was actually meant for Aissa, then shrugged.

"Danny offered to escort me home, so I might as well stay," she said, emphasizing the word home just a bit more than necessary.

"What's this about," Danny cut in before Aissa could respond. Something seemed to be going on between them, but he was too tired to let it play out.

A momentary look of irritation flashed across Aissa's face, but then she gave him a crooked smile.

"I understand," she said, reaching down into the open top of the wooden crate, "that you found a broken bit of this." She stood back up, cradling the Limelight copy of the Jade Phoenix in her arms.

"Where did you get that?" Danny demanded. He knew for a fact that his boys had collected it as evidence as soon as they'd arrived at the aerodrome. It was supposed to be in Captain Callahan's office right now for safekeeping.

"Relax, Lieutenant," Redhorn said in his official FBI voice. "We asked your Captain if we could borrow it for a few days."

Danny knew that would be the answer, but he didn't like it any better hearing it spoken out loud.

"What we need from you is the missing bit," Aissa explained. "Then Mike here," she nodded at Fitzgerald who gave her a winsome look, "will use a restoration rune to put back the missing piece."

"You know this thing's a fake, right?" Danny asked as he fished the broken piece of the statue from his pocket.

"She knows," Redhorn said with an inscrutable look.

Danny got the impression that Agent Mendes was on her own with whatever she was doing but he had no idea why. She and Redhorn were partners, after all.

As he set the broken tail feather on the desk, Danny remembered the tiny chips Redhorn had collected in Nick Maretti's library. When he needed his handkerchief to stop Sherry's bleeding, Danny had dumped everything into his suit coat pocket.

"Just a sec," he said, taking off his coat and turning the pocket inside out so he could carefully brush the green bits onto the table. The chunk he'd retrieved from Peter Grant's coffee cup, he put back in his pocket.

Aissa set the statue down on Sherry's desk right next to the broken piece and the glittering chips. Picking up the broken feather, she held it with the broken end out and moved around the statue trying to find where it had come from.

"Right here, I think," Sherry said, pointing to a spot where one of the bird's tail feathers seemed to stop short. She favored Aissa with a sweet smile and the FBI agent looked like she'd swallowed a frog.

"Yes," she declared after holding the bit up to the end of the short feather. "Okay, Mike, you're up."

She handed the bit of green Limelight to Mike, who stepped up to Sherry's desk. Setting the fragment next to the statue, he pulled out a navy-blue book that reminded Danny of Alex's red rune book. Paging through it, he eventually tore out a single sheet of flash paper and folded it into quarters.

"I didn't know you were able to write standard restoration runes," Sherry said as Mike picked up the fragment.

He laughed nervously, and shrugged.

"The boss gave me a few to use if the occasion came up," he said. "Agent Mendes here," he nodded at Aissa, "said the Bureau would reimburse us for the rune, so I figured it was okay."

Sherry looked like she was searching for a tactful way to object, but she just nodded in response.

Mike touched the folded paper to his tongue to moisten it, then pressed the damp spot to the statue. That done, he held the fragment against the spot it had broken from and grabbed a metal match from the touch-tip lighter on the desk. Pressing the match down on the sparkler, he lit it, then touched the flame to the flash paper.

Burgundy light flashed up as the paper burned and a twisted magical symbol hung in the air for a moment. Danny heard a loud click and the tiny green fragments leapt up off the desk, and adhered to the statue. After another moment, the reddish glow of the rune faded away.

"That ought to do it," Mike said, taking his hand away from the statue.

Aissa leaned in close, inspecting the formerly broken spot, then she grinned and nodded.

"That will do it," she said. Taking careful hold of the statue, she returned it to the straw-lined crate. When she had it situated to her liking, she stood and gave Danny a big smile. "Now you boys play nice while I'm gone."

The last half of that sentence was directed at Agent Redhorn, who stood as Aissa bent down to pick up the crate.

"Let me help with that," Mike said, grabbing the other side of the crate as Aissa lifted it.

She thanked him and, as Agent Redhorn held the door, she and Mike headed out into the hall.

"What was that about?" Danny demanded once Redhorn shut the door.

"The FBI still has to find the original statue of the Jade Phoenix," he said. "Agent Mendes is going to handle that while you and I look for Sadler."

"Wouldn't more eyes looking for a magical madman be better?" Sherry said.

"Don't worry, Miss Knox," Redhorn said. "Lieutenant Pak and I have legions of eyes at our disposal. We won't be at a loss for the lack of my partner."

Danny didn't like that answer, but he couldn't argue with it. Aissa was smart and capable, but to catch Sadler, they were going to have to cast a wide net. The loss of Redhorn's partner wasn't likely to matter.

"Well, I'm at a loss right now," he said. "I found the statue, but Sadler's still on the loose and even without the statue, he's got pounds of Limelight shards. Any idea what to do next?"

Redhorn motioned for him to sit, then waited until Danny did so before seating himself. For her part, Sherry just sat behind her desk, smoking a cigarette.

"We found where Sadler's been staying," Redhorn said, then proceeded to tell Danny about finding Alvida Grossman's little house and the alchemy setup in her basement.

"So Sadler wants more people to have access to magic, and he blames sorcerers for hoarding all the magic," Danny summarized. "We knew that already."

"Yes," Redhorn admitted, "but now we know he's trying to find a way to make those Limelight shards do their thing to groups of people instead of just one at a time."

"Great," Danny fumed. "So any restaurant or nightclub in the city could be a target."

"Not to mention train terminals, Empire Station, the Jersey Ferry, and the Statue of Liberty," Redhorn added.

"How can we hope to cover all that?"

"There is some good news," Redhorn said. "We lucked out and found a picture of Sadler from when he was a university professor. The Bureau is having a sketch taken from the picture and printed as we speak. We've also sent the image to the papers. With any luck the whole city will be looking for this psycho come morning."

Danny sighed and rubbed his eyes. He'd been so close in the aerodrome; if he'd only managed to wing Sadler, this whole episode would be over.

"My brain is getting fuzzy," he said at last. "Let's get together in the morning. Right now I need to go to bed."

"Why, Lieutenant Pak," Sherry said in mock outrage. "Is that what you had in mind when you offered to see me home?"

Danny was too tired to blush and simply chuckled at her joke.

"Correction," he said to Agent Redhorn. "I need to see Miss Knox safely home, then I need to go home to bed."

Sherry's apartment was in a clean, modern, women-only building on the east side's mid-ring. When Danny helped Sherry through the door, the building's matron glared at him until he flashed his badge and explained that Sherry had been injured.

"Don't be long," she growled as they boarded the elevator.

"Mrs. Phillips is a good watchdog," Sherry chuckled as the door closed. "She can hear the front door lock open from a deep sleep."

"I guess I don't have to worry about you getting shot here," Danny teased her.

She laughed and shook her head.

"No. I picked this building because I'll be safe here."

The way she said it suggested that this wasn't just an informed opinion but rather the result of her foresight. That thought drove something Danny had been wondering about to the forefront of his mind.

"It sure was lucky that you saw Sadler in time to knock me out of the way of his bullet."

"Thank God," she said as the elevator door opened on the sixth floor.

Danny took her arm and led her down to apartment six twenty-one.

"Funny thing about that," he said as Sherry dug her key ring out of her purse. "You were looking at me when Sadler shot, so how did you see him?"

"Out of the corner of my eye," she said without a pause.

She selected a key from her ring and slid it into the lock. With a twist, the door opened, and Sherry stepped forward.

"I don't think so," Danny said, lowering his voice. "Sadler was almost completely behind you. You knew something like this would happen, and that's why you pushed me into letting you come along."

Sherry turned and regarded him with a cold gaze. He wasn't going to fall for that, so he met her gaze and held it. After a moment, she stepped back from the door.

"Come inside," she whispered. "This hallway has ears."

Looking left and right, Danny didn't see any doors partially open, but Sherry would know her neighbors better than he would. Moving quietly, he stepped inside and Sherry shut the door behind him.

"Yes," she admitted. "I knew you'd be in danger, and yes, I felt it coming before Sadler shot at you."

"Facing danger is my job," Danny said, resisting the urge to yell at her. "You could have been killed."

"But so could you," she said, giving him a hard, earnest look.

"That can happen to me every single day," he countered. That wasn't exactly true with him being a mostly desk-bound Lieutenant now, but it was true enough.

"It can't," Sherry said, reaching out to grab his arm. "You don't understand, Danny. You don't know how important you are."

"I'm a cop, Sherry," he said. "I do important things, but if I was to die, someone else would step up and do my job."

Sherry shook her head slowly and her grip on his arm tightened.

"Being a cop isn't the job you need to do," she said. "Do you know how many friends Alex has? I mean real friends," she added before Danny could reply.

"Alex has lots of friends," he said. "He's got friends in shops and industries all over town."

"No," Sherry said. "Alex has associates, acquaintances even, but not friends. The only people he's really close to are Dr. Bell, Sorsha, and you."

"What about you, or Andrew Barton, or Charles Grier?"

Sherry just shook her head.

"Alex doesn't make friends easily," she said. "We're actually pretty close, but Alex has never invited me to dinner at the brownstone, or asked me to join him and Sorsha at a nightclub."

Danny wasn't sure where she was going with all of this, and it was too late to try to think it all the way through.

"Alex will be fine if he has to make a new friend," Danny said. "I don't want you putting yourself in jeopardy for the sake of your boss."

Sherry squeezed his arm again.

"I didn't," she insisted. "Alex knows more about magic than almost anyone alive right now, and he's going to learn more."

"How much more?" Danny asked without really thinking about it.

"I don't know," she admitted. "I've tried to see what he'll become but it's hidden from me. What I do know is that every time I look, I get this feeling. It terrifies me."

That sounded ridiculous. Sherry was right about Alex and his magic; he'd come so far since they'd first met, but he wasn't as powerful as a sorcerer.

"And he needs friends to what? Keep him grounded?"

"Yes, Danny," Sherry said, her nails digging into his arm. "He needs you. I don't know what it is about you that is so important for Alex, but without you...without you, I'm afraid for him."

Danny considered that. Sherry was right about him being Alex's friend. Both of them went out of their way to work with each other as often as they could. Danny had eaten over at Dr. Bell's many times over the years, and they often met for lunch to talk about their various cases. What Danny didn't get was how the lack of that interaction would cause Alex to change drastically.

"I know one thing that will change Alex," he said after a moment. "Letting his secretary get killed by taking her to dangerous crime scenes. From now on, if you think I'm in danger, just tell me."

"I don't expect you to understand," Sherry said with a sigh. Clearly, she had hoped that he understood something more than he did.

"Just take care of yourself and I'll do the same," he said, taking her hand off his arm and opening the door. "No more tagging along after bad guys."

He stepped out into the hall and heard the sound of a door close somewhere further down.

Ears indeed, he thought.

"Danny," Sherry said, stepping into the door frame. She gave him a look that was surprisingly shy, considering her usual confidence.

"What is it?" he said, managing not to sound as tired as he felt.

"I didn't come with you just to help Alex."

"Then why—" he began but before he could finish, she stepped forward, rising up on her toes, and kissed him. It wasn't a long or passionate kiss, just a quick peck on the lips, then she retreated back to her apartment.

"Good night," she said as she closed the door.

19

AFTER HOURS

Buddy Redhorn had been born in Maryland and lived there till he enlisted in the army at the age of sixteen. After the big war, he'd been mustered out in New York and found himself alone for the first time in a big city. His C.O. in Europe had been an investigator for the Pinkerton's Detective Agency before the army, and he'd given Buddy a glowing reference. Buddy parlayed that document into a job with the Federal Bureau of Investigation, and settled down in New York as a permanent resident.

Twenty years later, Buddy had a wife and a family and a tidy house in a quiet neighborhood in the east side mid-ring. It was actually fairly close to the Chrysler Building, which made his daily trip to work a breeze.

When he pulled up in front of his home, the street was dark except for the scattered street lights. His home was a two-story number made of red brick and hung with white shutters beside each window. A lattice of ivy covered much of the front of the house, with flower beds on the ground where his wife had planted bulbs in anticipation of next spring. The walkway that ran from the sidewalk to the front door was made of brown brick, and Buddy smiled when he saw it. He'd been given the bricks as a thank you from a masonry company when he'd caught their accountant embezzling funds. It had taken weeks, but he dug out the ground and laid the bricks for the walk himself.

Heels clicking as he strode along the bricks to the front door, Buddy slipped his key into the lock. As he turned it, the sound of his wife and children laughing along with Edgar Bergen and his wooden sidekick, Charlie McCarthy, washed over him.

"Dad!" Duncan yelled, leaping off the couch and rushing to embrace him. At twelve, he came up to Buddy's shoulder and Buddy had to hold back a chuckle as he realized that his son was almost as tall as Lieutenant Pak.

"Are your chores done?" he asked, knowing full well that his wife would never have permitted Duncan to listen to the radio otherwise.

Duncan started to report on the day's activities, when Jessica thumped into Buddy's side. Only eight, she stood just taller than his belt. Buddy rumpled his son's hair, then leaned down to pick up his daughter. Duncan looked like him, tall, lanky, with dark hair and blue eyes. Jess favored her mother, with a mass of curly red hair, dimples in her cheeks, and green eyes.

"Hollo, daddy," she said, burrowing her head into his shoulder.

He stood there for a moment, snuggling Jess, with his other arm around Duncan. Closing his eyes, he just let the peace of home and family wash over him.

"That's enough," his wife, Alexandra, said. "Your father needs to eat his dinner before it gets any colder. You two can go back to the radio."

Jess protested for a moment, then gave Buddy a hug around the neck and he let her slide down his leg to her feet. Duncan then took her hand and led her back to the couch.

"And where's my hug?" his wife said, stepping close and reaching up to encircle his neck with her arms. Buddy hugged her, then kissed her, sending a thrill through him. It was exactly the same as the first time he'd kissed her all those years ago in London.

"And how are you?" he asked when they broke apart.

She smiled at him with more teeth than usual. He knew that smile very well. It was the one that suggested that the children should be in bed early tonight.

"Frisky," she whispered, in case by some miracle he'd missed her signal.

She turned and led the way back to the kitchen, walking slowly in front of him so that he could observe her figure. Lexi was a round woman without being plump, all hips and bust and delicious curves. Buddy had loved her from the moment he'd first seen her.

"Now tell me, William," she said once she'd sat him down at the little table in the kitchen, "how was your day?"

She never called him Buddy, and she never said why, but he didn't mind. Lexi could call him anything she wanted and he'd love her for it.

"Busy," he said as she placed a bowl of shepherd's pie in front of him. It was his standard answer for things he wasn't allowed to talk about at home. As a member of the magical crimes unit, that covered most of what he did.

"And are you missing your attractive boss?"

Lexi had never really been a fan of his working for Sorsha, or his having Agent Mendes as a trainee, for that matter. He didn't blame her, but he put down his fork and took her hand.

"I forgot she was gone," he said. "Right now Director Stevens has me running all over town with Lieutenant Pak, he's one of Lockerby's friends."

Lexi listened patiently as he told her what he could about their joint case.

"So you've lost Agent Mendes too?" Lexi teased once he was done. "You must be destitute." Her tone was conciliatory, but that thrill-inducing smile was back.

Is it too early to send the kids to bed?

Buddy opened his mouth to suggest just that, but the telephone cut him off. His ebullient mood soured before the first ring ended. A telephone call at this hour meant that it wouldn't be his darling Lexi keeping him up tonight.

Parking his car a block south of Rockefeller Center, Buddy walked toward where two uniformed policemen were keeping back a crowd of bystanders. As he approached, Buddy had to push his way past several of them to reach the officers.

"I need to speak to whoever is in charge," he said, holding up his badge for the policemen to see.

Before the officers could answer, a young man in a brown suit standing to his left turned to face him.

"What's the FBI's interest in this?" he asked.

Too late, Buddy saw the notebook and pen in his hands. He was older than he first appeared, probably in his late twenties but with a youthful face. The dimple in his left cheek added to the effect, but the press badge tucked into the band of his brown fedora, on the other hand, set Buddy on guard.

"I thought this was some kind of accident," the reporter went on. "Is that not the case?"

Buddy looked the man full in the face and gave him his best 'business as usual' expression.

"The FBI always tries to help out our local partners," he said. "I saw the crowd and figured they could use a hand."

It was a standard answer, reasonable and sensible while revealing nothing of interest to the voracious press.

"Now, if you'll excuse me," Buddy went on, turning back to the closest policeman. "would you point me to the person in charge, please."

The officer stepped back so that Buddy could pass, then indicated a short man in a rumpled overcoat standing near the ice rink. Several dozen people were gathered in clumps around the edge of the rink, each talking with a uniformed officer who was taking notes. Beyond them, on the ice itself, was a dark spot as if the frozen surface had been burned. Radiating out from the burn were deep cracks and fractures surrounded by chunks of the still-frozen rink's surface. Most ominous were the gray blankets. Seven of them were spread around the burn mark, covering the bodies of the dead.

As Buddy descended the stairs down to the level of the ice rink, he took in the scene. One of the many light poles that illuminated the rink at night had fallen over and the light fixture atop it was torn open as if it had burst from inside.

Looks like Sadler had some leftover dynamite, he thought.

The detective in charge looked up just as Buddy reached the bottom of the stairs and he hurried over. He looked to be in his late thirties with bushy red hair and a plain, honest face that seemed to complement his rumpled appearance. Buddy wondered if he'd slept in his overcoat.

"Are you the FBI man?" he said before Buddy could speak. "My captain said someone from the FBI would come by to take charge. Is that you?"

Buddy held up his badge so the man could see it.

"I'm Special Agent Redhorn," he said. "What happened here?"

The detective shook his head and shrugged.

"I was hoping you could tell me," he said, producing his own badge. "I'm Detective Arnold, and I'll do my best to answer your questions, Agent Redhorn. What we know is that some kind of explosion happened at the top of that light pole." He indicated the fallen pole.

Buddy had assessed as much already, but he let the man keep talking. Detective Arnold turned back toward the front of the rink and began to walk as he talked, drawing Buddy along in his wake.

"Five people were killed by debris from the blast," Arnold went on. "Two more bled out before they could receive medical attention. All that is pretty straightforward. The part I don't understand is what happened afterward."

They reached a door that led back behind the skate rental desk. Arnold pushed the door open and came face-to-face with a short, broad policeman clutching a baton.

"It's just me," Arnold said. "How's our guest?"

"Still here," the cop growled, stepping back. He looked past Arnold to appraise Buddy, his eyes narrowing for a moment before he looked away.

Behind the officer was an open storage area with boxes along the walls and a pile of broken skates next to a workbench loaded with tools. An electrical heater sat on the concrete floor next to the bench, but it was unplugged and the coils were dark. Without the heat source, the workroom was just as frigid as the outside air.

Buddy's breath steamed as he looked at the room's other occupant.

He appeared to be middle-aged with slicked-back hair and spectacles. His brown coloring marked him as having Latin ancestry, but Buddy couldn't tell anything about his social status because, other than the spectacles, the man was entirely naked.

He sat, Indian style, on the bare floor, his body glistened with sweat. A trickle of blood ran from the meaty part of his right thigh where Buddy could see a small wound.

"This is Nick Papas," Detective Arnold said. "We found him in this state of undress, lying on the ice."

"In full view of everyone," the stocky policeman added with a snarl in his voice.

Buddy nodded, then crouched down in front of the naked man.

"How are you feeling Mr. Papas?" he asked.

The man looked up with bloodshot eyes and sweat dripping down his forehead.

"I wanted to go ice skating," he said in a thick Greek accent. "It was just so cold."

"What happened then?" Buddy asked.

"I had a drink or two," Papas admitted. "It helped for a while, but then something bit me on the leg." He pointed to the weeping wound on his thigh.

Buddy didn't have to dig out the shrapnel from Papas' leg to know what it was.

"And after that?" he prompted the naked man.

"I don't remember," Papas said. "The light fell over and I got a shock. When I woke, I was burning up."

"That's when he decided to get himself an indecent exposure charge," the cop offered.

"Are you all right now, Mr. Papas?" Buddy asked, ignoring the irascible officer.

The man took a deep breath, then nodded.

"Stay here and I'll have someone come and look at your wound."

"That's it?" the officer from the door complained. "How about getting him a towel, or at least a washcloth."

Buddy started to clench his fist but forced himself to relax.

"Shut your yap, Higgins," Detective Pak's voice came through the still-open door. It was followed a moment later by the man himself. He wore a blue suit, which was unremarkable except that when Buddy had last seen him, a few hours ago, he'd been wearing a brown suit.

When he offered to escort Lockerby's attractive young secretary home.

"Let me guess," he said, lowering his voice as he looked past Buddy, "he was cold right before the explosion?"

Buddy nodded.

"What kept you?" he couldn't help asking.

"Sorry about that," Pak said with a sigh. "After the day I had, I turned in right after I dropped Sherry off."

Buddy could usually tell when someone was lying and Pak's explanation had the ring of truth, so he let it go. He didn't much care where the Lieutenant was spending his nights, but Agent Mendes seemed to find him interesting. As her partner, it would fall to him to warn her if Pak were involved with Miss Knox.

"What did I miss?" Pak asked when Buddy didn't speak.

"Let's go for a walk," Buddy said, nodding toward the door.

He led Lieutenant Pak across the ice to where the cracks converged into the center of the burn mark. As he went, he recounted what he knew.

"I'm guessing the police moved the light pole when they got here," he finished. "This would be where it fell originally."

"We had to do that," Detective Arnold spoke up.

Buddy hadn't noticed the man following them. He must be more tired than he thought.

"The top of the pole where the light broke was sparking and popping so we had the manager here shut off the power and moved it off the ice."

"If it was in contact with the ice, how come only Nick Papas got shocked?" Pak asked.

"You know, I asked the manager about that," Arnold said, checking his notebook. "He said that electricity doesn't travel well in ice. Apparently it's different from just water."

Buddy looked at the burn mark and then at the covered bodies on the ice. Most of them were within ten yards of the center point.

"Did the pole fall and then explode," he asked, "or did it explode first?"

"I'm sorry, Agent Redhorn," Detective Arnold said, consulting his notebook again. "The witnesses are a little mixed up about that. Some of them say the explosion happened first, then the light pole fell, but some say it was the other way round."

"It exploded first," Pak said, pointing to the center of the burn mark. "If it had exploded down here, the blast would have blown a hole right through the ice."

Buddy shook his head. He should have seen that. As he mentally chided himself for not paying enough attention, the realization of what the burn mark meant popped into his mind.

"I think we've gravely underestimated Mr. Sadler," he said.

"Who is Sadler?" Detective Arnold asked, flipping over his notebook again.

"That's classified," Buddy growled, giving the little man his best 'go-away' look.

Arnold seemed impervious to the look and just stood there with his pencil poised over his notebook. Before Buddy could make his intentions better understood, Lieutenant Pak put his arm around the rumpled detective's shoulders.

"Thank you for all your help, Detective Arnold," he said. "Unfortunately Captain Callahan has asked that the details of this case be handled only by Agent Redhorn and myself. I'm sure you understand."

"Oh," Arnold said, hiding his disappointment well. "I'm sorry. I'll just make sure the men are finished collecting the witness statements, then."

"Before you do that," Pak said, "call back to the Central Office and tell Captain Callahan to get in touch with John D. Rockefeller."

"The sorcerer?" Arnold asked, somewhat alarmed.

"The very same. He's going to want to examine Mr. Papas."

Detective Arnold promised to make the call, then flipped his notebook closed and headed back towards the few groups of remaining people.

"He's a good man," Pak said once the detective was out of earshot. "He'll keep what he's heard to himself."

"He'd better," Buddy said with a sigh. "I'm worried."

That got a reaction out of the lieutenant and he looked up at Buddy with raised eyebrows.

"Why?"

"This burn mark," Buddy said, pointing down at the blackened ice. "I think we've seriously misread Gilbert Sadler. We've been operating on the assumption he's just some failed artist, but if I'm right, he's far more intelligent than we've given him credit for."

Pak looked down at the ice, then squatted down to rub the center with his thumb.

"Explain," he said after a long moment.

"Remember what Penny Walker said?" Buddy asked. "About how after things started to go badly in the homeless camp, she got burned?"

Pak stood up and nodded.

"She had a mark on her upper arm. It looked like a burning tree branch landed on her."

"Well, it wasn't a tree branch," Buddy explained. "What you saw was a very special kind of scar called a Lichtenberg figure."

"Never heard of it."

"Neither had I until I read the case files your captain sent over to my office," Buddy said. "In the first Limelight case, a young couple was found dead. Your friend, Lockerby, found Lichtenberg figures on one of the bodies and the coroner confirmed they'd died by electrocution."

"I'm still not seeing the connection," Pak said.

"Gilbert Sadler wants to give regular people magic," Buddy explained. "Every time he tries, it turns out just like the old Limelight cases."

Lieutenant Pak was nodding along now.

"Penny was the only one afflicted by the Limelight who survived, and she experienced an electric shock," he said. "And now Nick Papas reports that he was shocked right after being struck by what is presumably a chunk of solid Limelight."

"Somehow Sadler put the two things together," Buddy said, keeping his voice low. "He figured the shock had something to do with a permanent effect and he tried again here. He assumed the ice would carry the electric shock to everyone in the rink."

"Only he didn't count on ice being a bad conductor."

A shiver Buddy couldn't quite control ran across his shoulders.

"He's fixing his mistakes Danny," Buddy whispered, forgetting proper protocol and calling the lieutenant by his first name. "Next time he won't use ice."

The idea that Sadler had figured out how to permanently afflict people with bizarre and often dangerous magic was terrifying. The fact that the sculptor still had several pounds of the green stone just made it worse.

"You're right," Pak said, a determined look spreading over his sharp features. "But I don't think he's as smart as you think. Do you have that picture of Sadler you got at the university?"

Buddy wasn't sure what to make of the lieutenant's remark, but he seemed to be on to something, so Buddy took the photograph out of his pocket and passed it over. Pak took it, staring intently at the image of their quarry. After a long moment, he turned back to where the police were still keeping a crowd of onlookers at bay.

"He's not figuring this out because he's some kind of genius," Pak said, scanning the crowd.

"He's been watching us," Buddy said, catching on.

"Correction," Pak said, his eyes darting back to the photograph. "He *is* watching us."

Before Buddy could process what the lieutenant had said, the little man took off like a shot, running at full speed toward the stair that led to street level. Above him, on the promenade, a man fought free from the crowd, then turned and ran.

20

COLLATERAL DAMAGE

Buddy took off after the rapidly disappearing lieutenant. He was almost a foot taller than Pak, but the little man was much faster than Buddy would have given him credit for. By the time Buddy reached the stairs heading up to the street level, Pak was already at the top and out of sight.

Taking the steps two at a time, he vaulted his way to the top. As quickly as he'd gone, Pak was faster. Buddy barely caught sight of him disappearing around a corner half a block away.

Damn, he's fast.

Buddy took a deep breath, but before he could pursue the lieutenant, a woman's scream split the air.

"Help," the call came immediately after.

Buddy turned to find a well-dressed, middle-aged woman tearing across the street, heedless of the traffic or the crowd. She had the same wild-eyed look he'd seen on the faces of civilians in the war. The woman had seen something so horrific her only instinct was to flee.

"Help," the woman shrieked again, throwing herself into the chest of one of the policemen working crowd control. The officer reacted instinctively, pushing the hysterical woman away.

"How can I help?" Buddy said, raising his voice to just below a shout. The sound cut through the chaos of the moment. The woman's eyes focused on him, and she grabbed his arm, pulling him in the direction she'd come from.

"You have to do something," she said, her voice breaking. "He killed my husband. He's got a little girl."

Buddy resisted the urge to swear as the woman pulled on him.

"You two," he barked at the officers who had hassled him on his way in. "Go after Lieutenant Pak and back him up. He went that way." The two cops looked at him like he'd grown another head, but Buddy didn't have time to explain himself twice. "Now!"

The two officers jumped, then turned on their heels and ran off after Pak. Buddy turned back to the woman right as Detective Arnold came puffing up the stairs behind him.

"Grab some men," Buddy told him before he could say anything. "You're with me."

To his credit, Arnold didn't argue, just pointed at three more of the crowd control officers and waved them after him. The woman continued to pull on Buddy's arm and he allowed her to lead him. Since she had him by the left arm, he reached into his coat and drew his 1911, holding it down and away from the civilian. She was pulling him toward a restaurant on the corner of the Rockefeller Center building. The lights inside flickered, making it difficult to see anything, but one of the doors was blocked open by a body lying half in and half out.

"Stay here," he told the woman, pulling his arm from her grip and moving his hand to her shoulder. "We'll handle this."

His voice was lower, with no trace of anger or force but just as commanding. She looked up at him with tears pouring from her eyes.

"Help the girl," she choked.

"Stay with her," Detective Arnold said to one of the trailing officers.

Without the woman to hold him back, Buddy broke into a trot. He didn't want to outstrip his backup or startle whoever was inside, so he hurried as much as he could. As he approached, he saw that the body on the ground belonged to a man, who looked to be in his mid-forties.

Probably the woman's husband.

Grabbing the slide of his pistol, Buddy racked a round into the chamber, then swung the gun up in front of him as he rounded the open door. The scene inside the restaurant almost stopped him. He hadn't seen anything like this since the war. A man in a wool jacket knelt in the center of the open floor, cradling a little girl wearing a yellow coat in his arms. Around the pair were half a dozen bodies, obviously dead but without visible wounds. Terrified diners cowered in the far corners of the room, and a cook and a waitress peeked out from the kitchen door.

Buddy trained his gun on the kneeling man. Normally he would have demanded he drop the girl, but the way the man clutched her was protective, tender.

And the man was glowing.

Tendrils of golden energy flowed from the man to the child in his arms. She couldn't have been more than eight or nine, just like Jessica. At first, Buddy thought she was dead. A bright splash of blood stained the side of her yellow coat, but her eyes were partially open as the man whispered to her.

The sight finally brought Buddy to a halt. Before he could speak, the golden light passing between the man and the girl flickered.

"Stop what you're doing," Buddy commanded, leveling his weapon at the man.

He looked up, his eyes glowing the same golden color as the tendrils of light.

"Get a doctor," he said, his voice raw and full of emotion. "Please, my daughter's been wounded."

"Get a doctor," Buddy said to Detective Arnold. "You need to put her down," he said to the man. "We need to put pressure on her wound to stop the bleeding."

The girl coughed and blood sprayed over the man's coat.

"No," he gasped. His head jerked up and he reached out toward the cowering waitress. Almost before he finished moving, a tendril of golden light lashed out from his hand. Wrapping itself around the terrified woman's neck, it seemed to lift her up off the floor. Shrieking, the waitress tried to tear the light away, only to find it insubstantial.

The light pulsed and the waitress' cries weakened. At the same time the light passing between the man and the girl intensified.

"Stop!" Buddy demanded, leveling his weapon at the man's chest.

The glowing man looked up at him with an imploring look, but he didn't stop as the waitress' struggling grew weaker.

"I mean it," Buddy said. "We'll get your daughter help, but you have to stop this."

"If I stop, she'll die," he said, clutching the girl to his chest.

The moment seemed to slow down. The cries of the waitress and murmurs of fear from the other patrons faded into the background as Buddy focused on the glowing man. The look on his face told Buddy no words would stop him from doing anything to save his daughter. There was only one thing, one horrible thing, that could be done.

Buddy squeezed the trigger of his 1911. It was a deliberate motion, slow and steady so as not to spoil his aim. The gun kicked at the same moment the .45 slug tore a hole in the glowing man's head.

The glowing tendrils vanished, and the suddenly unsupported waitress fell, gasping, to the floor. The dead man slumped forward, and the girl slid from his arms to the floor. It was a gentle motion, as if he protected her even in death.

Buddy didn't hesitate. He ran forward, dropping to his knees over the girl. Dropping his gun beside her dead father, he pulled at the buttons holding her coat closed.

"Help me here," he called out as he heard running feet behind him. Detective Arnold dropped to his knees next to him and gently held the girl by the shoulder. "We've got to stop her from bleeding out," he said, though he was certain the detective had basic first aid training.

Buddy pulled open the coat and his blood froze in his veins. A piece of shrapnel from Sadler's explosion had punctured her back, low and on the side. Whatever her father had been doing was definitely keeping the child alive, and now her blood was pouring from the wound.

The shrapnel had hit her kidney.

Buddy clamped this hand over the wound, knowing as he did it that there was nothing he could do. Nothing in his training, nothing in his war experience could save this child.

"Don't worry daddy," the girl mumbled, her eyes unfocused and distant. She reached up and touched Buddy's cheek, clearly mistaking him for her dead father. "I love you."

Buddy didn't know what to say to her, but one look at her eyes told him it no longer mattered. In that moment, he saw his own daughter, remembered her hugging his leg. The echo of her own 'I love you' echoed in his mind and he clenched his fists so tightly that his joints cracked.

He stood up as if he'd been kicked.

"God, dammit!" he shouted, wishing he had something to throw, something to smash.

"Agent Redhorn?" the voice of Detective Arnold probed.

"I'm all right," Buddy said after a moment to master himself. He leaned down and picked up his gun, tucking it into its holster. "Have your men take statements, then call the coroner. I need to find Detective Pak."

Without waiting for an answer, Buddy strode from the restaurant. He didn't have to ask around to find out what had happened, it was patently obvious. Sadler's bomb had killed the little girl, and the father had been hit by the Limelight, too. In that moment, his only desire was to have the power to save his daughter, power the Limelight had granted him. He'd carried her to the restaurant, no doubt in search of a doctor or a phone, and used his newfound power to keep his girl alive at the expense of the restaurant patrons.

It wasn't his fault. All he knew in that moment was that his little girl was dying and he'd do anything, sacrifice anything, even other people's lives, to save her.

Buddy couldn't say for certain that he wouldn't have done the same.

The thought of Jess lying there, bleeding out because of a delusional madman, sent his blood boiling.

"Lieutenant Pak," he called as he approached the police by the stairs. "Please tell me you got our man."

Buddy wouldn't kill him, of course. Killing a suspect, even one as obviously guilty as Gilbert Sadler, would be unprofessional. Beating the man's teeth out, however, was left to Buddy's discretion.

As he reached the group of uniformed officers, he found the two he'd sent after Lieutenant Pak, but not the man himself.

"Where's Pak?" he demanded, perhaps a bit more sharply than he intended.

"We didn't find him, sir," the blond officer said. Something in his voice made the hairs on Buddy's neck rise up.

"What do you mean you didn't find him?"

"The only thing around that corner was this," the man said, handing Buddy a heavy chunk of rock.

As he turned it over in his hands, Buddy realized it wasn't a rock at all. It was a police issue .38, and it had been turned to stone.

"You and you," Buddy said, pointing to the same two men, "with me."

Not pausing to see if they would follow, Buddy turned and set off at a run toward his car parked in the next block.

Fifteen harrowing minutes later, Buddy mashed the brake of his FBI-issue car and tore off several layers of rubber as it skidded to a stop, bumping the curb in a quiet east-side neighborhood. Not waiting for the two policemen to pry their hands loose from the dash and seat back respectively, he opened the door and ran around to the sidewalk. His destination was an unassuming brownstone in the middle of the block with a sandstone staircase running up to its front stoop.

Leaping up the stairs two at time, Buddy strode to the heavy door and began pounding on the ornate stained-glass window in its center. Normally he never would have risked such a beautiful window by banging on it, but Buddy knew for a fact that a bomb had gone off outside this door a few months ago and the window survived.

"Come on, Doc," he said, pounding again.

This time several panes of the stained glass popped free and fell inside the vestibule beyond. At the same moment, light flared up inside and a moment later the inner vestibule door opened.

"Who's there?" a robust voice came from inside.

"It's Agent Redhorn," Buddy answered. "Dr. Bell? I need your help right away."

"Just a moment," Bell's voice replied.

Buddy saw movement and the crunching of broken glass as the man moved to the front door. A moment later it opened, revealing an old man in a rich red smoking jacket and tweed suit pants. His face was craggy and lined but his eyes were sharp, if a bit tired, and his bottle-brush mustache twisted into a smile.

"Agent Redhorn," he said, "it's nice to see you again. How can I assist..." he paused as his eyes went wide. "Are you injured?" he suddenly demanded.

Buddy looked down at the dried flecks of blood on the backs of his hands and the scarlet stains on his formerly white shirt cuffs.

"No, I'm fine," he said. "Listen, you trained Lockerby, didn't you?" Redhorn asked, his tone a touch too urgent.

"Why don't you just tell me what you need," Bell said in a soothing voice.

"Okay," Buddy said, forcing himself to remain calm and professional. "Lieutenant Pak and I are on the heels of a madman who can turn things to stone. Pak went after him, and I think the bad guy grabbed him. How long would it take you to write a finding rune?"

"Having worked with Alex for years now, I always keep a finding rune or two on hand," Bell said, reaching into his smoking jacket and withdrawing a small, green screw-post book. "We'll need something belonging to Danny, though. I know where he lives, let me get my coat."

"Will this do?" Buddy said, holding out the stone service weapon. "The cops found it where the lieutenant disappeared. I'm sure it's his."

Bell reached out and took the weapon. Buddy expected him to falter a bit under its unexpected weight, but the septuagenarian doctor handled it with ease, turning it over in his hands. Buddy hadn't seen the man in close to a year but now that he was paying attention, the doctor actually looked younger than he remembered.

"It looks like the one Danny carries," he said with a nod, passing the gun back to Buddy. "It's worth trying it first. You and your boys better come in, but mind the mess."

Bell stepped back so that Buddy could enter along with the two policemen who had managed to extract themselves from the car and come up behind while the Doctor was talking. As he passed through the vestibule, Buddy nearly tripped over something. As he looked down, he saw that a second set of tiles seemed to be sitting atop the tiled map of Manhattan on the floor. For a mind-bending minute, Buddy thought there were two floors.

"As I said," Bell cut through his thoughts, "I'm redoing the wards that protect my home. It can have unusual side effects until it's done."

Shaking the strange sight out of his mind, Buddy continued into the brownstone's central foyer. He'd been in the doctor's home before and knew that there was a cozy library to the right with a large kitchen just beyond that. Straight ahead, a stair led to the upper floors.

"Through to the kitchen, Agent Redhorn," Bell said, following the policemen inside.

Buddy turned and passed through the library to the little hallway beyond. A coal fire burned in the library grate and he could smell the smoke of a fine Cuban cigar permeating the room. Clearly they had interrupted the doctor's evening of quiet solitude.

In the kitchen, Buddy reached to the right of the door and flipped on the light as he entered. A heavy chandelier of green metal lit up above a table big enough to seat a dozen people. Beyond the table was a large ice box and a china cabinet, with an enormous stove and oven to the right side. Gleaming pots and pans hung from hooks above the tiled counters on either side of the oven, and an open pantry door filled the space to the extreme right.

"Everyone sit," Dr. Bell said, entering last. "I need to get a few things from my vault."

Buddy pulled out one of the heavy chairs that matched the massive table and sat while Bell opened a door set into the wall next to the opening they'd come in through. The door should have opened into the narrow hall they'd just passed, but instead, when Bell pulled it open, Buddy could see a vast room. From his vantage point, he couldn't see the entire space, but he did see paintings on the ceiling and luxurious furniture. Buddy knew what runewright vaults were, because he'd been inside Lockerby's, but Dr. Bell's vault put Alex's to shame.

A moment later, Bell returned, shutting the door behind him. He carried a leather bag exactly like the one Lockerby carried to crime scenes.

Looks like Lockerby picked that trick up from the Doc, he thought.

Suddenly he felt a lot better about his decision to come here for a finding rune. He could have gone back to Alex's office, but it was almost nine so no one would be there. Now that he thought about it, Buddy didn't have home numbers for Ms. Knox or Mike Fitzgerald. If this hadn't worked, he would have had to try Lieutenant Pak's captain and hope he knew how to track down a good runewright.

Dr. Bell put his bag down on the end of the table, then opened it. In quick succession, he pulled out a thickly folded stack of paper, a square wooden tile with a runic drawing on it, and a compass that reminded Buddy of the one he'd used in the war. Setting the tile in the middle of the table, Bell unfolded the paper, revealing a map of Manhattan Island, and placed it on top of the tile. The compass went on next, right over the position of the wooden tile.

"Put Danny's weapon in the center of the map," Bell said as he opened his green, screw-post book, "right on top of the compass."

Buddy did as instructed, then sat back.

"All right, Agent Redhorn," Bell said, tearing a rune paper from his screw-post book. "I need you to think about Danny." He folded up the rune and set it gently atop the petrified pistol, then looked at Buddy. "Ready?"

Buddy nodded and Bell took a gold lighter from his pocket and ignited the rune paper. It burned away in seconds, leaving the rune itself behind, floating in the air. Buddy didn't even dare to breathe; he'd seen this before and he knew the rune was trying to locate Lieutenant Pak. Once that happened, the rune would connect with the compass below it. Once it had the link, there wouldn't be any place in the city that Sadler could hide Lieutenant Pak.

"Did it work?" one of the policemen asked, only to be shushed by his companion.

The rune burst in a shower of light and Dr. Bell reached in to slide the compass along the map. Buddy stood up and leaned over so he could see the needle.

It wasn't pointing north.

As Dr. Bell slid it along the map, it began to spin in lazy circles. Bell picked it up, then pointed to the spot underneath.

"Danny is there," he said indicating a spot near the rail yards. "Go get him, Agent Redhorn."

He held out the compass and Buddy took it with a growl.

"You may be certain of that," he said, turning and heading for his car.

21

MOSES

Danny started awake and found himself sitting at a table in a small room. A bare bulb hung from the ceiling just above him, and he blinked his eyes repeatedly to get them used to its stark light. His head still hurt from being hit, but he wasn't dead, so he'd gladly take the sore head in stride.

Part of him resented the fact that Sadler got the drop on him so easily. When Danny rounded a corner to a side street, the sculptor had just been standing there on the sidewalk. Danny ordered him to throw up his hands, but instead the man charged him. Without any choice, Danny had fired twice but Sadler's skin shifted to gray and he'd bashed Danny in the face with a fist turned to stone.

Looking around now, he found the room sparse, with a sink on one side and a tiny counter and a bed and dressing table on the opposite. The absence of an icebox or any other furnishings told him this was a rented room, probably in a boarding house.

"How the hell did he get me in past the landlord?" Danny wondered out loud.

It was far from his most pressing problem, so he let the thought go. What his addled brain did finally latch on to was the fact that other than himself, there wasn't anyone else in the room.

"Time to go," he said, reaching for his jacket to see if he still had his service revolver. When he couldn't seem to reach his jacket, he looked down at himself for the first time and almost screamed.

His hands had been turned to stone.

He'd expected to find himself handcuffed, but Sadler hadn't bothered. Sticking out of his suit coat, Danny's hands weren't his usual tan color, but the pure white and black of marble.

Heart racing, he closed his eyes and breathed deeply. He knew a few sorcerers, more than most people, they should be able to fix this.

You hope.

A fresh wave of panic washed over him, and he breathed deeply again.

Calm. You aren't helping yourself like this. Calm down and think.

After a few deep breaths he was able to open his eyes again and actually look at his hands. They didn't appear any the worse for wear for being stone. If he could get out of here, there was a pretty good chance a sorcerer could change him back.

He started to stand up, but his fingers dragged across the table with a disturbing grinding noise. It wouldn't do to break off a finger; if that happened, a sorcerer might not be able to stick it back on. Sitting down again, he tried to think. His hands weighed enough to make movement difficult, and he certainly couldn't open any doors.

As he sat, pondering, the sound of a key scraping in the lock of the solitary door reached him. A moment later the door opened, and Gilbert Sadler strode in with a paper bag of groceries in his arms. He was a squat, broad-shouldered man, with dark, slicked-back hair, upturned nose, and blue eyes behind a pair of round spectacles. Danny could see a broad, calloused hand holding the grocery bag. It looked powerful and worn, just what one might expect from a sculptor.

"Oh, good," Sadler said when he noticed Danny. "You're awake." He shut the door behind him and moved to the table to deposit his paper bag. "I was worried I'd hit you too hard."

Danny remembered that Sadler had hit him with his fist, a fist that was suspiciously solid and rock-like. A quick glance at Sadler's hands revealed that neither of them was currently made of stone.

"I take it that means you can undo this," he nodded down at his hands.

Sadler looked confused for a moment, then he smiled.

"Of course I can," he said. "The enchanted jade has given me power over stone."

He reached out and touched the back of Danny's left hand and warmth immediately flowed over it and up his arm. Thousands of pinpricks washed over the formerly afflicted flesh and Danny grunted against the sensation.

"Now," Sadler said, sitting down across the little table form Danny, "If you behave yourself, I might just be persuaded to release your other arm."

He began taking things out of his bag, including a loaf of bread, a bottle of milk, and a piece of some kind of meat wrapped in butcher paper. Last of all, he pulled out a two-foot length of metal rod and set it on the table. When he finished, he folded the paper bag and set it aside. Danny watched as Sadler took a large carving knife from the tiny counter by the sink and proceeded to make a sandwich from the bread and what turned out to be a small piece of roast beef.

"Would you like one?" he asked as he set the completed sandwich on a paper napkin.

"No thanks," Danny said. Quite apart from the fact it was very late, his stomach was still a bit queasy from having his hands turned to stone.

"Your loss," Sadler said, wrapping up the meat and the bread and moving them to the counter with the knife. When he returned, he reached under the table and withdrew a small cardboard box, setting it next to his sandwich. He took a bite and began chewing before looking at Danny.

"Holding me here is a bad idea, Mr. Sadler," Danny said at last. "The DA is going to want to hit you with a kidnapping charge."

Sadler shrugged and wiped his mouth with a napkin.

"I'm sure your DA wants to charge me with murder," he said, setting his sandwich down, "so I hardly think kidnapping will matter."

"Why did you bring me here?" Danny asked. "Obviously you could have killed me at any time, so clearly you wanted to talk."

Sadler grinned and reached into the box, pulling out Danny's badge. It was similar to the badges carried by detectives, but it had the word 'Lieutenant' stamped across the top.

"Very good," he said. "I don't wonder that a smart man like yourself made Lieutenant, Daniel. Do you mind if I call you Daniel?"

"If you like," Danny said, keeping his voice friendly and even. Sadler clearly wanted something, but he was also playing some kind of mind game, dancing around his point as if he wanted Danny to guess it. Not really having the stomach for games, Danny decided to come straight to the point.

"So why am I here?"

A look of irritation crawled across Sadler's face, but he seemed to banish it quickly.

"I need someone to understand," he said after a pause. "I need someone to know why."

"You want to be an alchemist," Danny said with a shrug, "but you don't have the talent, so you blamed sorcerers for some reason. Now you think that giving regular people random and potentially dangerous magical abilities will somehow change all that."

Sadler sighed and shook his head.

"I suppose I had that coming," he said. "I was that person not so very long ago."

"So you've changed?"

Sadler's sad face transformed into an energetic grin that bordered on mania.

"Oh, yes, Daniel," he said. "My mind and my vision have been greatly expanded. It all started, as you well know, when I bought that block of jade from Peter Grant. The moment I first touched it, I knew it was special. What I didn't know, what I couldn't have known, was how it would change everything."

"I know," Danny said. "It's a philosopher's stone, some kind of magical battery."

"Oh, it's so much more than that," Sadler said. "That stone doesn't just hold magic, it bestows it on anyone in contact with it. At first as I carved the bird, I didn't know what I was feeling, but gradually, the truth became clear to me. In the shards of that stone, is the power to bring magic to the masses. No more will our countrymen live in a society of the mundane proletariat ruled by the magical aristocracy, finally we will fulfill the promise of our founders. Finally all men will be made equal."

Danny had heard this kind of talk before; it was common among proponents of Karl Marx and his communist philosophies. He'd never heard anyone speak of magic that way, but there was a first time for everything.

"It's true," he admitted, "not everyone has magic, but we don't have magical lords ruling over us either."

"Don't we, Lieutenant?" Sadler smirked. "You have but to go outside and look up to see the flying homes of our betters. They put them up there to remind us who is mighty and who is not."

"And you're going to fix all that by giving unsuspecting women shark teeth and a taste for human flesh?"

Danny was trying to provoke a reaction, to keep Sadler talking, but instead the sculptor turned away.

"That was a regrettable mistake, Daniel," he said. "I hadn't figured out how the jade worked yet."

"At least thirty people have died because of you and that stone, Mr. Sadler," Danny said, sensing weakness. "How many more have to die so you can carry on this war against a few sorcerers?"

"You don't understand," he snapped, whirling back to Danny with his face contorted in a snarl. "You don't have magic so you can't see what it's like for those of us who, how did you put it? Those of us who don't have the talent." He turned and spat on the floor. "Do you have any idea what it's like to have a gift, to be able to do extraordinary things, but then be told that whatever level of skill you've reached is all you'll ever have? To be told that you've reached the end of your abilities and no amount of work or study or practice will make the slightest bit of difference?" He slammed his fist down on the table. "Do you have any idea what it's like to be Moses, sitting on top of Mount Nebo?" His voice broke and he slumped back in his chair. "You're able to see the promised land, but you're forbidden from entering it?"

"I'm sorry, Gil," Danny said in a quiet voice. "I get it, I do. I'm an

American citizen, but there's things I'll never be allowed to do just because of who my father was."

Sadler snarled and scooped up Danny's badge.

"But you are doing them, Daniel, aren't' you?" He held up the badge with 'Lieutenant' printed on it to emphasize his point. "You've broken through your barriers; all you had to do was work harder than everyone around you. But I...I will never be the alchemist I dreamed of being, no matter how hard I work."

"But you don't have to be an alchemist," Danny implored him. "You copied the Jade Phoenix, a famous sculpture, and your work fooled everyone. You might not be a great alchemist, but you are a great sculptor, one of the best."

"I never wanted to be a sculptor," Sadler said, tossing the badge down in front of Danny. "All I ever wanted to be was an alchemist."

"And Moses wanted to enter the promised land," Danny countered. "We don't always get what we want, Gil. It isn't fair, but that's life."

Sadler gave Danny a penetrating look, then picked up the box from which he'd taken Danny's badge. Turning it over, he scattered dozens of chunks of alchemical jade across the table.

"Not anymore, Lieutenant," he said with a widening grin. "With this, I can balance the scales, take power from those strutting peacocks in their soaring castles, and give it to the people. No one will be left outside the promised land ever again, Daniel."

"Except for Peter Grant," Danny countered. "I saw the name Gil Sadler in his books. Not Gilbert, but Gil. That's what you call a friend. He was your friend and he died by literally painting himself to death. That was because of you, Gil. You did that to him."

Sadler hung his head under the weight of Danny's accusation.

"I never wanted that," he said. "Pete was my friend. I wanted him to share this wonderful gift with me."

"Just like you want to share it with the rest of the city," Danny said. "If you do this, all you're going to have is more regrets."

"I know you believe that," Sadler said, scooping up a handful of the limelight stone shards, "but this time you're wrong."

As he spoke, he squeezed the shards in his hand and Danny could see them begin to mold like clay.

"I've learned from my mistakes," he went on, picking up the length of metal rod he'd taken from his grocery bag. "I saw how the powers imparted by the philosopher's stone depended on what the recipient wanted at the moment they were affected." He flattened out the clay-like stone, then wrapped it around the end of the rod. "I saw how the powers needed electricity to make them permanent." Rolling the stone between his hands, he fashioned it down to a tapering point with just the tip of the rod sticking out. "Now I understand that the power must be received willingly, as a gift, not imparted unwittingly or by force."

"How are you going to manage that?" Danny asked.

In answer, Sadler reached across the table and touched Danny's right hand, transforming it back to flesh.

"Who would refuse the gift of magic, Daniel?" he said, spreading his arms theatrically.

Put that way, Danny could see his point. All Sadler had to do was set up on a street corner and invite people to try his magical wish granting machine. His mind raced. With Sadler's abilities, there was no way to overpower him; the sculptor could turn him to stone on a whim. What Danny needed was a gun, but his service weapon had been turned to stone and he was pretty sure Sadler didn't have one he could borrow.

"Don't look so flustered, Daniel," Sadler said, sweeping the remaining jade fragments back into his box. "This really will be for the best."

Before Danny could tell Sadler what he thought of that idea, a woman's voice came echoing up through the floorboards. Danny couldn't hear what she was saying, but he could tell by the tone that she was angry.

"It sounds like your friends have found you," Sadler said, standing and picking up the box and his mostly uneaten sandwich. "With friends like that runewright detective, I knew they would. I just wanted to explain myself to you, to make you understand that everything is going to be okay. Better than okay."

The sound of thundering feet on stairs reached them and Sadler turned to the room's lone window.

"Do tell Agent Redhorn and that Lockerby fellow that I said hello," he said, then opened the window and jumped out. Just before he disappeared from sight, Danny saw his skin change from light tan to slate gray as Sadler turned himself to stone. A moment later he heard a heavy impact from the street below, and the sound of the room's single door being kicked in.

"FBI," Redhorn shouted as he entered. "Nobody move."

"He's gone," Danny said, picking up his badge from the table. "Jumped out the window just before you got here."

Redhorn looked at the open window, then back to Danny.

"You're not tied up," Redhorn observed. "Why didn't you stop him?"

"He turned my hands to stone so he could have a chat with me," Danny explained. "I didn't want to see what he'd do if I tried to stop him without a weapon."

Redhorn looked angry at that, but said nothing as he holstered his 1911.

"What kept you?" Danny asked when the big man didn't speak. "I expected you much earlier."

Redhorn whirled on Danny and looked like he might shout, but after a moment to compose himself, he related the story of Donald Parsons, the man with the little girl.

"I'm sorry," Danny said when Redhorn finished. "You did the only thing you could."

"Yes," Redhorn growled, his eyes flashing with momentary emotion. "But that doesn't make it any easier. How did you make out with Mr. Sadler? Did he tell you anything we can use?"

"I think we might have caught a break with that," Danny said, then he related their conversation.

"Why does he think giving regular people magic will affect the New York Six?" Redhorn asked.

Danny could only shrug at that.

"He seems to ascribe communist theories about scarcity to magic," Danny said. "Somehow the sorcerers are hoarding magic and must be deposed so that magic can be redistributed to the masses."

"That's crazy," Redhorn said.

Danny could only shrug in agreement.

"It also doesn't tell us where he's going to strike next," Redhorn growled. "You said it yourself, he could just set up on a street corner."

"No," Danny countered. "He needs a source of electricity, and not just what he can get out of a power outlet."

"If he tries to commandeer a sky crawler station, he won't have much time to work his come-get-magic song and dance," Redhorn said. "Every station has a cop standing guard and if he turns the guard to stone, he'll just start a panic."

"He needs a place with a lot of electricity where he can give his message to a large group of people in a short amount of time," Danny said, then he looked at Redhorn with a smile spreading over his face. The big man looked back and nodded knowingly.

"Empire Station," they said together.

22

THE GADGETEER

Buddy Redhorn groaned at the pain in his head as his alarm clock dragged him to wakefulness. He knew without looking that it was six-thirty, time to get up. Since complaining wouldn't do anything useful, he carefully extracted his arm from under Lexi's shoulder and sat up.

He didn't stand yet, but he did have the presence of mind to silence his mechanical tormentor before it woke his wife. As he sat, rubbing his eyes, Buddy had just enough resolve to silently curse the universe for being unfair. Between the incident at the diner and tracking down Lieutenant Pak, it had been well after midnight before he'd been able to wrap his wife's sleeping form in his arms and finally rest.

That seemed like mere minutes ago.

Baring his teeth in a silent snarl, he stood and headed to the bathroom to wash his face and shave. He was certain that Pak's guess about Sadler's target was correct. The sculptor would try to use the immense energy of Andrew Barton's power projector to send his Limelight energy all over the city. The only saving grace was that Empire Tower wouldn't open to the public until seven, and it wouldn't be crowded enough for Sadler to make his move until eight or nine.

"You didn't wake me," Lexi said, appearing behind him in the mirror as Buddy wiped the remnants of shaving cream from his jaw. She laid her arm over his shoulder, pressing her cheek to his shoulder.

Buddy smirked at her reflection.

"I see you managed anyway," he said.

"Well, I went to bed without my husband," Lexi said, a red eyebrow rising to accompany a sardonic smile. "It was very rude of you to make me wake in that same condition. Naturally I had to get up to properly chastise you."

She squirmed under his arm, and pulled him down for a passionate kiss. Finally Buddy had to pull away. Lexi had a way of making a man lose track of time.

"See what you miss when you don't come home on time," she whispered in his ear. She returned the smirk he'd given her, then turned. "I'll go make something for you to take with you."

"Lexi," Buddy said, grabbing her arm to prevent her from leaving. "As soon as I'm gone, get the kids up, pack a bag, and go visit my mother."

"You know I don't like that woman," Lexi said with a grin, but her expression melted away as she looked at his face. "What is it?"

"You know I can't say," he said.

"But you have to stop...whatever it is."

"I will," he said, touching her cheek. "But it will be easier if I know you and the kids are safe."

Lexi held his gaze for a long moment, then put her hand on top of his.

"Then I'll go see the old bag," she said, with her patented smirk.

Buddy gave her a grin. His mother had always disliked the Irish and he'd gone and married one. To be fair, his mother had tried to be polite, but she still hadn't fully divested herself of her old ways.

"Thank you," was all he said.

He remained a moment, watching Lexi sway her hips for him on her way to the kitchen, then turned to the closet to put on a suit. When he finished, he checked his 1911, pulling out the magazine to check it, then replacing it and tucking the weapon into the holster under his left arm.

Turning from his dresser, Buddy went into the hall and cracked the door to Jessica's room. All he could see was a lump under her covers and a mop of red hair hanging out and over the edge of the bed. It was enough and he smiled before silently shutting the door.

Duncan's bedroom was downstairs, so Buddy headed down and through the front room to the kitchen where Lexi was sliding a fried egg off a spatula and onto a bit of toast. To that she added a slab of ham and another piece of bread.

"Some Irishwoman you are," he chuckled. "Not a potato in sight."

She laughed at that, her face splitting into a wide grin. Buddy loved making her laugh.

"It was you Yanks who invented hash browns," she said.

"Morning, Dad," Duncan said, staggering into the kitchen with a yawn.

Buddy hugged his son, kissed his wife, then took his sandwich and headed out to his car.

When Buddy pulled up in front of the Central Office of Police, he found Lieutenant Pak standing on the sidewalk waiting for him. Next to him was the large figure of Captain Callahan, a cigarette in one hand and a grim look on his face. What he didn't see was the two dozen police they would need to secure Empire Terminal and the lobby of Empire Tower. The only other person in sight was a uniformed officer who leaned against a police flying unit nearby, reading the paper.

"You look like I feel," Pak said as Buddy exited his car. "You remember Captain Callahan."

Buddy nodded and managed to stifle a yawn.

"Captain," he said. "I take it there's been a change of plans."

"Agent Redhorn," Callahan acknowledged him. "I'll cut to the chase. I spoke to Mr. Rockefeller after I got Danny's report last night."

That surprised Buddy. Callahan must have serious fortitude to wake a sorcerer up in the middle of the night.

"He said he wanted to see both of you in his office."

Buddy glanced to the flyer, now understanding the reason for its presence. Having worked for Sorsha for almost five years, he'd ridden in flying cars many times before. Unfortunately, that didn't mean he liked it.

"What does Mr. Rockefeller want with us?" he asked.

"I imagine he's got some insight on how to apprehend Mr. Sadler," Callahan said. "In any case, what Rockefeller wants, he gets, so get going."

Pak shot Buddy a wide grin, then headed for the floater as the uniformed officer slid behind the wheel. Reluctantly, Buddy followed, pausing long enough to slip his arm through the leather loop mounted to the door. It was supposed to keep passengers from sliding around while the floater operated, but to Buddy it was a lifeline.

"I hardly got any sleep," Lieutenant Pak confessed as the floater jumped several feet straight up.

"Sorry," the officer said over his shoulder. "The verticals are a bit sticky this early in the morning."

"How about you?" Pak went on as if nothing had happened.

"Barely a wink," Buddy confessed. "What do you think Rockefeller wants?"

When Pak didn't answer, Buddy looked over at him to find the man leaning against the door, fast asleep.

Lucky bastard, he thought as the floater dipped unexpectedly.

All Buddy could do was put a stoic look on his face and take a white-knuckle grip on the leather loop as the floater climbed slowly upward, toward the flying mansion of Sorcerer John Rockefeller.

Only five of the New York Six had flying castles that circled the city. Most were built exactly like they sounded, a medieval style structure cut out of a massive chunk of rock by magic. Rockefeller's home was the exception. It still flew high above the city, but instead of building it by magic, Rockefeller had a palatial mansion built on a remote plot of land, then simply lifted it up into the sky, ground and all.

Buddy nudged Lieutenant Pak as the floater drifted down over the circular drive that still existed in front of the massive, white marble building. A moment later they stood on the imposing front porch. To

Buddy's great surprise, their knock on the door was answered by Rockefeller himself. He wore an expensive suit and he looked as if he'd been up for hours.

"Well, here you are at last," he chided, mild irritation flashing briefly across his face. "Come in."

Rockefeller stepped back, pulling the door with him, and ushered Buddy and his temporary partner into a grand foyer that was bigger than Buddy's entire house. Greenish marble covered the floor with a whitewashed oak staircase along the back wall curving up to the second floor. Light-colored furniture had been tastefully arranged throughout the space with vases of fresh cut flowers positioned under magelights that made them appear to glow.

Buddy took off his hat, but before he could even look around, if popped out of his grip and floated over to a hat stand behind the door. A moment later the lieutenant's hat joined it and Rockefeller clapped his hands together.

"I must admit," he said, leading the way toward a door in the back wall, underneath the curved stair, "it has been some time since I had visitors up here. I used to throw big parties years ago, but these days I find I prefer solitude."

Buddy exchanged a look and a raised eyebrow with Pak.

"I don't mean to be rude, sir," Pak said, "but there's a very dangerous man on the loose and we need to catch him."

Buddy wondered if Rockefeller would be offended by the lieutenant's thinly veiled attempt to hurry him along.

"Fear not, Lieutenant Pak," the sorcerer said with a wry chuckle. "I spoke at length last evening with Captain Callahan and I think you might be looking in the wrong place."

The fog that still enshrouded Buddy's mind broke with a snap that brought his head up. He was pretty sure they had Gilbert Sadler figured out and he hated when he missed things.

Passing through the door at the end of the foyer, their host led them to a hallway paneled in light-colored wood with a door on the right side.

"This is my workshop," he said, touching the door with his finger.

Buddy heard a rattling clack as the door unlocked, then Rockefeller pulled it open.

"Probably best if you don't touch anything," he continued as he ushered Buddy and Pak inside. "Some things in here still have a residual magical charge."

The room beyond was two stories high, with glass windows all around the top that allowed golden morning light to illuminate the space. Along the walls were shelves full of parts and random junk, interspersed with pegboards full of hanging tools. Workbenches filled the center area of the room, and a crane on a metal support beam hung above.

Covering most of the tables were strange objects that looked familiar at first glance, but weren't on closer inspection.

"What is all this stuff?" Pak asked, pointing to something that looked like a pocket-sized version of a flashlight.

"It's a light," the sorcerer said, picking it up. The moment he touched it, an intense beam of white light erupted from the front end. It was so bright that Buddy could see its circle on the wall despite the daylight pouring down from above.

"That's amazing," Pak said, an enthusiastic smile blooming on his face.

"Why don't you market those?" Buddy asked. "I know the FBI would buy one for every agent we've got."

Rockefeller sighed and tossed the contraption to Buddy, who caught it deftly. As soon as it left the sorcerer's hand, however, the light vanished.

"What's wrong with it?" Buddy asked.

"Nothing. It requires magic to work."

"You mean like charms?" Pak asked.

Charms were physical objects made by sorcerers that usually carried powerful, limited-use magical spells on them. They could sometimes be bought from high end shops, but they were always in limited supply and very expensive.

"It's exactly like a charm," Rockefeller said, "and that's the problem." He held out his hand and Buddy handed him back the flashlight. "If I charge this thing up, it'll go for a good while, a few hours at most, then I'd have to charge it up again. I could make a fortune with it, but I'd spend all day recharging them."

He tossed the flashlight back onto the workbench with a sigh.

"That's the case with most of this junk," he said. "But as you pointed out earlier, you have a madman to apprehend, so let's get on with it."

He walked over to a workbench that was uncharacteristically clean. Reaching out, he tapped his finger on the table and instantly a thick fog rolled out from the spot.

"Captain Callahan brought me up to speed about your Mr. Sadler," he began. "He told you that he intends to use electricity to energize the Limelight stone in order to give magical powers to the people of New York."

Lieutenant Pak nodded.

"Naturally, you assumed he meant to employ Barton's power projector on top of Empire Tower." He raised his hand and a replica of the tower leaped up out of the mist.

"Stands to reason," Buddy said. "It's exactly what he needs to achieve his goal."

"You aren't wrong about that," Rockefeller said, "but your Mr. Sadler would have to be desperate to try it." He waved his hand again and a portion of the top of the tower illuminated. "This is Barton's antenna. In order to reach it, Sadler would have to gain access to the private elevator that goes to the upper floors."

"Giving security ample time to trap him in the elevator," Buddy said, catching on.

"And call Barton back from Washington," Lieutenant Pak added. "That would cook his goose for sure."

"What Sadler needs," Rockefeller said, "is access to a powerful source of electricity that's not heavily guarded."

"Are you suggesting he'll use the crawler lines?" Buddy asked.

"He could do his 'what do you wish for' routine on a crawler full of people," Pak suggested, though his expression said he doubted it. "But that seems too small for Sadler's ambition."

"I agree," Rockefeller said, snapping his fingers. As he did, the mist changed. Empire Tower shrank down, and the skycrawler lines ran out from it. As they went, the buildings of Manhattan grew up beneath them until the entire island was revealed. "Most of the crawler lines have a dozen stops before they reach Empire Station," the sorcerer explained. "That doesn't give your man much time to use his magic wand. Every two minutes the crawler will stop at a new station. However," he snapped his fingers again and two rail lines lit up, "these two are express lines."

Pak was nodding along, and Buddy felt a smile spread across his face. The express lines ran up to the Bronx and out to Brooklyn, and the ride took about fifteen minutes each way. That gave Sadler plenty of time, but there was still the problem of his audience.

"That still doesn't help him grant magic to the people," Pak said, echoing Buddy's thoughts.

"You're stuck on the idea that he cares if people get magical abilities they want," Rockefeller said.

"He said he did," Pak protested.

"I'm sure he'd love to do it that way," the sorcerer said, "but if what you told your Captain is accurate, he's a fanatic. He's not going to let a little thing like informed consent get in his way."

Buddy looked back at the ethereal map of Manhattan and the skycrawler network. The rails that carried the express crawlers ran through the heart of the city, over neighborhoods and around apartment buildings. It wasn't even half the island's population, but Buddy would have bet it represented a third.

"He's going to hang his antenna off the bottom of the express crawler," Buddy guessed. "It will affect everyone nearby as it goes along its route."

As he spoke, the streets below the express routes and the buildings nearby began to glow softly.

No one spoke for a long moment, then Lieutenant Pak cleared his throat.

"He still has to get on the crawler," he said. "That's where we can set up to stop him."

"He could get on at any stop before or after Empire Tower," Buddy countered. "We'll have to put a man in every crawler."

"Wait a minute," Pak said. "If you're right about how he'll use his device, he could take any train in the city, not just the express."

"I don't think so," Rockefeller said. "You already have an officer in every station, so every time the crawler stops, he has a chance to get caught. The express is the choice a smart man would make, and while Sadler may be insane, he's proven he's also smart."

"We should still put men in every crawler," Buddy offered.

"That'll scare him off," Pak countered. "If Sadler's ridden the skycrawler before, he knows there's police in the stations but not on the trains. We should put an extra man at every station to help watch for him."

"And if they see him?" Rockefeller asked.

"They shoot to kill before he can turn himself to stone," Buddy answered without hesitation.

"What about us?" Pak asked.

"You two should position yourselves in Empire Station," Rockefeller said. "That's the most logical place for Sadler to board the express. There's usually only one policeman there, and there are hundreds of people. It's the best chance he has of slipping on the crawler unnoticed."

Buddy sighed. There were too many things that could go wrong with this plan, but he had to admit, it was the only plan they had. No matter what, stopping Sadler from turning a third of the city into Penny Piranhas or worse, the life-draining father, was his only priority.

"All right," he said. "I guess we'd better get going."

"Not quite yet," Rockefeller said. "I've got something here that might help."

23

THE LEAP OF FAITH

Buddy Redhorn checked his watch for the fifth time in as many minutes. This wasn't his first stake-out by any means, and he prided himself on his ability to remain calm and patient while he waited for the bad guys to reveal themselves. This time was different. Gilbert Sadler was a monster, destroying peoples lives with the reckless abandon of a drunk in a brewery. He simply didn't care who he hurt while he was tilting at his personal windmills.

Reflexively, Buddy touched cold steel beneath his jacket, sliding his finger down until he felt the rough grip of his Navy Colt 1911. One way or another, Sadler's reign of terror ended today.

Resisting the urge to check his watch again, Buddy picked up a newspaper and pretended to read it. This familiar surveillance activity calmed him as he focused his eyes over the top of the paper. He'd been sitting on this bench in Empire Terminal for three hours now. Across the wide central aisle, Lieutenant Pak sat in the terminal's cafe, pretending to read a paperback novel. As if he sensed Buddy's glance, Pak looked up and gave him the minutest bob of his head.

Both of them had been on this stake-out since early morning. Buddy had started at the express station in Brooklyn, watching the sky bugs as they started their journey into the city. Pak had been at the station in the Bronx. Neither one of them had seen Sadler so, when the last inbound express ran, they boarded it and met here at Empire Station.

The end of the line.

Or it will be for Sadler, he growled in his head.

Now all he and Pak had to do was wait for Sadler to attempt to board an outbound express. Those trains would start running any minute now.

As if to punctuate his thoughts, a chime sounded from the north side terminal platform. A large sign above the platform listed the available trains and an electric bulb lit next to the name, *Brooklyn Express*.

Across the terminal, Lieutenant Pak stood up and tucked his book into the outside pocket of his jacket. He moved to the north platform along with a dozen or so others, waiting for the crawler to arrive. While he moved in close, Buddy stood to the side, watching the potential passengers as they approached the platform.

Buddy pulled the copy of Sadler's picture from his pocket and scanned it quickly to reacquaint himself with the sculptor. Looking up, he searched the faces of the men and women moving toward the platform. So far, none of them were Gilbert Sadler.

As he watched, Buddy heard the crawler arrive at the platform behind him. He knew without turning that Lieutenant Pak had moved close to the crawler's door, to check everyone boarding. From the rumble of unimpeded boarding, it sounded like Pak was having just as much luck as he was.

When the last passengers passed Buddy on the way to the platform, he turned to watch them board. About twenty people were spreading out, taking seats on the upper and lower decks. Grinding his teeth, Buddy was about to turn away when the car conductor leaned out of the driving compartment window, looking back to make sure all the passengers had finished boarding.

It took Buddy a whole second to understand what he was seeing. The man driving the crawler was Sadler. In that time, the conductor leaned back and the boarding door closed. As the crawler's energy legs began to glow, Buddy charged, running all-out toward the car. He dashed past Danny and leaped up onto the bottom step that stuck out past the closed boarding door. The crawler surged as it began to accelerate properly, and Buddy barely managed to seize the brass handrail before he was swept out of the station, three stories above the street below.

Danny whirled as someone ran by him. Belatedly he realized it was Agent Redhorn, who jumped up onto the outside of the crawler car just as it accelerated out of the station. The FBI man's gray fedora was blown off his head and landed on the terminal platform right at Danny's feet.

His mind wanted to review the memory of the passengers, but there wasn't time for that. He did spare enough time to swear as he bent down and scooped up Redhorn's hat, then he took off running toward the east side of the terminal.

The offices of Barton Electric occupied the upper floors of the tower and the elevator that went up there was protected by a manned security station.

"What is it, Lieutenant?" Stan Green, one of Barton's regular security men asked as Danny came running up.

"Telephone," Danny demanded.

Stan retrieved the phone from behind the counter and Danny scooped up the receiver.

"New York six, twenty-three-hundred," he told the operator. A moment later Rockefeller answered.

"Did my gizmo work?" he asked.

"I haven't had a chance to try it yet, but we've got bigger problems," Danny said. He quickly explained Buddy's actions. "The only reason he would have done that is if he saw Sadler on the crawler. I need you to get ahead of that car and stop it." When Danny finished speaking, there was silence on the line. "Hello?"

A sound like a child's balloon popping startled him and when he turned, Rockefeller was standing at his elbow.

"Hang up, Lieutenant," the sorcerer said. "Now is it the Brooklyn or the Bronx crawler?"

"Uh, Bronx," Danny said, putting the phone receiver down.

"All right," Rockefeller said, grabbing Danny's elbow. "Hold on to your lunch."

"My wha—?" Danny tried to ask, but before he finished the question, they were both gone.

Danny had never teleported before, but he'd heard Alex's stories about the process. His friend's description hardly measured up to the reality of the experience. It felt as if his body was being stretched on a medieval rack, just well beyond what would be physically possible. When Rockefeller had grabbed him, Danny's eyes were open and his brain struggled to process what he was seeing. In his right eye, he could see Stan, frozen in open-mouthed shock as Danny vanished right before him. On his left side, he could see a blur of motion that ended abruptly at what appeared to be an open air skycrawler station. All his mind seemed to be able to grasp was that his body had somehow been stretched between the two locations, existing for a split second in both.

Then everything snapped back to real time. His body lurched, folding in on itself in an instant, and Danny felt his guts twisting and wrapping together in his middle. Worse, his brain seemed to slosh inside his skull, giving him the nauseating feeling that he was falling while knowing that he stood on his feet.

The sensation vanished like a soap bubble on a needle, but the twisting in his guts and the nausea stayed behind. Danny dropped to his knees and vomited up the sandwich he'd eaten at the Empire Station cafeteria.

"Oh, God," he gasped when his stomach had finished heaving. "Don't ever do that again."

"Come on, boy," Rockefeller said, a note of compassion in his voice. "Pull yourself together. The express crawler will be here in a minute or two."

"Right," Danny managed, forcing himself to his shaky feet. "What's the plan?"

"We can assume that if Agent Redhorn has control of the situation, he'll have the driver stop the crawler."

"What if Sadler killed the driver?" Danny asked. It would make sense that Sadler didn't want any chance of being interrupted while he put his plan into action.

"Good point," Rockefeller admitted. "As soon as the car comes into sight, I'll manipulate the controls and bring it to a stop in this station."

"Can't you just...I don't know, pick it up off the rail?" Danny asked.

"Don't be absurd, young man," Rockefeller scoffed. "A crawler is an immensely complex magical machine; I can't just go throwing powerful spells on it. If one of them reacts badly with something, the whole crawler could explode, or jump off the rail and go crashing down to the street. I could pick it up as a last resort, but it's best if I try something subtle first."

Danny hadn't really considered how much magic must be bound into a crawler to make it move like it did. Since Rockefeller was the sorcerer that created it, he resolved to take the man at his word.

"Let's hope Agent Redhorn has everything under control, then."

Buddy held on to the crawler's railing as the vehicle accelerated to nearly sixty miles per hour. Once it reached its cruising speed, Buddy was finally able to lean out enough to grab the door mechanism. It was a folding panel that was opened and closed by means of a pneumatic mechanism controlled by the driver.

Buddy shoved the fingers of his free hand into the gap between the edge of the door and the body of the crawler and pulled. The door started to fold inward, but the pneumatic piston prevented it from moving more than an inch. He had a momentary thought of breaking the vertical pane of glass in the door, but it was too thin for him to squeeze through in any case.

Frustrated, Buddy looked up.

Since it was December, all of the open-topped crawlers had been parked until spring. That said, the upper level had large windows, the kind he could easily fit through.

Determined not to look down, Buddy put his foot up on the angled handrail that led up to the door. Above him there was a decorative rail that ran all the way around the body of the crawler. It wasn't meant to be used as a safety feature, but he had no other options.

Heaving himself upward, he lunged for the bar and caught it with his left hand. Saying a quick prayer that the railing would not break off the moment it held his whole weight, Buddy let go of the handrail on the right side of the doorway and took hold of the decorative rail with both hands. Using his foot for leverage, he hauled himself up, putting his right foot on the rounded top of the vertical handrail.

The window was right in front of him now, and he could see the upper deck of the express crawler. What was more, he could see Sadler. The man was walking along the aisle toward the rear of the car. Not considering the risk, Buddy let go of the rail with his right hand and grabbed his pistol. Drawing it, he pressed the top of the slide against his shoulder and pressed down and forward to cock it.

It wasn't possible for Sadler to hear the noise of the pistol being cocked, but he turned in Buddy's direction nonetheless. The sculptor's brows knit together as if his brain couldn't process what he was seeing. It was a moment of hesitation the madman couldn't afford.

Buddy lashed out with his weapon, shattering the window. Ignoring the shards of glass that showered over him, he drew a bead on Sadler and fired twice. The first round caught the man in his thigh, and he cried out in pain, falling down onto one of the seats behind him. The second shot was only seconds behind the first, but that was long enough for Sadler to shift his body to one of stone and the bullet ricocheted off his arm and into the ceiling.

Buddy was vaguely aware of screaming from the passengers in the crawler but there was no time to take control of the situation. He could hear the ones from the upper deck go pounding down the stairs to the lower. That, at least, would keep them out of the way. As he cleared the broken glass with his 1911, Sadler was struggling to stand. Apparently having his body turned to stone didn't negate the wound in his leg.

Cursing the ill luck of not hitting the rogue sculptor somewhere more vital, Buddy grabbed the widow's edge, put his foot on the decorative railing and launched himself through the open hole. He rolled when he hit the floor, careening into the seat on the far side. As he scrambled to right himself, Sadler loomed over him.

"You are a persistent fool," he growled, raising his stone fist over his head and bringing it down with force.

Buddy barely managed to roll out of the blow's path as it crashed down, splintering the wood planking of the floor. He kicked out with his foot, hitting Sadler's thigh. Buddy knew it wouldn't hurt the man; instead Buddy pushed against him, using him as leverage and sliding out from beneath the threat. He rolled backward, landed on his feet, and fired two more shots one-handed. They bounced off Sadler's stone chest, but it gave Buddy time to drop his left hand into the outside pocket of his suit coat.

Lacing his fingers through what felt like a glorified set of brass knuckles, Buddy pulled out the little device Rockefeller had given him. Where your typical knuckle duster had a narrow edge to concentrate the force of any blow, the sorcerer's version widened out into a flat oval that held a dampening spell.

"That isn't going to work, flatfoot," Sadler chuckled, brushing the lead slugs from his lapels. "Normally I'd turn your legs to stone so you could watch my triumph, but you've already cost me too much time."

Sadler lashed out, trying to grab Buddy's arm. At the same time Buddy punched with his left hand, intercepting Sadler's stone one. Where the damper met the stone hand, Sadler's digits turned back to flesh. Buddy didn't hesitate, he brought his heavy 1911 up and bashed down on Sadler's hand. The sculptor howled in pain as several fingers broke.

Buddy followed up the blow by punching Sadler in the chest, causing the stone surface to retract again. This was the opportunity Buddy had been waiting for. He raised his pistol, intending to shoot the unprotected chest.

"No," Sadler roared, grabbing Buddy's gun with his mangled hand. Broken fingers or not, his magic was still working, and the gun began to turn grey. Buddy could feel the petrifying power tingling in his hand, and he let go of the pistol before he lost the ability to use his hand. Sadler reached for him, but Buddy wasn't going to be fooled twice. He lashed out with the damper, smashing its considerable bulk into the freshly broken hand.

Sadler howled, cradling the wounded appendage against his chest. Buddy pressed his advantage, driving Rockefeller's brass knuckles right between Sadler's eyes. His head snapped back, and he fell into the seat. Buddy tried to follow up, but the sculptor surprised him. Sadler reached out with his wounded hand and managed to endure his broken fingers enough to grab Buddy's wrist. Numbness spread up Buddy's arm before he could jerk his hand free. When he did, his arm pulled him off balance for a moment; it had been turned to stone up to his elbow.

Fear tickled Buddy's spine, but he ignored it. Either Rockefeller could fix his arm or he'd have the perfect perch for his stone parrot; in the meantime, he had a formidable weapon to replace his petrified pistol. Buddy hefted his stone fist and clubbed Sadler over the head with it.

Sadler cried out and rolled away from a follow up attack. Buddy tried to get in another swing, but his arm was too heavy to move quickly. With an incoherent scream of fury, Sadler kicked out, forcing Buddy to step back to avoid his foot. At that moment the crawler turned on its rail and the floor shifted under Buddy's feet. He fell but didn't stay down, pushing up to his knees just in time for Sadler to grab his shoulder. Excruciating pain shot through Buddy's shoulder, but he didn't have time to react as numbness immediately flowed down into his chest and up through his neck.

A moment later Buddy didn't feel anything as his body had been entirely turned to stone.

24

THE FALL

While Rockefeller prepared to take control of the sky crawler, Danny squinted into the distance. He'd already checked that his service revolver was loaded and that the magical damper the sorcerer had given him was secure in the outside pocket of his suit coat. Rockefeller told him it would be able to hold off the effects of Sadler's Limelight rod, at least until it was out of power. Hopefully he wouldn't need it, assuming Rockefeller could stop the crawler.

Preferably without blowing it up.

In the distance, sunlight flashed on metal and Danny shaded his eyes.

"Here he comes," he told Rockefeller.

The sorcerer closed his eyes and extended his hand toward the oncoming crawler as it raced north along Central Park West. A moment later his face contorted in irritation.

"Damn," he muttered. "Your boy Sadler has frozen the controls, probably turned the levers and joints to stone."

"Can't you change them back?"

"No," Rockefeller growled. "I mean I can, but I'd have to physically see them."

"What about teleporting onto the crawler?"

"At that speed?" Rockefeller scoffed. "You might get a young pup like Kincaid to try that, but I don't want to be splattered all over the inside of a crawler going sixty miles an hour. Might as well jump in front of a speeding locomotive and save ourselves the trouble."

Danny ground his teeth. It was never wise to provoke a sorcerer, but the express crawler was getting closer every second.

"Can you divert the electricity in the rails?" he asked. "Take away Sadler's source of power?"

"Now that's not a bad idea," Rockefeller said. "The car would drop down on the rail and grind to a stop. It might jump the track if I did that, but as long as I'm there to catch it, everything should work out."

"Great..." Danny started, then caught the look of doubt on the sorcerer's face. "What's wrong?"

"It'll take me a few minutes to set up the spell I need," he said. He turned to Danny with a sudden light in his eye. "If I can get you on that crawler, do you think you could keep Sadler busy while I rig up the spell?"

Danny looked down at the approaching express. He could see it clearly now, its purple energy legs churning as it surged forward. Assuming he hadn't fallen off, Agent Redhorn was on board, but even if he'd found a way to subdue Sadler, he hadn't managed to slow the crawler.

"All right," Danny said. "What do you need me to do?"

"Get on the far platform. Just before the crawler gets here, I'm going to slow it down enough for you to jump on as it goes by."

Danny unbuttoned his overcoat and slipped it off, folding it before he set it on the tiled floor of the station. On top, he added his hat.

Next to him, Rockefeller closed his eyes again for a moment, then grinned. "I've opened the door for you," he said, opening his eyes and giving Danny a wink. "Sadler didn't bother locking down that control. Now get going, it's almost here."

Danny turned and ran to the skybridge that went above the twin rails of the crawler line. The express ran on a third line on the far side of the outside platform. Even though the crawler didn't make stops at this station, the line was designed so that people could exit onto the platform in the event of an emergency.

The crawler was so close now that he could see frightened-looking people crowding onto the lower deck. That meant Sadler must be on top. That made sense, for that was where the driver's compartment was located. Still, the fact that the people wore looks of terror as the crawler sped toward him meant that, assuming Agent Redhorn had managed to get inside the crawler, he had not yet subdued Gilbert Sadler.

Danny moved to the end of the platform, giving himself room to run in case Rockefeller couldn't slow the car enough for him to simply hop on. He shook his arms, trying to keep himself loose as the speeding crawler came uncomfortably close. Glancing to the left, he spared a quick look at Rockefeller who was holding his hands out in front of him like he intended to physically catch the crawler.

The sideways glance almost cost Danny his life. Without warning, a mass of air hit him from behind. Unprepared for the sudden rush, he spun around, throwing his arms around the support pillar to keep from tumbling into the crawler's path. In a moment the wind died down, or rather focused, because now Danny could see it, a horizontal tornado about two feet wide, hovering over the electrified crawler rail.

The onrushing crawler hit the end of it and immediately slowed as if it had suddenly encountered water. The closer the car got, the more resistance it met, but as he watched, Danny knew it wouldn't be enough to fully stop the express. As the car entered the station, Danny took off, running along the platform until the boarding stair came hurtling by.

With a silent prayer that it wouldn't be the last thing he ever did, Danny jumped. Grabbing the railing, he swung himself inside and through the open doorway. Almost immediately the car leapt forward as the wind vanished, and Danny was slammed back into the stairwell. Down by his feet, he could see cars and people moving along Central Park West far below, and he shivered at the sight.

"Get yourself together," he mumbled out loud, rolling so his knee was on the stair. His hand shook as he grabbed the butt of his .38 and drew it.

Moving up to the top of the stairs, he looked over the lower deck. Two dozen people or so were packed against the front of the car, all of them wary of his brandished weapon.

"I'm a cop," he hissed in as low a voice as he dared.

"Someone was fighting with the driver," an old man in a blue suit said, pointing at the upper deck. For someone on a speeding crawler where the driver might be in trouble, he seemed remarkably calm.

"Stay here," Danny said, and continued up the stairs.

He was hoping to find Agent Redhorn with Sadler in custody. As he came around the top of the spiral star, he felt a momentary surge of hope as Redhorn himself came into view.

A moment later he swore, as he realized the FBI man had been turned to stone. He was in a kneeling position with one hand out, as if holding something back with the other hand raised, fist closed, ready to lash out.

Danny forced himself to look away from the statue. He hoped that Rockefeller could undo Sadler's magic, but right now he had to stop Sadler.

Or delay him.

All he really had to do was keep the sculptor from unleashing his weapon until the sorcerer figured out a way to stop the crawler without killing everyone.

Easy, right?

Moving as quietly as he could, Danny crept up the rest of the stairs to the upper deck. Unlike street level crawlers, sky crawlers had the pilot's compartment on the upper deck, which made sense because the driver didn't have to steer, just control the vehicle's speed as they came to stations.

The door to the driver's compartment stood open and Danny could see a shadow moving back and forth inside. He tightened his grip on his pistol as he slid into the center aisle between the seats and started moving forward.

"Lieutenant," Sadler's voice assaulted him as the man suddenly peered out of the open door.

Danny raised his pistol, but the sculptor's skin changed from pale to slate gray in a flash.

"Don't bother," Sadler said. "You know there's nothing you can do to stop me. Frankly, I wonder why you're trying."

"You're going to kill thousands of innocent people," Danny said, his tone clearly implying that if Sadler had been sane, that point would have been obvious.

Sadler just shrugged at that.

"You're being dramatic, Daniel," he said, reaching down and picking up his Limelight lightning rod from the floor of the driver's compartment. A heavy gauge wire was attached to the back end and ran back into the compartment, so presumably Sadler had wired it into the crawler's controls. "Once I activate this, the people all over the city will begin to receive the gift of their own magic. It's true a few of them might die, but we must serve the greater good."

"Whose greater good?" Danny asked. He'd already heard the man's communist rhetoric, but the longer he kept the sculptor talking, the more time it gave Rockefeller. "I doubt the people you're about to kill will see it that way."

"You're wasting my time," Sadler said, holding up the rod. "Now that this is charged, however, you can be the first recipient of its power."

He was grinning manically now, the light of fervor burning in his dark eyes. Danny twisted his upper body, extending the pistol forward. This had the effect of hiding his left arm from Sadler's view as he reached into his coat pocket for Rockefeller's magic damper.

"I want you to think, Daniel," he went on as he pointed the green spear-tip end of the rod squarely at Danny's chest. "Think about the magic you want the most. What is it that you most desire?"

As he spoke, the green stone flared to life, glowing brightly in the confines of the crawler's upper deck.

"Now hold that thought," Sadler said.

He thrust the rod forward just as Danny brought the damper around. Golden light flared from the rod, but as it crossed the distance to Danny, it seemed to collapse on itself, squeezing back into a narrow beam that was absorbed by the damper.

Sadler's maniacal grin vanished.

"Your stone friend had one of those," he snarled. "It didn't help him any more than yours will help you."

He lashed out with the rod again and once again the golden light was drawn into the damper.

Come on Rockefeller, Danny thought as he gritted his teeth for another attack. *You told me yourself that these gizmos of yours don't last long*.

Sadler's face was flushed red, and he bared his teeth as he took the rod in both hands. This time the burst of light was so bright, Danny had to force his eyes to stay open. The light flickered around the damper for a moment, and sparks popped along the charm's edge.

Hold on, Danny implored the device as he tightened his grip.

Across the room, Sadler cried out in frustration, then the light pulsed brighter. It blinded Danny for a moment, and he feared the damper had failed, but the little device rallied and once again the light was drawn into it.

Sadler cursed and dropped the rod.

"I wanted you to join me," he shouted, flecks of spittle flying from his mouth. "But now I have to destroy you. I can't waste any more time on your delays."

Danny didn't wait for him. His revolver was still in his right hand, and he fired at Sadler while darting forward. Even though he was made of stone, Sadler instinctively flinched away from the bullet. It wasn't much, but by the time Sadler recovered, Danny had closed the distance.

Lashing out with the damper, Danny slammed it into Sadler's face. The stone skin flickered and the skin around the blow turned pink. Raising his revolver, Danny fired. Sadler seemed to sense the shot coming even as he staggered under the blow from the damper. He brought up his hand to cover his face just in time to deflect the incoming bullet.

Undaunted, Danny punched Sadler's arm as the man tried to turn away and the damper absorbed the magic that made it stone. This time Danny's follow up shot from his revolver hit the mark and Sadler screamed in pain as the bullet sliced through the muscle of his arm.

Sadler swore incoherently, spinning back toward Danny. This time he led with his stone right fist, catching Danny in the shoulder.

Reeling as if he'd taken a hit from a sledgehammer, Danny fell back, landing on the floor of the upper deck. Sadler loomed over him and drove his fist down on Danny's left arm. Something snapped, and Danny winced in pain.

Sadler raised his fist again, stretching up to his full height so he could drive it down with the added benefit of his weight.

"You never should have defied me," he growled.

The stone fist came down.

Danny brought his revolver up, hoping to use his remaining bullet to force Sadler's blow off course. As his finger tightened on the trigger, however, the floor was suddenly pulled out from under him.

The gun boomed and Danny spun sideways, slamming face first into the glass of the front window. His broken arm burned with pain and he grit his teeth to keep from crying out. Beside him, Sadler landed heavily, sending spiderweb cracks spiraling across the surface of the magically enhanced glass.

Below, Danny could see the electrified rail the crawler was supposed to be running on. Now the vehicle was suspended by its back end, hanging in the air.

"It's about time, Rockefeller," he wheezed as the car began to slide sideways and descend down toward the winter brown grass of Central Park.

"What have you done?" Sadler roared, scrambling to sit up.

Being carful of his broken arm, Danny rolled to his back. He dropped his empty .38 and reached across his chest to take the damper from his left hand.

"No," Sadler howled as he realized what had happened. He turned from the window with murder on his stone features.

This time Danny was ready for him. Ignoring the pain in his arm, he lunged up and drove the damper right into the sculptor's nose. Sadler's head rocked back as his face turned back to flesh. Danny didn't hesitate; he struck Sadler again.

"Stupid boy," Sadler slurred as he tried to fend off another blow. "Your gun is empty! You can't kill me."

Danny hit him again, changing his entire head back to flesh.

"I'm not going to kill you," Danny growled, raising the damper over his head, "gravity is."

He brought it down with all his force onto the enchanted glass of the crawler's front window. The damper hit like the blunt instrument it was, but it also pulled out the magic keeping the glass together. With a report like a gunshot, the glass shattered.

Opening his hand, Danny dropped the damper, lashing out with his arm to grab the brass rail that ran along just above the floorboards. The weight of his body jerked his arm tight, threatening to pull it out of its socket, and pain exploded in his broken arm. It was a miracle, but Danny clung to the rail despite the pain.

Taken by surprise, Sadler had no chance to avoid falling. With a scream of terror, he plummeted out of the crawler. Danny watched as his stone body slammed into the frozen ground fifty feet below. As he hit, Sadler's head exploded as his stone body came down on top of it, cutting his scream off with sudden finality.

"Hold on, Lieutenant," Rockefeller's voice pulled Danny's attention away from the gruesome sight below.

Looking up, Danny saw the sorcerer, hovering above him in the air as the crawler car drifted slowly downward. He had his arms out and sweat ran down his craggy face, but he also wore a roguish smile.

A wave of exhaustion washed over Danny, and his hand began to ache.

"Just another few moments," Rockefeller called encouragement at him.

Danny wanted to tell him where he could stick his encouragement, but he worried that the strength required to open his mouth would sap his grip and kill him. He was about to try it anyway when a grinding, tearing noise erupted behind him. Before Danny could even wonder about it, the stone form of Agent Redhorn slammed into the seat above him, and went spinning out the window.

"No!" he shouted, but there was nothing he could do. The FBI man plummeted down, landing right on top of Sadler's remains, and shattered into a million pieces.

25

PATCHING UP

Light slowly crept into Danny's consciousness. For a moment he thought he was dead, which would make the light Heaven beckoning. A moment later the pain hit him like an express crawler, and he knew without a doubt that he was still alive. A curse escaped his lips as he tried to push himself up into a sitting position. That turned out to be a mistake as his arm erupted in pain and he swore again.

"Take it easy, sir," a familiar voice said, and Danny felt a hand on his shoulder.

"Crenshaw?" he managed, forcing his eyes open. The young detective was kneeling beside him.

"There's an ambulance on the way," Crenshaw said, "don't worry."

Danny didn't feel like he needed an ambulance. Gilbert Sadler had broken his arm, but that could be mended quickly with the right alchemical draughts. He smiled as he remembered that no amount of mending, alchemical or otherwise, would get the mad sculptor on his feet again. Danny had seen to that.

He'd managed to hold off Sadler until Rockefeller had arrived. Apparently, the sorcerer decided the only thing he could do was risk picking the crawler up off of the still-electrified rail. He'd almost dumped Danny out of the front window with that move, but at least the car hadn't exploded.

"Buddy," he gasped, forcing himself to sit up without the aid of his broken left arm.

"Easy, Lieutenant," Crenshaw said, trying to ease Danny back down on the grass.

Danny swatted the detective's hand away but made no further attempt to rise. He didn't need to.

About ten yards to his left was a pile of broken stone. Danny could see a shoe-shaped rock sitting on the dead grass just beyond the pile. He remembered it in perfect detail, the remaining bits of jagged glass smashing as Agent Buddy Redhorn's petrified body crashed through and fell down to shatter on the remains of Gilbert Sadler.

Just looking at the pile of broken rock, Danny knew there was nothing that could be done. If Redhorn had remained intact in the crawler, Rockefeller would have been able to put him back together, but this?

"Where's Rockefeller?" he asked Crenshaw, determined to try to restore the FBI man.

Crenshaw jerked a thumb over his shoulder. Behind him, the sorcerer hung, suspended in the air with his hands extended toward the crawler car. As Danny watched, the car's purple legs flared into existence, scrambling as if they wanted to run, to propel the car forward, but before they could get purchase on the ground, they faded away again. Inside the crawler, the lights flashed on and off for a moment, then the entire thing seemed to settle on the ground, melting the few bits of snow that remained in this windswept part of the park.

"Help me up," Danny said, offering Crenshaw his good arm. The detective stood, then, using his own good arm, grabbed hold and pulled Danny to his feet. As he rose up, Danny became aware of the crowd that surrounded the area. People had packed in from the street and spread out in a circle around the space, from the look of it at least a hundred or more. Uniformed policemen were engaged trying to keep the bystanders back, and Danny saw the occasional flash bulb go off, from a reporter's camera no doubt.

Pushing those details from his thoughts, he marched over to where Rockefeller was still hovering over the downed crawler.

"Lie back down," the sorcerer said without even looking. "You fell out of the crawler just before it touched down; you might have internal bleeding or a concussion."

"I'm fine," Danny growled. "Is the crawler stable?"

Rockefeller sighed and rotated in the air before drifting down to stand before him.

"Yes," the sorcerer said. "Despite my worries, it seems to have survived being yanked off the rails, though we'll probably have to decommission it for safety reasons. And now that you know everything is in hand, go back and lie down."

"I'm fine," Danny reiterated, "but Agent Redhorn needs our help."

Rockefeller looked around as if he were confused.

"Didn't he get off with the passengers?"

"No," Danny said, then hesitated. "He got off before I did." Danny tuned and nodded toward the rock pile.

Rockefeller blinked, not understanding for the briefest of moments.

"That's not good," he said, striding across the frozen ground to the pile.

"Yuck," he said when he caught sight of the fleshy remains of Sadler's head.

"That's Sadler," Danny explained. "He fell out first with most of his body made of stone, but not his head."

Rockefeller looked up with interest in his eyes.

"You used my magic damper?"

Danny nodded.

"Splendid," the sorcerer said, then he looked back at the rock pile. "So where is Agent Redhorn?"

Danny explained about Redhorn being turned to stone and then falling out of the crawler.

"You need to fix him," he concluded.

Rockefeller picked up a piece of what looked like an arm and weighed in his hands, then he turned with bad news in his eyes.

"What is it?" Danny asked.

"I can restore these pieces to flesh, of course," he said, "but that wouldn't be much use with Agent Redhorn in his current condition."

"But you're a sorcerer," Detective Crenshaw protested.

"My power has limits," Rockefeller said. "For me, magic is about what I can conceive in my mind. I don't know how Agent Redhorn's body was put together before, so I have no way to know how to reassemble it."

"But," Danny interjected, "if Agent Redhorn were in one piece, you could change him back, right?"

Rockefeller gave him a penetrating look, then nodded.

"I'll take care of the first part," Danny said, "but it will take me half an hour at least."

"I need to stay with the crawler until an engineer from Manhattan Crawler Lines gets here to help me get her back on the rail so we can take her to the yard."

"That'll work. I need to find a phone, then I'll be back."

Danny turned, but before he could head toward the street to find a phone, Rockefeller put a hand on his shoulder. Instantly, Danny's overcoat appeared on his body, and Danny realized he had been cold. He turned back to thank the sorcerer, but Rockefeller wasn't done; reaching into thin air, he extracted Danny's brown fedora.

"Don't forget your hat, son," he said with a kind smile.

"Thanks."

Danny dropped a nickel in the slot of the pay phone in the back of Hardman's Drug Store.

"Lenox Hill five, sixty-six fifty-four," he said when the operator came on. A moment later, Dr. Ignatius Bell answered. "I need a favor, Dr. Bell," Danny said. "A big one."

"You know I'm always happy to help, lad," Bell said. "What do you need?"

"Agent Redhorn was turned to stone by our bad guy," Danny explained.

"I have an extensive medical background," Dr Bell said, hesitancy in his voice, "but I can't reverse petrification."

"I've got that taken care of," Danny went on. "My problem is that after he was turned to stone, his body was shattered."

There was a long pause on the line and Danny felt his stomach sinking with every passing second.

"When you say shattered, do you mean exploded into shards or merely broken in pieces?"

"He fell about twenty feet onto a hard surface," Danny explained. "I've seen Alex use a restoration rune when he reassembled the plague jar from that thief's apartment."

"I recall," Bell said. "It's possible, provided your men haven't contaminated the scene too much."

Danny couldn't resist a dark chuckle at that. Thanks to the smashed head of Gilbert Sadler, the cops were giving the rock pile a wide berth.

"Can you help?" He tried to keep the urgency out of his voice.

"I can't make you any promises, Danny, but I will bring my bag of tricks and do the best I can. Now tell me where you are."

It was almost half an hour to the minute when Dr. Ignatius Bell stepped out of a cab at One Hundred and Fourth Street and Central Park West. He tipped the driver handsomely, then withdrew his medical bag before shutting the door. There was no need to ask directions to Danny and the shattered remains of Agent Redhorn, as a large crowd had gathered in the park, gazing up in wonder.

The reason for their awed looks became readily apparent as Iggy crossed the sidewalk and stepped off it onto the frozen ground of the park. Rising up from a spot inside the ring of people was an entire sky crawler. Its front windscreen had been broken out, but other than that, it seemed in good order.

As Iggy watched, the car turned so it was facing south, then floated overhead to the innermost rail of the sky crawler system. Bell knew from experience that the recently added express trains ran exclusively on the inner rail so they would not conflict with regular traffic.

Tearing his attention away, he made his way through the crowd until he encountered a uniformed policeman with bushy eyebrows over hard, disagreeable eyes.

"I'm here at Lieutenant Pak's request," Iggy said in his most brusque and officious voice. He'd learned over many years that the low men in any organization usually wanted nothing to do with the higher-ups. Men of uncertain authority were always a risk to the grunt level worker since it could not be readily discerned just how much damage they could do if offended.

True to form, the uniformed officer decided that he had no desire to find out how much trouble Iggy could make, and he stepped back.

"He's down there," the man said in a Bronx accent so thick, Iggy could barely understand him. Nevertheless, he thanked the man and pushed through the opening.

Once beyond the ring of people, Iggy could clearly see a large pile of rock that had to be the remains of Agent Redhorn. Beyond that, Danny was sitting on a park bench talking with several of his men while another took notes. The sorcerer, John Rockefeller, stood to one side, his hands raised in the air as he directed the overhead flight of the errant sky crawler.

"Dr. Bell," Danny said as soon as he caught sight of Iggy's approach. "Thank you for coming." He stood and indicated the rock pile. "He's over here."

As he led the way, Danny explained about Redhorn's landing on the recently deceased sculptor, Gilbert Sadler.

"Oh, yes," Iggy said when he stepped around the pile. At the bottom was an absolute mess of skull fragments and brain matter. Young Danny had done an excellent job of dispatching the villain.

"What do you think, Doc?" Danny asked as Iggy continued to examine the rocks.

"I think restoring Agent Redhorn might be possible," he said after a moment. "But we're going to need to separate his bits from what's left of your sculptor."

Danny turned and called over one of his detectives.

"How will we know which bits are which?" he asked.

Iggy didn't answer; he just set down his medical bag and opened it. Taking his green rune book from his inside jacket pocket, he paged through until he found a finding rune and tore it free, then he did the same for a linking rune. Replacing his book, Iggy next took a vial of turquoise-colored liquid from his bag. Being careful not to spill any of the contents, he dabbed the bottom of the rubber stopper on the linking rune, then folded it and the finding rune together.

"I need a bit of Agent Redhorn," he said as he worked.

"Uh," Danny replied. "How am I supposed to know what bits are him and what ones are Sadler?"

Iggy sighed and looked up from his preparations.

"Well, you could find a bit of face," he said. "A nose, perhaps? Since Mr. Sadler's face has been rendered into a pulp, that would have to be Agent Redhorn by default, correct?"

Danny didn't reply. From the look of it, he was trying to catch up to Iggy's explanation.

"But, to save time," Iggy went on, "you can just hand me that bit of sleeve." He pointed to a piece of smooth, oval stone with the pattern of a suit coat sleeve cuff on it.

"How do you know that belonged to the FBI guy?" the Detective with Danny asked.

"Because, according to your lieutenant, Gilbert Sadler wasn't wearing his suit coat when he fell out of the sky crawler. Since I can see sleeve buttons on that bit of stone, it clearly came from Agent Redhorn."

"Now I see where Alex learned that annoying skill," Danny said, picking up the bit of petrified arm and handing it to Iggy.

Iggy ignored that comment and set the stone on the ground, making sure it wasn't in contact with any of the other petrified body fragments. Setting the packet of rune paper on the rock, he lit it, sending an amber-colored finding rune spinning in the air. After a moment, it turned a light blue, like the liquid in the vial, then it popped, sending a shower of sparks down onto the bit of arm. As soon as the sparks touched it, the rock began to glow turquoise blue.

The detective whistled and pointed at the rock pile. Now dozens of the fragments were glowing as well.

"Have your men comb through that pile and remove every glowing rock they find," Iggy said. "No matter how small. Have them pile them over there." He indicated a spot of open ground about ten feet away.

"You heard the man, Crenshaw," Danny said to the detective. "Get a detail together and take care of it."

Crenshaw nodded and hurried away in the direction of several uniformed officers. Danny turned back, but Iggy perceived a brief look of pain pinch his face. It was only for a second, but Iggy knew he hadn't imagined it.

"You're hurt," he said, not as a question but as a statement of fact.

"Broken arm," Danny confessed. "It's okay for now."

"I understand you're quite a good detective, Danny," Iggy said in his scolding voice. "But unless you've become a doctor in your spare time, I'll thank you to let me be the judge of whether or not you are 'okay.' Now sit down on that bench and let me have a look."

Danny did as he was told, but stopped before sitting down to get awkwardly out of his overcoat and his suit jacket. Shivering in the cold, he finally sat down. Iggy hesitated for a moment, but the reality that he couldn't have his patient shivering during an examination won out over his desire to protect Alex's secrets. After all, Danny knew quite a lot of secrets and had proven trustworthy.

Opening his green rune book, Iggy tore out a climate rune, unceremoniously licked it, and stuck it to the brim of Danny's hat.

"Uh, Doc?" Danny began but Iggy lit the paper with his gold lighter in answer.

Danny shivered again, then seemed to relax. Iggy knew from experience that the climate rune was making the lieutenant feel perfectly comfortable despite the December weather.

"That's some bag of tricks you've got, Doc," Danny said.

"Actually, Alex cooked that one up," he said proudly. "It's terribly useful, but we're keeping it under our hats, so to speak."

"Mum's the word," Danny said. "Though I wouldn't mind getting a handful of those myself."

Iggy chuckled at that. The climate rune was something everyone would want if they knew about them. Of course, they'd also wonder how Alex had come up with them and that might lead the Legion to conclude that he had access to the monograph, which would be very bad for both of them.

Well, not as bad as it would have been last week, Iggy thought, a self-satisfied smile spreading across his face.

"I'll see what I can do," he said to Danny. "Now let me see your arm."

It was obvious as soon as Iggy rolled up the lieutenant's sleeve that the arm was indeed broken. Fortunately, only the radius bone had broken. It hadn't punctured the skin, but it would still have to be set, which would be unpleasant.

Reaching into his medical bag, Iggy withdrew a small piece of shriveled paper.

"Put this under your tongue," he said, handing it to Danny.

"Is this paper?"

"Yes," Iggy replied, "but it's made of refined seaweed so it's safe to eat."

Danny did as he was told while Iggy fished a small, stoppered bottle from his bag along with a flask of whiskey and a jar of yellow powder.

"Give me your arm," he said. Once Danny had complied, Iggy took it in a firm grip. "This will hurt, but you need to stay still."

Once Danny nodded and closed his eyes, Iggy jerked the bone back into position. Danny grunted in pain and Iggy kept a tight grip on the arm that turned out not to be necessary.

"All done," Iggy said, letting go. "Now drink this." Iggy handed over the small, stoppered bottle. "That's a healing draught; it will accelerate your body's natural healing."

While Danny drank the potion, Iggy poured one finger of the whiskey into a tin cup, then added a teaspoon of the yellow powder and stirred it into the brew.

"This is bone powder," he said passing it over. "It will ensure your arm heals nice and strong."

Danny tipped the cup back and grimaced, then returned it.

"Is that it?" he asked.

"Are you hurt anywhere else?"

Danny shook his head.

"Just the arm."

Iggy took out some gauze and wrapped it snugly around Danny's arm. Once he was done, he sprinkled hardening powder on it and set it with a curing rune.

"That will do," he pronounced after a quick inspection. "Come see me next week and I'll take that off. Now put your coat back on and we'll go see how your men are doing."

Danny stood and dressed himself, while Iggy picked up his bag and headed down to where Crenshaw and the officers were picking through the pile that was Sadler looking for more glowing pieces.

"I think we've got everything we can see," Crenshaw said as they approached.

Iggy knew that was probably true, but it wasn't correct. There were doubtless hundreds of tiny bits too small to detect in the afternoon light. It didn't matter. For what he had in mind, having the big bits in close proximity would do.

With a sigh of regret, Iggy opened his rune book for the third time and paged all the way to the back. There, on the next to the last page, he found what he was looking for. Unlike normal rune paper, this one was yellow in color. It got that way from having been soaked in some very expensive alchemical solutions. Then there was the ink, which used dust made from a five-carat diamond. It was, with only one exception, the most expensive rune Iggy had ever created.

He'd done it several months ago, after Paschal Randolph had tried to blow up the brownstone and he and Alex spent the next few days writing major restoration runes to repair the damage. It had taken time to put the brownstone back in order after the blast, and that bothered Iggy. If Randolph or the Legion had tried a second bomb right after the first, it would have destroyed a major part of his home, not to mention giving them access to the secrets inside.

Iggy had decided right then that he needed a way to repair the entire brownstone at once, and thus the greater restoration rune had been born. A major restoration rune cost about five hundred dollars to make, but thanks to secrets in the Monograph, his cost was lower by half. As far as Iggy could guess, the greater restoration rune had cost him around two thousand dollars in materials.

Tearing the rune free from his book, Iggy set it on top of the pile of softly glowing stones. He hesitated a moment as he pulled his lighter from his trouser pocket. He wasn't worried about the money; he had quite a lot of the stuff, but this was the first time he would ever use this rune. It had made sense when he thought it up, and when he designed it, and when he wrote it, but this was where the proverbial rubber met the road.

Dear God, I hope it works.

With that cheery thought, Iggy lit the rune paper, then quickly stepped back.

26

UNBROKEN WILL

Danny flexed the fingers on his left hand, feeling the tendons move smoothly past the break in his arm. The area of the break was warm, almost hot, but he knew that was a result of the healing draught, so he tried to ignore it.

As it turned out, ignoring his arm was a fairly easy thing to do. He'd seen runes work before, many times, but none of his experience with Alex prepared him for what was happening in front of his eyes. The rune paper Dr. Bell had put on the rock pile that was Buddy Redhorn didn't just burn like he'd seen runes do before. This one burst into streaks of fire, then seemed to shoot out burning lines, like fireworks. It burst into a secondary pattern of blues and golds before resolving into a circular pattern behind the base rune, like the rose window of a cathedral.

Once it was fully constructed, the rune blazed with so much light that Danny had to shield his eyes. It wasn't as bright as one of Alex's flash runes, but it would do in a pinch.

"Is it working?" he asked the doctor, still blinded by the brightness.

"Shush," Bell hissed back at him.

As Danny watched, the light began to fade, but it did not so much dim as break apart into floating motes. They drifted like silver fireflies, falling and looping slowly downward in a shower of incandescent light.

As the sparks descended, a clacking and rattling sound began to emanate from the rock pile. One by one, the petrified pieces of Agent Redhorn began to rise, floating upward from the pile. Each lazy, drifting mote of light eventually came to rest on a rising stone, causing it to pulse with the same turquoise light they had seen before. When the stones changed color, they also began to rotate, spinning lazily in a counter-clockwise direction.

Danny knew something was happening, he just had no idea if it was something productive. He resisted the urge to ask Dr. Bell again, since the old man was staring at the reaction as if he were analyzing every tiny aspect of it. Instead, all Danny could do was wait and hope Bell knew his business.

Who are you kidding? Everything Alex knows, he learned from Bell.

As the motes of light became fewer and fewer, the base rune faded away. At the same time the spinning stones moved faster and faster until all the pieces were in motion.

With a sudden clap like thunder, two of the pieces slammed together in the center of their orbiting brothers. The edges where the bits came together glowed for a moment, then the new piece hung still in the air as if it were held up on a rod. Danny jumped at the unexpected sound and took half a step back. It turned out to be a good choice as suddenly the swirling rock pieces swung out into a wider orbit before they began crashing into the solid pieces in the center.

It sounded like someone firing a tommy gun, a staccato series of bangs as each piece attached to the middle bit, growing it outward; first into a torso, then moving up and out, building arms, legs, and finally a head. When the last bit slammed home, completing Agent Redhorn's right foot, the cracks blazed again, then vanished, leaving the petrified body whole again.

In the aftermath of the magic, there was a long moment of utter silence. The police and the crowd just stood without talking or shuffling, and even the noise of the street seemed muted.

"My God," Rockefeller's voice seemed to boom in the unnatural silence. "That was some impressive magic."

Bell seemed startled by the compliment, but he rallied quickly.

"I understand the rest is up to you," he said, turning to Rockefeller and extending his hand to him. "Doctor Ignatius Bell."

The sorcerer shook it and nodded.

"John Rockefeller," he replied, even though Bell clearly knew who he was.

"Can you turn him back?" Danny asked. The statue looked just as it had when he'd first seen it on board the crawler, but that didn't mean it was whole.

"That's not the problem," Rockefeller said, turning to Dr. Bell. "Do you think you got all the bits?"

"There's bound to have been some loss," Bell replied, setting his doctor's bag down and opening it. "Tiny fragments and bits of dust probably blew away. I estimate a one percent loss."

Rockefeller stroked his chin as his brows furrowed.

"That's not good," he muttered, more to himself than anyone. "I can de-petrify him, but he might just die if something important is missing."

Danny watched this exchange with mounting anxiety.

"Is there any way to make it safer?" he asked, directing his question to both men.

"Patience, Danny," Bell said, digging around in his bag. He withdrew a stoppered bottle, then a metal shaker of the kind Danny had seen in high-end clubs. Finally, Bell took out several bottles and a long, thin measuring spoon.

No one spoke as Bell measured out the powders, spooning precise amounts into the shaker. When he finished, he added the contents of the stoppered bottle, then he took out a brown bottle and added a splash of that liquid. Satisfied, he returned the brown bottle and the powders to his bag, then capped off the metal cup and shook it like a high-class bartender. When he finished, he popped the top off and swirled the liquid around in the steel mixing cup.

"What's that?" Danny asked.

"It's a restorative made from a major healing draught," Bell said. "I've modified it a bit so that it will quickly regrow missing tissue. Once John here returns Agent Redhorn to his proper form, I'm going to need you to get him in a sitting position and hold him. I need to pour this down his throat, so you're going to have to hold on tight."

"How long?"

Bell gave him a hard look.

"Until he tells you to let him go or he's dead."

A cold knot settled in Danny's gut, but he held the Doctor's gaze and nodded. He waited until Bell nodded back, then walked around behind the statue of Agent Redhorn.

"Are you both ready?" Rockefeller asked. "This should only take a moment."

"Ready," Bell said, standing to the side and holding the metal cup protectively in both hands.

"Ready," Danny said, shaking his good arm. He'd have to get his left arm around Redhorn's neck so his broken arm wouldn't be a hindrance. That would leave his right arm free to pin the FBI man.

Rockefeller stepped up to Redhorn and said something Danny didn't understand. When he spoke, his voice was deep and echoed as if he were yelling into a well. As the sound faded away, he touched Redhorn's forehead and pink flesh began to spread out from the spot. The magic washed over the FBI man's body in a few seconds, and he gasped as his lungs returned to normal.

Danny didn't wait to see the effects of the transformation. Reaching around Redhorn, he seized him by the throat and grabbed his left hand, pulling it to the right and trying to restrict the right arm as well. Instantly Redhorn began fighting him; his breathing was coming in ragged gasps and he tried unsuccessfully to speak.

"Hold him still," Bell said, stepping forward and jamming his thumb into the side of Redhorn's cheek, forcing his mouth open.

Danny looked to Rockefeller for help, but the Sorcerer was leaning on his knees, panting heavily.

"Agent Redhorn," Dr. Bell said, his voice suddenly military and forceful. "Drink this." He pressed the metal mixing cup to Redhorn's lips and tipped it up.

The FBI man spluttered and gargled but seemed to get most of the liquid down. As soon as Dr. Bell stepped away, Redhorn collapsed, and Danny found himself bearing the man's entire weight.

With a grunt, Danny relaxed his grip and let Redhorn slide down his torso until he could lay him on the ground.

"What now?" Danny asked.

"We wait," Bell said. "It shouldn't be long."

"How long?"

"Did we win?" Redhorn gasped, sounding like a man with a five pack a day habit.

Danny looked around at the crowd and the pile of bloody rock and chuckled.

"Yeah," he said. "I think we did."

"Sadler?"

"Dead."

Redhorn closed his eyes and sighed.

"How do you feel, Agent Redhorn?" Bell asked.

"Buddy," he said. "My name is Buddy."

Danny didn't mean to, but he chuckled.

"What?" Buddy said, opening a bloodshot eye to look up at him.

"What kind of a name is 'Buddy?'"

"I lied about my age to get into the big war," he said. "I was just a stupid kid. Tried to be everybody's friend, so they just called me Buddy. It stuck."

"I thought you were an investigator for the army," Bell said.

"That came later," Buddy said, closing his eyes. "Speaking of investigating, did you secure the device?"

"It's in an evidence locker in Detective Crenshaw's car," Danny said. "Captain Callahan will take charge of it once we get it over there."

"It needs to be destroyed," Buddy said.

"Are you sure about that?" Rockefeller said. "Sadler may have been insane, but if that rod he created actually works, we could give magical abilities to our policemen or our soldiers. That's a very potent possibility."

"No," Danny said. "Agent Redhorn is right. The reason Sadler was insane was because of his exposure to that Limelight stone." He looked between Bell and Rockefeller. "It affects people with magic. If either of you came in contact with that rod, it could affect you, too. We simply can't risk that."

"So how do we destroy it?" Rockefeller asked. "I could do it, of course, but if you're right about how dangerous it is, I shouldn't touch it."

"Have Detective Crenshaw put it on the ground right there," Dr. Bell said, pointing to a patch of open ground near the bench Danny had been using.

"What do you have in mind, Doctor?" Buddy said, his voice tired and his eyes still closed.

Bell didn't answer, but knelt by his bag and opened it. Danny took the opportunity to call Crenshaw over and tell him to go get the Limelight rod. As he hurried off to comply, Danny turned back to find Dr. Bell removing a black bottle with a skull and crossbones on it from his bag. The lid had been sealed with lead and a heavy cord was wrapped from the top to the bottom and back several times.

"What's that?" Danny asked.

"Universal solvent," Bell said. "It's an alchemical base so powerful it can dissolve almost anything."

"Except that bottle?" Danny asked with a note of skepticism he just couldn't suppress.

Dr. Bell looked at him with a raised eyebrow and a half smile.

"That bottle cost more than your car."

"You sure that stuff will do the job, Doctor?" Buddy asked, pushing himself up to a sitting position.

"I'm more concerned about what your superiors are going to say," Bell responded.

"I don't care what they'll say," Buddy said.

"Once the rod is destroyed, it won't matter what they say," Danny said, standing up. "So, let's get on with it."

As if on cue, Crenshaw returned, and Danny had him put the rod on the ground.

"Now what?" he asked.

Dr. Bell pulled a pair of heavy leather gloves from his bag and passed them to Danny.

With a skeptically raised eyebrow, Danny took the gloves and pulled them on.

"How big is that bag, Doc?"

Bell smirked back at him.

"It may actually be bigger on the inside than on the outside," he said, but he didn't elaborate.

Danny wondered about that since he knew Dr. Bell had a runewright's vault and that a runewright could only have one of those at a time.

"Now be careful with this," Bell said, passing the black bottle over. He'd taken the strings off, but the lead seal was still intact. Using the seam of the heavy glove as a pry surface, he pulled up the edge of the lead, then peeled it away from the cork stopper.

Tossing it away, Danny walked carefully to where the Limelight rod lay. Kneeling down, he took hold of the stopper and twisted it carefully, working it back and forth until it popped free. A wave of acrid odor threatened to make him cough, but he didn't dare.

Holding his breath, Danny positioned the little vial over the green stone tip of Sadler's device. Tipping it carefully, he poured a steady stream of sickly yellow syrup down on the stone. Everywhere the liquid touched, it ate away at the alchemical jade. Billows of toxic smoke rose up, forcing Danny to abandon the empty bottle and step away.

Finally able to breathe again, he bent over and coughed until his lungs felt clear. When he finally turned back to the device, all that remained was a bit of the metal rod. The solvent had even eaten a small hole in the ground.

"That's not going to China, is it?" Buddy asked.

Danny looked at him askance.

"Was that a joke?"

The ghost of a smile crossed the big FBI man's lips before he answered.

"No," he said.

"The solvent will run out of steam soon," Dr. Bell said, motioning for Danny to return his heavy gloves. When Danny passed them over,

Bell moved to the abandoned cork stopper, then picked up the black bottle and carefully pushed the stopper back inside.

All of these things went back into his bag, and he stood with a self-satisfied expression.

"How are you feeling, Agent Redhorn?"

"I'll be okay," Buddy said, extending his hand to the doctor. "Thank you."

With that, Dr. Bell excused himself and headed back toward the street to catch a cab.

"If you'll excuse me as well," Rockefeller said, "I'm going to share a cab with the good doctor."

"Can't you just teleport home?" Danny asked.

Rockefeller gave him a sour look.

"I'm exhausted, Lieutenant," he said, a bit indignantly. "Would you like me to teleport you home in my current condition?"

Danny held up his hands to ward off any such attempt.

"Point taken," he said, then he reached into his coat pocket and withdrew Rockefeller's magic dampening knuckle duster. "Thanks for this," he said, handing it back. "It held out long enough to save my life."

Rockefeller nodded and accepted the device. He moved to tuck it into his pocket but hesitated, holding it up and squinting at it.

"I dropped mine somewhere," Buddy sad. "Sorry."

"Not to worry, Agent Redhorn," the sorcerer said. "I found it in the sky crawler."

With that, the man turned and headed to the street to catch up with Dr. Bell. Once he was out of sight, Danny turned to Redhorn.

"You want a lift back to your car?" he asked. "I imagine you'll want to get a head start on the paperwork that will explain all this."

"Yeah," Buddy said.

Five hours later, Buddy Redhorn eased his sedan up to the curb in front of his house. Detective Pak had been right about the paperwork, it, and the obligatory meetings that went with it, took most of the rest of the day. On the plus side he had time to call Lexi and deliver her from his mother.

Getting turned to stone and broken in a million pieces had a way of giving a man perspective.

Stepping out of the car, he took a deep breath, holding it for a moment, then let it out. He'd work long and hard to buy his little slice of the American dream and he loved everything about it.

Moving around to the back of the car, he opened the trunk and hefted out the heavy cage.

"Trust the stone," the petrified parrot squawked.

"Lexi is going to hate you," he said with a grin, then he shut the trunk and lugged the cage up the walk to his front door.

"What are you doing home?" his wife asked as he entered, a curious smile on her face. The smile faded a moment later when she spotted the bird cage. "And what is that?"

Buddy explained about the parrot, talking fast.

"It's the perfect pet for the kids," he concluded. "It doesn't need to be fed, you don't have to clean up after it, and it only talks when you move it or talk to it."

Lexi folded her arms beneath her substantial chest and gave him the look she'd used to wilt lesser men. Buddy simply stood, holding the cage, with a smile fixed on his face.

"William," she said, her voice husky and dangerous, "if you're lying to me..."

She let the sentence drop off, but Buddy took her meaning.

"Scout's honor," he said.

She held the look for a long moment, then shook her head.

"It's a good thing I love you," she said, her scowl still in place.

Buddy set the cage on the kitchen table and drew his wife in to a bear hug that ended in a passionate kiss.

"What do you say we have dinner early, then we can listen to the radio with the kids. The Shadow is on tonight, they love that one."

Lexi looked up at him with questions in her eyes.

"You hate that show," she said.

"But I love you and the kids," he said, "and I'm home early."

Lexi's hard look melted into a dazzling smile.

"So you are," she said, snuggling up to his side. "And I seem to remember the last time you came home on time, you got a call that interrupted our evening."

Buddy looked at his beautiful wife for a moment, then went to the phone and took it off the hook.

27

FLYING SOLO

Buddy Redhorn was late to work the next day, but frankly, he didn't care. He'd stopped a madman from turning a third of the city into a magical time bomb, after all.

That ought to be worth coming in late once in a while.

He expected Director Stevens to come by his desk to have a word about his tardiness. Stevens wouldn't care, but appearances had to be maintained for the less productive agents. Once he'd been at his desk long enough to fill out a few of his long-overdue reports, he began to wonder where the Director actually was.

Getting up from his infrequently used desk, he crossed the open floor to Steven's office door. A small table sat next to the door with several wire baskets arranged on it. Buddy found the one marked for after-action reports and dropped his paperwork into it. No noise came from inside the office, and he was forced to conclude that the Director was out.

He was a little disappointed, to be honest. It wasn't often that Buddy was in the main office, especially after closing a major case. He wasn't a glory hound, but it was nice to be acknowledged by the boss every once in a while.

On his way back to his desk, Buddy suddenly realized that the entire office was quiet. On his first day back while Sorsha was out of town, he'd been besieged by agents who didn't think training a girl, or working for one, was a suitable assignment for a federal agent. Now everyone was studiously ignoring him.

He had a momentary impulse to stop by Agent Unger's desk and try to provoke him. Buddy abandoned the thought almost as soon as he had it. Unger wasn't worth the effort.

"There you are," the chipper voice of Agent Mendes came from behind him as he sat back down at his desk. Buddy had a momentary feeling of embarrassment; he'd been so busy reveling in his success in foiling Sadler that he'd forgotten his partner and her mission to locate the real Jade Phoenix.

"Agent Mendes," he said, giving her a nod. "I'm sorry I wasn't in this morning to help with your case. Where are we?"

Mendes moved around and sat on the corner of his desk. She wore her usual dark gray suit and burgundy tie. Buddy expected her to look harried, but she had a surprisingly serene expression on her face.

"I think you were right," she said.

When she didn't elaborate, Buddy asked her what she meant.

"You said that the higher-ups in DC wanted me gone," she explained.

"I think they want to shut down the magical crimes task force as well," Buddy said. Realistically, the task force was just himself, Agent Mendes, and Miss Kincaid, but Buddy liked working these kinds of cases, and Sorsha was an excellent boss. She listened to his ideas and gave him a free hand to pursue leads and suspects without looking over his shoulder every minute. He was about to mention that when he clued in to what Mendes had said.

"Why do you think DC wants to shut us down?" he asked, glancing at the Director's empty office. "Did Director Stevens say something to you?"

Mendes sighed and blew a strand of her unruly hair out of her face.

"He came by this morning," she said. "He took my badge."

Buddy never would have expected that. If Steven wanted to fire Agent Mendes, he should have discussed it with him first. He was her trainer, after all.

"Don't worry," he said, glancing at the empty office again. "As soon as Director Stevens returns, I'll speak with him."

"I'd rather you didn't," Mendes said, reaching into her coat pocket. "Because he gave me this." She withdrew her hand, producing a folding leather wallet.

Inside was the gold FBI shield of a full agent. Stevens had taken her silver trainee one.

"You passed your training period?" Buddy asked. Then the full meaning of that fact occurred to him. "You found the real Jade Phoenix," he said. It wasn't a question, he was sure of it. No other action could have led to Stevens making her a full agent.

Mendes' face split into a wide grin and she suddenly beamed.

Buddy felt a rush of excitement and a pang of loss at the same time. He was proud of his protégé, but her achieving the rank of full agent meant she wouldn't be working with him any more.

"Tell me," he said, allowing a grin to spread across his own features.

"Well..." Mendes hesitated for dramatic effect. "Once I had the fake statue, I took it straight over to the Devereaux Gallery. Mr. Devereaux was very glad to get it back."

"The fake statue?" Buddy asked. After all, Devereaux knew the statue taken from his gallery was a forgery.

"I told him we recovered the original," she said, fixing him with the smoldering look she reserved for convincing men to trust her. "He was very grateful and put the fake right back on display, this time with around the clock guard."

Buddy considered that for a moment, then shook his head.

"But we never cleared William Devereaux," he said. "He could be the one who paid Sadler to make the fake."

"No, he couldn't," Mendes said. "When you sent me all over talking to art galleries, a few of the curators told me about how difficult it is to forge a statue. From what they said, you can only make a passable copy from photographs. It will look okay in a display case, but it won't stand up to close inspection."

"And an avid collector like Nick Maretti thought it was the genuine article," Buddy said with a nod. "So the fake was damn near perfect."

"In order to get the fake to the point where it would fool someone like Maretti, Sadler would have to have access to the original. He'd need to compare the original and his fake side by side."

Buddy nodded as he understood.

"Devereaux never had the chance to give the real statue to Sadler," he said. "During the day it wasn't on display, and at night there where three guards keeping an eye on it." He regarded Mendes with his best teaching expression. "What if the guards were in on it?"

Mendes shook her head.

"If you were a guard in on a scheme to swap out a piece of art with a fake, what would you do if the fake was stolen?"

"I'd think one of my co-conspirators had hung me out to dry and I'd skip town."

"Exactly," Mendes went on. "You remember when we talked to the night guards, they didn't seem suspicious or nervous, they were shocked."

"So Devereaux isn't our man," Buddy admitted. "How does giving him the statue help find the original?" He had a pretty good idea where she was going, but this was her show and he intended to let her have the glory.

"If Gilbert Sadler had to have the actual statue in his possession to refine his forgery, there's only one window of opportunity for that," she said. "When the statue was returned to Trevor Hardwick while the gallery was being repaired."

"It was supposed to be in Hardwick's vault," Buddy said.

"But it was in Sadler's studio," his protégé declared. "Hardwick wouldn't steal his own statue, so that only leaves one person who could have given the statue to Sadler."

"Brent Cooper, his valet," Buddy said.

"That's the way I figured it," Mendes said, starting to speak quickly as her excitement grew. "When I returned the statue to Devereaux, I had him tell the press that the statue had been authenticated, that it was the original."

"That must have made Cooper's buyer very nervous," Buddy chuckled.

Mendes was so excited that she was practically bouncing.

"I got a warrant and tapped the phones at Hardwick's home," she explained. "Pretty soon that collector from Colorado called, demanding to meet with Cooper. We staked out the meeting and when the collector showed up with the real statue, we scooped them all up. Cooper and the collector are awaiting trial and the real Jade Phoenix is on its way to Brunei. Not only did I close the case, I staved off an international incident."

Buddy nodded where he sat. He took some pride in her victory, but that was the pride of a teacher. She'd earned this one all by herself.

"The sad thing is that Cooper did this because Hardwick promised to give the statue to him years ago. He thought that Hardwick forgot but when the lawyer read the will yesterday, the old man left Cooper one hundred thousand dollars in the will."

"Sounds like Cooper will be hiring a good lawyer," Buddy said as he pushed back his chair and stood. "Agent Aissa Mendes," he said, sticking out his hand for her to shake. "Let me be the first to welcome you to the FBI."

She hesitated a moment, then threw her arms around him in a big hug.

"Thanks, boss," she said.

"Not for much longer," Buddy said as she let him go. "You're a full agent now. I'm sure when Director Stevens gets back, he'll have a shiny new assignment for you."

For the first time, Mendes electric smile faltered.

"Actually," she said, a touch of hesitancy in her voice. "The Director already told me I'll be staying with the Magical Crimes Task Force."

Buddy looked over at the empty director's office. If Mendes wasn't moving, that would mean he was. If he was honest, he wasn't exactly thrilled about leaving, but Mendes could handle the task force beside whoever they paired her with. He only wished he knew where Stevens was and what his boss had decided about his fate.

Danny Pak arrived at the Central Office of Police bright and early the morning following the death of Gilbert Sadler. There had been quite the story in the previous day's evening papers. The tale was a sensational bit of fiction detailing the untimely heart attack of an express crawler driver and the heroic intervention of a pair of unnamed policemen and the sorcerer John Rockefeller.

He'd been worried that someone would remark on Dr. Bell's runewright skills, but the papers attributed all the magical goings on to Rockefeller, so that was good. Danny was one of the few people who knew about the Archimedean Monograph and who currently possessed it. He wanted to make sure that list stayed exclusive.

Danny didn't mind the omission of his name; the powers that be needed to keep the existence of Gilbert Sadler quiet, never mind the Limelight. What bothered him was the loss of time in his regular job. If he didn't get his division running like a Swiss watch, and soon, he wouldn't stay a lieutenant.

"Morning, boss," Detective Wilson said, sticking his head through the office door. "I've got some paperwork for you."

Danny resisted the urge to sigh.

"Put it on the pile," he said, indicating his stack of folders.

Wilson grinned and dropped the folder right on top of the papers Danny was working on.

"I think you're going to want to see this," he said with an enigmatic grin.

Danny opened the file and began to read. With every line, his eyebrows went up.

"You caught the whole gang?" he said, looking up at Wilson's grinning face.

"Yes sir, they're downstairs in the cooler as we speak."

"And you got a signed confession," Danny said, picking up one of the papers.

"Once they knew the jig was up, they all wanted to roll on their pals for consideration from the DA."

Danny closed the file and moved it to his completed cases basket.

"Great work, Wilson," Danny said, meaning every word. "I'll get you something new in a few minutes."

"That's okay, Lieutenant," the Detective said. "I've already got another case."

That didn't surprise Danny too much; after all his boss was supposed to cover for him while he'd been on assignment.

"I guess Callahan's still got it when it comes to running this division," he said.

"Callahan?" Wilson said. "I haven't seen the Captain down here since he wanted you to meet him on the docks."

"Then where did you get a case?"

"Johansson brought it to me."

"Officer Johansen?" Danny asked. "Big, blond guy?"

"He wants to make detective, but he bit off more than he could chew, so I'm helping out. I think he's onto a gang of counterfeiters."

Danny was impressed. He'd made Detective the same way, by digging up his own case.

"Help Johansson as far as you can go," he said. "If you break this, we'll have to call the Secret Service for the wrap up, but I'd like you two to make the arrests if possible."

"We'll work on it," Wilson said. "Anything else?"

"Yeah, tell Crenshaw I want to see him."

"He's not here," Wilson said. "He said something about breaking that bicycle theft case and ran out of here like a bat out of hell."

Now Danny was impressed. Crenshaw needed a win and Danny had been keeping him from his case all week.

"Well, if you see him," he said as Wilson headed for the door.

"I'll let him know."

Danny looked at the closed case file Wilson had brought. It was a big win for Division 5. If Crenshaw did indeed solve the bicycle case, that'd be two this week.

"Maybe you'll get to stay a lieutenant for a while after all," he said out loud, though he did take an extra moment to knock on the wooden top of his desk.

He spent the rest of the morning getting caught up on his paperwork. To his surprise, it went faster than he expected. After considering that strange fact for a moment, he realized he wasn't second-guessing his decisions as often.

"If this keeps up," he said to himself, "you might have time for a real lunch."

He picked up the next folder in his 'to do' stack, then put it down. He decided then and there that it didn't matter how much he managed to get done.

Picking up the phone, he gave the police operator the number of Alex's office.

"Lockerby Investigations," Sherry's cheerful voice greeted him.

"How's your side?" he asked.

"Much better," she replied. "I'll be a little stiff for another day or two, but it's healing up nicely."

The line went silent for a minute while Danny tried to maneuver toward the reason for his call.

"Is that why you called?" Sherry asked. "To check up on me?"

"Well, yes," he admitted. "But I was also wondering if you'd like to have lunch with me."

"Why Lieutenant Pak," she said with a smile he could hear in her voice. "How could I say no to such a smooth talker?"

"I can be over there in fifteen minutes," he said, checking his watch.

"I'll be ready," she said.

Danny hung up, then grabbed his overcoat and hat on his way to the elevators. When he woke up that morning, he was worried he might not have a job by dinner, but now, everything seemed to be going his way.

28

THE CONSPIRACY

Doctor Ignatius Bell stood at the window of his library, looking out at the street. He wore his best tweed suit, though he'd removed the coat and replaced it with his red velvet smoking jacket. He was waiting for some guests to arrive at the brownstone, and he was a bit nervous about this group.

Being set in his ways, Iggy didn't like visitors in general, but he definitely didn't make a habit of inviting sorcerers to his home. Of course, he hadn't invited John Rockefeller to his home as much as the sorcerer had invited himself. He had something on which he wanted Iggy's opinion and that made it difficult for the doctor to say 'no.'

Once the sorcerer had called, Iggy got another call from Captain Callahan. The Captain wanted to ask Iggy about magical crimes and he wanted to bring Adam Stevens with him. Stevens was the regional director for the Federal Bureau of Investigation.

Iggy turned to look over his shoulder at the bookshelf on the left side of the hearth. The Archimedean Monograph sat there on one of the upper shelves, doing its level best not to be noticed. It was the primary reason Iggy didn't want two high-ranking representatives of the state and federal government and a sorcerer in his home at the same time.

Still, Sorsha Kincaid had been right here in this very living room on several occasions and hadn't noticed the book. Iggy was relatively sure it would be safe on its shelf.

Still, he didn't like it.

The first to arrive was Rockefeller. Instead of materializing on the sidewalk outside, the sorcerer arrived in a cab. He wore a pinstriped suit and carried a walking stick as he climbed the stoop with a spring in his step.

Without waiting for the man to ring the bell, Iggy abandoned the window and moved through the vestibule to the door.

"Doctor Bell," Rockefeller said, taking off his hat as Iggy opened the door.

"Welcome to my home, Mr. Rockefeller. Please come in."

"Call me John," the sorcerer said, stepping into the vestibule.

"And you may call me Iggy."

If Rockefeller found Iggy to be strange moniker for a septuagenarian doctor, he made no comment. Iggy was about to close the door, but a second cab pulled up to the curb and two men got out. The six-foot three frame of Police Captain Frank Callahan was easy to recognize. The other man Iggy had never met, but based on the tailored Italian suit, he could only be Regional FBI Director Adam Stevens.

"Thank you for hosting this little clam bake, Doc," Callahan said when he and Stevens mounted the top step. He turned and introduced Director Stevens before Iggy invited them in.

"Let's have this meeting in the kitchen," Iggy said as he shut the door.

A moment later the four men were gathered in the brownstone's kitchen. Iggy had laid out tea and he took a moment to pour out before taking his seat.

"I'd like to thank everyone for coming," Callahan said. "I hate meetings, so let me cut to the chase. Everyone's been briefed on our misadventures with the late sculptor, Gilbert Sadler." He looked around the table and everyone nodded. "I have reason to believe that his case isn't closed."

That took Iggy by surprise. From what he saw, Sadler was about as finished as it was possible to be.

"If you are referring to the statue made out of Alchemical Jade," Stevens said, "my agents took it into custody this morning. It's secure."

"It needs to be destroyed," Iggy spoke up.

"I agree," Stevens said. "I'll arrange to have it delivered here so you can destroy it."

Iggy surpassed a shiver at that statement.

"I'd prefer you didn't," he said. "Limelight affects magical practitioners, and it seems like this solid version is capable of affecting people just by being near them. It's best if it isn't near me."

"Danny can take care of it," Callahan said.

"I think," Rockefeller piped up, "that you might not want to let Daniel near the statue, either."

"Why not?" Iggy asked. "I've known Danny for years, and I can assure you he isn't magically talented."

"I'm sure he wasn't," Rockefeller said. He reached into thin air and pulled out something that looked like a pair of brass knuckles, then dropped it on the table. Before anyone could ask a question, he repeated the process, dropping a second brass knuckle on the table.

"These are charms I made," the sorcerer explained. "I gave one to Daniel and one to Agent Redhorn."

"Why?" Callahan asked.

"They're magic dampeners," Rockefeller explained. "I figured they would give each of them an edge if Sadler tried to use his toy on them."

"Apparently they worked," Stevens said.

Iggy noticed the slight hesitation from Rockefeller.

"What's wrong?" he asked.

"Like all charms," Rockefeller explained, pointing to the two devices, "these are only effective as long as the spell that powers them has energy."

"The more you use the device, the weaker it gets," Callahan said with a nod. "Eventually the spell runs out and the charm is useless."

"Precisely," Rockefeller said. "Now this one," he indicated one of the devices, "is inert. The spell that powered it is completely drained. But this one," he indicated the second device, "this one has a full charge. It's like it was never used."

"But," Callahan interjected. "We know both Agent Redhorn and Lieutenant Pak used your dampeners on Sadler."

"Yes," Rockefeller said with a solemn nod. "We do."

"This one," Iggy said, pointing to the one Rockefeller said was fully charged. "It belonged to Danny, didn't it?"

The sorcerer nodded and Iggy felt a knot form in his gut.

"Why is that important?" Director Stevens asked.

"Mr. Rockefeller thinks Sadler used his device on Danny," Iggy said. "As I understand it, the Limelight grants the recipient the power to do what they most desire, Danny thought he was protecting a car full of innocent people. I'd wager at the time, his innermost desire was that the charm not run out of power."

"You think Lieutenant Pak can...charge up magical charms?" Stevens said, skepticism ringing in his voice.

"That is exactly what I think," Rockefeller said. "If I'm right, Daniel has become a sort of magical battery."

"What about his mind?" Iggy said. "In our experience, people granted real power by Limelight tend to wind up killing themselves."

"I don't think young Daniel is any danger," the sorcerer said. "If his abilities work the way I think they do, they can only rejuvenate a weak spell. He could re-power charms, but that's about the extent of it."

"Does he know?" Iggy asked. He was having trouble not being angry that Rockefeller hadn't told anyone about his findings.

"Not yet," Rockefeller said, then he turned to Callahan. "I'd like your permission to work with him, to test these abilities and, if necessary, teach him how to control them."

"I'm sure I can make that happen," Callahan said, "but we may have a bigger problem." He waited as all eyes at the table turned to him. "Since yesterday, the department has received three calls regarding crimes involving unusual magic. In one case an eyewitness reported that a young man walked through the back wall of her jewelry store and into her safe, then made off with approximately a thousand dollars' worth of stones. Another report claims a man stole a bronze bust of Abraham Lincoln, weighing five hundred pounds, by picking it up and carrying it off."

"You're thinking the people on the sky crawler were affected between the time Agent Redhorn was turned to stone and when Daniel boarded the sky car," Rockefeller said.

Callahan nodded, then looked around the room.

"I thought it was unusual when Lieutenant Pak reported that none of the hostages in the car stuck around to be interviewed by the police, or even the press."

"So, Sadler got to them somehow?" Stevens said. "How did he manage to give them powers and convince them to...I don't know, commit crimes? Why would he do that?"

"According to Danny," Iggy began, "Sadler was a devote of Marx. According to that philosophy, peace and a utopia will come when the people rise up against the government. Sowing the seeds of chaos is a good way to start that process."

"Chaos like a bunch of magical criminals running around the city," Callahan agreed.

"How could Sadler convince a crawler full of regular people to behave that way?" Stevens asked. "It still seems a bit far-fetched."

"Not necessarily," Iggy said. "We know that there are magics that can affect the mind. We also know that exposure to Limelight makes the recipient some kind of magical genius. It's entirely possible that Sadler planted the idea of a life of crime into his hostages, gave them magical abilities, then instructed them not to talk to the police."

Stevens sighed and rubbed his temples.

"So what do we do about this?" he asked. "I've got my own magical investigations unit, but Sorsha Kincaid runs that and you said she shouldn't know about this."

"Danny," Iggy said. "He's already been affected by the Limelight, he's a damn good investigator, and he understands how to fight magical criminals."

"What about his duties as a lieutenant?" Stevens asked. "That's a big responsibility, and he won't just be able to go running off after one of these affected criminals."

"I can cover for him," Callahan said. "But we'll need to keep these cases quiet. If word gets out that there are a score of criminals, all with magical abilities, we could have a panic on our hands."

"Well, he seems to work well with Agent Redhorn," Stevens said.

"I'll have him assist the lieutenant whenever one of these cases arise. They'll handle them discreetly and both our departments will know what's going on."

"I like it," Callahan said. "It's simple and hopefully quiet."

"I'll want to work with Daniel too," Rockefeller added. "Dr. Bell was quite right; we need to make sure his abilities won't kill him."

"Agreed," the two lawmen said in unison.

"There's one other thing you haven't considered," Iggy said. "This new arcane crimes unit you've created must be kept secret; from the press, from their fellow agents, and most especially from Alex, Sorsha, and Andrew Barton. Under no circumstances are they to learn that there might be more Limelight out there in the world."

"I can arrange that," Callahan said.

"As can I," Stevens affirmed.

Iggy sighed. He didn't like any of this, but he understood that it needed to be done. If he was right about Sadler using mind control, the former passengers from the crawler would have to be stopped—gently if possible.

"All right," he said at last. "The first order of business is to dissolve the statue." He turned to Director Stevens. "Get a bottle of universal solvent over to Redhorn along with the statue. After that, Redhorn and Danny need to get started on these three special cases. Did I miss anything?"

No one spoke as they looked around the room.

"Then let's get going. The sooner Lieutenant Pak and Agent Redhorn find these affected people, the sooner things can go back to normal."

THE END

You Know the Drill.

. . .

Thanks so much for reading my book, it really means a lot to me. This is the part where I ask you to please leave this book a review over on Amazon. It really helps me out since Amazon favors books with lots of reviews. That means I can share these books with more people, and that keeps me writing more books.

So leave a review by going to the Blood Relation book page on Amazon. It doesn't have to be anything fancy, just a quick note saying whether or not you liked the book.

Thanks so much. You Rock!

I love talking to my readers, so please drop me a line at dan@danwillisauthor.com — I read every one. Or join the discussion on the Arcane Casebook Facebook Group. Just search for Arcane Casebook and ask to join.

The adventures of the Arcane Irregulars will continue next year. In the mean time, look for Alex's continuing adventures in Arcane Casebook #8, coming soon. (Go to www.danwillisauthor.com to preorder it right now)

ALSO BY DAN WILLIS

All books available at Amazon unless otherwise noted.

Signed copies available at danwillisauthor.com/shop

Arcane Casebook Series:

Dead Letter*

In Plain Sight

Ghost of a Chance

The Long Chain

Mind Games

Limelight

Blood Relation

Capital Murder

* Dead Letter is the prequel novella to the Arcane Casebook series. Available for free at danwillisauthor.com

---

Dragons of the Confederacy Series:

A steampunk Civil War story with NYT Bestseller, Tracy Hickman

Lincoln's Wizard

The Georgia Alchemist (Forthcoming)

Other books:

The Flux Engine

ABOUT THE AUTHOR

A former programmer, Dan Willis started his writing career with the long-running DragonLance series. He is currently the author of the Arcane Casebook series, the new Arcane Irregulars series, and the Dragons of the Confederacy series.

For more information:
www.danwillisauthor.com
dan@danwillisauthor.com

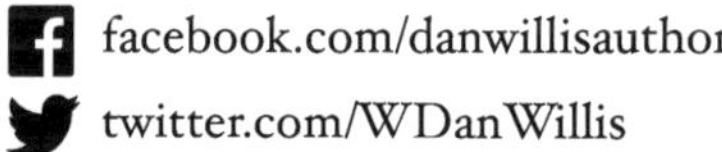
facebook.com/danwillisauthor
twitter.com/WDanWillis

Made in the USA
Middletown, DE
05 November 2021

51735893R00165